The First Stone

By

Gillian Jackson

'Whoever among you is without sin, let him cast the first stone.'

John Chapter 8 vs 7

Published in 2014 by FeedARead.com Publishing

Copyright © The author as named on the book cover.

The author or authors assert their moral right under the Copyright, Designs and Patents Act, 1988, to be identified as the author or authors of this work.

All Rights reserved. No part of this publication may be reproduced, copied, stored in a retrieval system, or transmitted, in any form or by any means, without the prior written consent of the copyright holder, nor be otherwise circulated in any form of binding or cover other than that in which it is published and without a similar condition being imposed on the subsequent purchaser.

A CIP catalogue record for this title is available from the British Library.

Acknowledgements

Many thanks to my husband, Derek for his endless patience and support and to all my family for their encouragement and enthusiasm.
Thanks again to DS Sean Jackson for his insights and answers to my questions and to Kate, my daughter in law for her proof reading skills.

This book is a work of fiction. Names, characters, places and incidents are a product of the author's imagination. Any resemblance to actual people is entirely coincidental.

The First Stone

Chapter 1

'Jenny, come here quickly, I think we've won the lottery!' Malcolm's voice rose in both pitch and volume until he sounded as if he was choking.

'Come on love, you say that every week, it's not funny anymore.'

'No, honestly we've got six numbers, come here and see for yourself.' Waving the lottery ticket in front of his wife's eyes Malcolm Grainger was half laughing and half crying with a face flushed from excitement as he stared again at the numbers on the television in disbelief. Jenny snatched the crumpled pink ticket and turned to the screen trying to memorise the numbers before they disappeared. Fumbling with uncooperative reading glasses she just caught the final line up of numbers as they were displayed in order.

'Seventeen, twenty one, thirty...oh Mal, you're right we've won the lottery!' With trembling hands Jenny's arms snaked around her husband's ample waist as he squeezed until she could hardly breathe.

'We'll have to ring the kids.'

'No, not yet, let's just think about it for a while shall we? We don't even know how much we've won. It was a roll over, wasn't it?'

'Yes, but we might have to share it. Perhaps you're right; we shouldn't count our chickens and all that. What does it say on the website, is there a number to ring or something?'

Malcolm brought their laptop and searched for the lottery site, scrolling down slowly and hovering over the bright red numerals which announced the week's jackpot of eight point two million pounds. Bouncing up and down on the worn sofa like an excited schoolboy he was barely able to control the mouse to search the site properly.

'Here, let me.' Jenny wrestled the laptop from him. 'Here it is, get a pen and write this number down!'
Jenny and Malcolm looked at each other, huge grins splitting both their faces.

'You ring them, I can't stop shaking,' she said.

'I need a drink first!' Taking a can of beer from the fridge he offered one to Jenny who shook her head, laughing.

'Champagne would be more appropriate, pity we don't have any but I'll put the kettle on.'
Malcolm began dialling the number while Jenny returned and perched on the edge of the sofa, holding her breath and listening to one side of the conversation. A series of stuttering noises were impossible to interpret but Malcolm was nodding and smiling so the news must be positive. He eventually recited their address and telephone number before mumbling monosyllabic words of thanks and replacing the phone.

'We're the only winners, eight point two million and only one winning ticket!' Malcolm's breathing was erratic, his previous ruddy face suddenly pale.

'Sit down love before you fall down. So, what happens next?'

'Someone will ring tomorrow and arrange to come and meet us. They said something about verifying the ticket, advisors and publicity. I couldn't take it all in but they'll explain everything tomorrow.'

The hiss of the kettle from the kitchen prompted Jenny to her feet, moving automatically to make a pot of tea, the proper thing to do in all circumstances. Malcolm was sitting in the same spot when she returned with two steaming mugs, his face expressionless.

'I'm going to ring the kids now.' Jenny announced, unable to contain the delight any longer and desperately wanting to share their good news.

'No, let's leave it 'till tomorrow when we know more.'

'What more do we need to know? We've won the lottery all our worries are over and for the kids too! We can pay off their mortgages and have a family holiday to Disney World like we've always dreamed. I'm going to ring them now.'

'Pull the other one Mum.' Kate groaned, 'Another tenner is it?'

'No, it's eight point two million pounds actually.' Jenny grinned knowing Kate would assume it was a joke, just as she had done with Malcolm.

'Are you serious, because if you're not and this is a wind up, I don't think it's particularly funny?'

'I'm serious girl! Someone's ringing from the lottery tomorrow but they've confirmed that there's only one winning ticket and we've got it.'

Kate eventually accepted that her mother was speaking the truth, incredible though it seemed. They chatted for only a few more minutes as Jenny wanted to ring their son, Matthew, which she did as soon as the phone disconnected. Matthew too expressed similar disbelief taking even more persuading than Kate that this was not some kind of joke. Both children promised to come round first thing the next day, if it hadn't been so late and their own families were not in bed they would have dashed round immediately but celebrations would have to be postponed until morning. Jenny, flushed with excitement went to find Malcolm who had gone upstairs while she was on the telephone. He was getting ready for bed as if it was just a normal Saturday night.

'What are you doing? We can't go to bed now, there's too much to talk about and plan. It's not every day you win millions on the lottery.'

'I know love, but I think we're getting a bit carried away with it all. What do you want to do, go out shopping already?'

'I would if the shops were open! Come on, we should be celebrating, this is the best thing that's ever happened to us and I know I won't be able to sleep tonight.'

Reluctantly Malcolm followed his wife downstairs. Jenny would happily climb up on the roof top to tell the whole world of their good fortune, but warning bells were beginning to sound in his head. Perhaps the win would bring more than only good things into their lives. After Malcolm's initial euphoria and as reality began to dawn, he knew that broadcasting this news could potentially bring untold damage to their family.

Jenny woke to the sound of 'Joy to the World' as the doorbell chimed its anthem repeatedly until she staggered downstairs to open the door. She had slept surprisingly well, which could have been due to the bottle of wine she had polished off before eventually turning in, and was therefore completely unaware of her husband's restless night and the number of times he had got up to make a milky drink or simply to stare into the inky blackness of the night from the bedroom window, his stillness masking an inner turmoil.

Matthew took his finger off the doorbell.

'Appropriate tune Mum!' He entered the hall grinning, giving Jenny a bear hug and lifting her tiny frame right off the ground. The reality of the lottery win began to dawn on a still sleepy Jen once again and she squealed with excitement, brown eyes suddenly wide with delight. Malcolm appeared beside them bemused by their pleasure and they moved automatically into the kitchen. Jen put the kettle on, flopped down at the table propping an aching head in her hands and asked.

'Well, what do you think love?'

'Amazing, fantastic... what do you think? Tell me how much again, I don't know if I dreamt it or not?'

'Eight point two million and we're the only winners! It hasn't quite sunk in yet!'

'Get away! You had most of it spent in your head last night. I think you could sort out the country's economy single handed now. Better buy some shares in M&S son, their profits are about to take an upturn.' Malcolm was pleased at the excitement shared by his wife and son, the win couldn't have come at a better time, particularly for Matthew who had been made redundant from work a month previously and was beginning to worry about the bills he could no longer pay.

'You won't have to downsize now, and young Tom can still go to that private school you'd set your heart on.'

'Thanks Dad, that's good of you to say but we don't have any expectations you know, this is your win.' Matthew spoke from the heart, although a windfall would be more than welcome, he wasn't going to assume any rights to his parents' winnings.

'You know we'll see you right, there'll be as much pleasure in watching you enjoy the money as in spending it ourselves. Now where's Kate, it's after eight o'clock, I thought she'd be battering the door down at daybreak?'

'She won't want to wake Daisy if she's still sleeping. They've had a few rough nights with teething lately.' Jenny rose to make the tea, squeezing her husband's shoulder affectionately in passing. Malcolm was saying all the right things but something didn't quite add up and his smile didn't seem to reach his eyes. Perhaps he was still in some kind of shock which would account for it. When it was all confirmed by the lottery people it would sink in and then they could really celebrate. As if hearing her name, the door bell rang again and Matthew jumped up to let his sister in. More hugs and squeals followed from Kate and her husband Mike. Baby Daisy grinned happily, enjoying the mood of the adults whilst totally oblivious to what had caused it. Tea was poured and Malcolm watched as his delighted family began to talk simultaneously,

'We'll book a table at The Grange tonight, early enough for the children to be able to come.'

'What time are you expecting the lottery people to ring?'

'Have you told Auntie Christine yet Mum?'

'We could eat out every night now if we wanted to!'

'Are you going to see your Dad and let him know Mal?'

'Let's slow down a bit here shall we? We haven't actually got the money yet so there's no need to broadcast it is there?' Malcolm became the voice of reason, nursing his own fears and hoping to steer his family in a different direction to the one in which they were blindly heading.

'Don't be a killjoy Mal, this is the best thing that's ever happened to us, I want to shout it to the world and his wife!'

'Perhaps Dad's got a point Mum. They give you the 'no publicity' option for a reason. There are always people who'll try to take advantage in a situation like this, con artists who write begging letters and such, there's that to consider surely?'

'Stuff and nonsense!' Jen replied. 'We know who our real friends are and the rest can go and jump for me.'
Malcolm's brow furrowed as he busied himself with the cornflakes. An agreement on this matter was not going to be reached easily.

'Have you thought about what you'll spend it on yet? Do you think you'll move?'

'We haven't had time to think of anything yet have we love?'

'No, it's too soon.' Malcolm's unenthusiastic response didn't go unnoticed by Jenny who was concerned at such lack of enthusiasm.

'Why don't you go to the home and have a chat with your Dad? He'll be thrilled for us I'm sure.'

'Yes, I thought I'd go later today after we've heard from the lottery people.' Her husband managed a smile which went only a small way in reassuring Jenny that all was well.

Chapter 2

The journey from Fenbridge in North Yorkshire to the little border town in Scotland where Maggie's parent's lived was not an arduously long one but the pressures and time constraints of their working lives prevented Maggie and Peter Lloyd from visiting as often as they would wish. They had however reserved this particular weekend in October for a visit, determined to make the effort, certainly before the bleak Scottish winter set in. It had always been easier for George and Helen Price to travel to their daughter's home but during the last few months George had been unwell and his wife thought it prudent not to travel too far.

The drive was uneventful with only moderate traffic and surprisingly no road works to contend with. Their car was heavy laden, not because Maggie hadn't mastered the art of travelling light but rather that their dog, Ben and cat Tara, needed almost as many items as they did themselves. Tara was resigned to travelling in the carrier basket and slept for nearly the whole journey but Ben, with more of an understanding of what a car journey meant, was quite excitable at times, even attempting to squeeze into the front seat with his mistress, which was an impossibility due to his gradually expanding middle.

'Nearly there now boy.' Maggie patted his head reassuringly and as they pulled into the driveway of her parent's cottage, Ben began to bark. During the last few miles of their journey, the weak sunshine of the autumn afternoon had vanished, replaced by the grey light of evening and the all too familiar gathering rain clouds. But even such gloomy conditions couldn't detract from the scenery through which they were passing. The purple heathers and dry brown ferns spread out to each side of the winding road, so atmospheric with the distant fog rolling in from the coast, sitting heavily on the darkening landscape. Maggie took it all in, understanding exactly why her parents had chosen this part of Scotland to retire to. The cottage also evoked that Celtic atmosphere, thick grey stone walls keeping the cold outside and the warmth of open fires in. Standing in an idyllic cottage garden which was her father's pride and joy, Maggie too had come to love this place and the calm atmosphere it afforded.

Helen had been watching from the window and rushed out to embrace her daughter with the usual affection lavished on her only child.

'Come in where it's warm both of you! Yes, you too Ben, the biscuits are in the kitchen.' At times Peter could swear that dog understood every word as his four legs carried him inside ahead of the others, his claws slipping on the stone tiles and his nose leading him straight to the kitchen.

'Your Dad's in the lounge, supposedly watching the news but I think he's nodded off. He gets very tired these days.' Helen led the way through the hall to the cosy lounge where George, disturbed by the noise of their arrival was waking up. He grinned at the sight of Maggie who responded with the same smile and hurried over to hug her father.

'How are you Dad?'

'Oh, fine... as ever.' George winked, the old twinkle of humour still apparent in his brief answer.

'You must be starving, the kettle's not long since boiled and I've got some nice ham and eggs for supper.' Helen assumed all visitors arrived at their door with empty stomachs and that it was her role in life to meet that need.

'I told you not to worry Mum. A sandwich would have been fine.'

'Nonsense, it's no trouble and I'm sure you will have been far too busy to bother much today?' The question was also a statement and no more was said. Maggie knew it was pointless arguing with her mother over food so she smiled her acquiescence and followed Helen to the kitchen while Peter carried their bags to the room at the end of the hall.

'How has Dad been?' Maggie asked when they were out of earshot of George. Helen found Ben the promised biscuit then busily began setting the table as she answered.

'He's had quite a good day today. He certainly understood that you were coming and has helped me make up the bed, yes... not a bad day at all.'

'And are there many bad days now?'

'I think it's about half and half. There's no point in trying to hide it from you Maggie, you'll see for yourself that he's getting worse but on the more lucid days we get on fine.'

'So what does the doctor say?'

'There's medication we can try but it'll take time to find one that suits him. They've been very good but the Alzheimer's seems to have taken hold rather quickly. We got a prescription for a drug called Donepizil to try out but I only got the prescription filled yesterday so he's only had one day on it so far. Hopefully there'll be no side effects but I'm rather glad you're here now, at least if there are any problems you'll be able to help.'

'Of course Mum, but let's not anticipate any. Dad's in good physical health isn't he? That should help surely.'

'Yes, you're right love, but it's still grand to have you and Peter around, for Dad as well.'

As the four sat to eat together at the little kitchen table it was not at all apparent that anything was wrong with George. The meal was a pleasant occasion after which

Peter took Ben for an evening walk while Maggie helped to clear away.

'Game of scrabble next Dad?' she grinned as he nodded and went to get the board ready.

'The doctor said it was good to keep his mind active and as I said it's a good day today so off you go and see if you can win.'

'I don't have a good track record against Dad, but if I get lucky with picking out some good letters, who knows?'

When Peter returned and the kitchen was up to Helen's fastidious standard of tidiness, the game became a foursome as Peter teamed up with George and Helen with her daughter. After an hour, the women conceded, blaming a run of bad letters. The game was cleared away and the television switched on for the late evening news.

Later, in bed, Maggie related what Helen had said earlier about George's worsening condition.

'He seemed on good form tonight, I certainly didn't have to carry him in the game of scrabble.'

'Yes, Mum said it was a good day but the bad ones are becoming more frequent now, about half the time apparently.'

Peter pulled Maggie closer, knowing how this must be affecting her, she was very close to both parents.

'We'll be able to get a feel of how things are this weekend and then perhaps talk to your Mum about how we can best help. You know whatever you want to do will be fine by me don't you?'

'Yes, I know and thank you, I really appreciate that. It's one of those situations you never think will happen to your own family and I'm not sure what exactly we can do for them.'

'Let's see how things go and perhaps have a chat with your Mum before we leave shall we? She's a strong woman and knows her own mind but hopefully she'll also know when it's time to ask for help.'

The next morning, although bright and sunny, was cold with a heavy frost. Winter always came sooner in Scotland than it did in Fenbridge. Maggie and Peter wrapped up well to take Ben for an early walk. Their dog was elderly now so walks were not as long or energetic as they used to be. Maggie had walked full circle around the fields surrounding her parents' house more times that she could count, with Ben doing even more miles as he ran ahead sniffing at the unfamiliar scents and excited by the open spaces. Their walks now were more sedate and Ben was happy to return home after barely half an hour, seeking a warm spot beside the fire. Helen had cooked breakfast and George was still in the bathroom as the others sat down to eat.

'He'll be out in a few minutes, just get on with yours why don't you,' she instructed. Maggie thought her mother didn't look too rested so asked,

'Did you have a good night Mum?'

'Not really, your father couldn't sleep. Too much excitement I think which is a sorry state of affairs when scrabble is the highlight of the day.'

'Ah but it was the exceptional company that made it so exciting.' Peter grinned.

Laughing, Helen began pouring the tea and right on cue George came into the kitchen to join them. Conversation drifted to previous visits to Scotland,

'Do you remember the first time I brought you here Peter? It was so cold and I don't think you'd believed me when I told you how bad it can get.

'Of course I remember, you made me so welcome that I knew I'd found my new family.'

'Ooh, how cheesy!'

'And what about that Christmas when we took you to Gretna and Sue was there?' Helen began to reminisce too, referring to her daughter's closest friend whose husband had arranged a secret wedding in Gretna and even Maggie had been kept in the dark.

'Ah yes, Sue, such a nice girl.' George joined in the conversation. 'Has she found herself a husband yet?' Good looking girl but a bit of a flirt.'

The others were silent for a moment before Maggie answered, trying to sound as casual as she could.

'Sue got married at Gretna that Christmas Dad, don't you remember? They've got a little girl now, nearly three and her husband's a policeman.'

George looked puzzled so Helen added,

'She married the policeman, you know, the one who got shot last year. We've met them often when we've been down there love, Alan he's called and their little girl is Rose.'

'Shot? Is he dead then?'

'No, he's fine now, back at work and fit as a fiddle.' Helen answered. There was sadness in her eyes as she looked at George and a weariness which was so unlike her usual self. The conversation was steered to other topics but her father's lapse in memory troubled Maggie. His conversation seemed so fluent and he'd appeared to be his usual self the night before but his memory was obviously affected. Maggie's heart ached for him and for her mother who had to live with the reality of this cruel disease which was slowly, piece by piece taking her husband away from her. The rest of the weekend passed without incident but saying goodbye was difficult. In spite of reassurance that she'd be fine, Helen struggled to hold back the tears as Maggie and Peter left. It was obvious that their visits to Scotland need to be more frequent, a thought that occupied Maggie's mind during the journey home.

****

The clouds were moving quickly, each one becoming more ominously grey as they passed overhead. A storm was likely thought Malcolm as he tapped in the security number and pushed open the heavy doors to Willow Dene Nursing Home, the wind at his back swirling crisp brown leaves around his feet to land on the door mat. The stuffy heat hit him immediately in contrast to the cold autumn gusts outside and the smell of boiled vegetables lingered in the corridor, remnants from the usual Sunday roast lunch. It wasn't a bad place for his father to be in, the nursing staff, although always busy, were cheerful and efficient and Bill Grainger seemed as content as it was possible to be in such circumstances. Sunday afternoon was the time his son visited alone and the two spent a couple of hours in each other's company, Malcolm taking the Telegraph crossword puzzle for them to tackle together. It was remarkable how Bill's mind remained so alert considering the little stimulation his present life afforded. A stroke four years previously had robbed him of his active retirement, denying him the simple pleasures of life such as tending his allotment and visiting family at times which suited him. Now, trapped in a body which stubbornly refused to regain its former physical strength, life was lived entirely within his own mind and the confines of a ten foot square room. Bill had no mobility and could use only a limited amount of muscles in the right hand side of his body. His face too had only half of its previous movement, permitting nothing more than lop-sided smiles and winks rather than blinks. Malcolm could never decide if it would have been preferable for his father's life to have ended on the day of his stroke allowing him to be reunited with his beloved wife who had been dead since Malcolm was eight years old, or if the old man enjoyed this very limited existence. Communication was usually restricted to single words which, with great effort, Bill attempted to verbalise or tap out on the electronic note pad by the bed-side, an equally tiring effort, so a discussion on the topic of quality of life was never going to happen.

'Hi Dad!' Malcolm fixed on the usual smile and the old man responded with his best effort at mirroring the expression. Pulling up the chair, the Telegraph was brought out and Malcolm launched straight into the first clue. The silence of their thoughts was broken only for the usual messages from the family to be offered.

'Jen sends her love and will be in on Wednesday evening as usual and we saw the children this morning, they're both well and send their love. Matthew will probably pop in later in the week, he's busy looking for jobs at the moment but he'll get in soon.' Malcolm was sticking to the usual script, procrastinating to avoid what he really needed to say. Bill smiled and then raised his arm to tap the keyboard, *'Mongoose'* he typed.

'Oh yes, one across, a small flesh eating mammal, eight letters. Mongoose, very good Dad.' He filled in the first answer to their puzzle wondering how to tell his father what was weighing so heavily on his mind.

'We've had a bit of a win on the lottery Dad.' Should he give the watered down version or be honest? Bill's right eyebrow arched in a gesture of surprise.

'Well, it's more than a bit of a win, eight point two million in fact. I don't think it's actually sunk in yet.' Is this how a lottery winner should be acting, as if it had been no more than a tenner? Malcolm went on,

'The fact is that Jen and the kids are so excited and want to broadcast it to the world but I'm not so sure. Of course it's great news and means financial security for us all but I'm inclined to play it low key, opt for the no publicity option, you know?'

Bill slowly nodded his head, eyes misting over as he understood the implications his son had in mind. Slowly he moved his right arm to the rest attached to the side of the bed from where he could reach the keyboard and tapped a single word, 'remember.'

'Yes Dad,' Malcolm nodded slowly, 'I remember.'

Chapter 3

Malcolm Grainger worked as a security guard at Fenbridge town hall and rang in on Monday morning to tell them that a family situation necessitated him taking the day off work. In a round about way it was true, he needed to be with his family when the lottery representative came to see them, goodness knows what would happen if he wasn't there to represent the voice of reason. Kate and Matthew would be coming round too, work being no problem for his son and job hunting now relegated to the last thing on his mind. By ten thirty the atmosphere in the Grainger's small lounge was electric. The four of them, rarely alone together without grandchildren and spouses, laughed like they had in years gone by. Malcolm felt somewhat on the periphery, delighted to see them so happy but with that same little voice in his head urging caution. The doorbell chimed its anthem and Jenny jumped out of her seat like a horse from the starting gate to dash to the door.

'I hope one of the first things you buy is a new doorbell Mum, that one is so embarrassing!' Matthew called out before silence replaced the previous jollity as the three listened to the sound of their visitor being welcomed into the house. Jenny returned to the lounge, face flushed and grinning like a schoolgirl to introduce not one but two visitors, a man and a young woman. The man was shorter than his companion with a round face and equally round spectacles sitting on the bridge of his nose. His body resembled a figure eight, squeezed in at the middle by a rather uncomfortable looking belt. The smartly dressed woman seemed more poised and oozed efficiency in a friendly kind of way. After introductions,

'Please call me John and this is Bea,' the family looked eagerly to the pair, willing them to get down to business.

John, holding a bottle of champagne, was rather gushing, offering congratulations in several different ways having obviously had plenty of practice, until Matthew could hold the question back no longer.

'When do we get the cheque?' He asked rather bluntly, earning a reproachful look from Jen. Bea took over the conversation in a quiet, simple manner.

'Well, today we need to see your ticket to confirm its validity, and then there are some forms to be filled in and if everything is in order the money will be paid into your bank account by the end of the working week. We don't actually give you a cheque, only one of those huge ones for publicity purposes, electronic transfer is much safer and quicker all round.' Bea smiled at the family, enjoying the role of bearer of such good news.

'So, do you have the ticket?'

Jen was up first to retrieve the precious scrap of paper from under the mantle clock which had been acting as a temporary paperweight. It was folded in a rather crumpled envelope having spent two nights under her pillow, just in case. She handed it over to Bea, who opened a smart leather brief case to reveal a neat laptop computer and began to type away on the keyboard. Matthew made a mental note of the laptop maker's name, thinking he'd quite like to have one of those, along with many other things he'd been dreaming about over the weekend. John too had a briefcase, his containing a small bundle of forms which he offered to Malcolm for inspection. After a quick read through and seeing nothing to concern him, Malcolm began to fill in some of the required details, digging into his trouser pocket for his cheque book to copy the details carefully onto the form.

'You mentioned publicity' he asked casually, handing the forms back to John. 'What's the expectation regarding this?'

'Well it's entirely up to you. From our point of view we would be delighted to arrange one or two press conferences, it's a sizeable win and obviously newsworthy, we find most winners are only too pleased to do a few publicity shots.' John sounded eager.

'I'm not so sure. My inclination is to keep it quiet. There'll be another winner next week so I think we'll give the publicity option a miss.'

'But Mal, we hadn't decided yet. What's the problem with sharing our good news? People are going to find out anyway sooner or later.' Jenny quite fancied having her picture in the nationals and couldn't understand Malcolm's reluctance. Bea was quick to offer her opinion,

'You don't have to decide anything now, we appreciate that it's probably not quite sunk in yet and you'll need time to think. I'll ring tomorrow, we'll still have time to arrange something then and it will give you a bit more time to discuss it. Naturally we would appreciate the publicity, there's nothing like a happy family picture with a huge cheque to sell more lottery tickets but please, don't feel under any obligation.'

John pushed the bottle of champagne towards Malcolm,

'Congratulations again Mr Grainger, shall we leave this with you then?'

Malcolm took the hint and offered their visitors champagne which was readily accepted before they eventually left.

'Gosh, champagne before lunch, I could get used to this!' Jenny giggled. 'But why no publicity love? I rather like the idea of our picture in the paper.'

'We'll talk about it later.' Malcolm closed the subject for the moment but knew he had to make a decision soon.

'Mike's Mum has Daisy for the day so I thought if anyone was up for a bit of celebratory shopping, today's the day!' Kate looked at her mother, knowing what the answer would be.

'Ooh yes, count me in! What about you boys?'

'I could quite fancy checking out that new computer superstore at the retail park, how about it Dad?'
Malcolm smiled at his son, nodding in agreement and the four arranged to meet for lunch after going their separate ways.

'We went to Debenhams and asked for one of those personal shoppers Dad, we certainly got the five star treatment after that!' Kate's excitement gave her an attractive glow.

'And I can see that she found plenty of clothes that you wanted to buy.' Malcolm smiled at his daughter and wife, who, if the number of carrier bags was any indication, had obviously had a great time. Neither were women who would normally be extravagant so it was good for them to spoil themselves now that they could afford it. Matthew too had bought a new laptop and a fancy phone, something which Malcolm wouldn't have a clue how to use but Matt was happy with his purchases too.

'Didn't you find anything you wanted love?' Jenny asked.

'Not really, there's nothing I particularly need but I did think we could look on the net to see about a holiday, somewhere warm where we could all go together, Florida perhaps?' His words brought a squeal of delight from Kate,

'Disney World!' she said, 'I've always wanted to go, it'll be fantastic!'
Malcolm could see how this money could bring the family happiness. None of them lived beyond their means so a few extravagances were in order. This was also put into practice when they chose their meals as they all had what

they would like without checking the price on the menu first. Ordering a steak, Malcolm decided that for the rest of the day at least he would try to enjoy their good fortune without crossing bridges and anticipating events which might never happen.

****

That same Monday morning, in mid October, found Maggie Sayer back at work and preparing for the first client of the day. 'Sayer' was Maggie's professional name, that of her first husband, Chris, who had died suddenly after they had been married for only three short years. It was an event which, although the nadir of her life, was also the catalyst which had changed her future and from which she embarked on therapeutic counselling as a profession, channelling those dark, traumatic experiences into helping the many clients who came her way. Thoughts of her parents and the problems they were facing had been disturbing Maggie since their weekend visit. During the journey home from Scotland she and Peter discussed George's worsening condition. It was becoming unwise for him to leave the house alone which added pressure to Helen's increasing responsibilities. George had usually been in the habit of walking to the village shop to buy a paper each morning and as it was less than a mile down the road, the exercise was good and he always had the news to read if the weather made his other passion of gardening impossible. Helen appreciated the first hour of the day to organise her own tasks and even if George stopped to chat to friends he was generally back within the hour. It had been an anxious time therefore when, about a week before Maggie's visit, George had been gone for over two hours. When he did return, looking as if he hadn't a care in the world, concern made Helen snap at him, a rare occurrence. He was however genuinely puzzled and couldn't explain why it had taken twice as long as usual to fetch the paper, his grasp on time was slipping away. The milk she'd asked for had also been forgotten. Sharing this with her daughter and son in law, they agreed that perhaps it was no longer safe for George to make these outings alone as the missing hour had never been accounted for. Now, reflecting on the episode Maggie felt the enormity of the burden that this was going to place on her mother's shoulders as well as her own ineffectiveness to be able to offer any practical help due to the distance separating them. Dismissing these worries for now, Maggie re-read the details of her next client, wanting to focus solely on the young woman she was about to meet for the first time. She memorized the doctor's brief notes, finished the nearly cold coffee and then opened her door to see if Alice Greenwood had arrived.

Alice was a tall, graceful young woman, thirty one years old according to the notes and suffering from mild depression, possibly due to the recent death of her father. She offered Maggie a neatly manicured hand as she entered the room, smiling pleasantly from an oval face with huge blue eyes. Smartly dressed in a dark trouser suit and crisp white blouse gave the appearance and air of a capable, intelligent woman, someone who was comfortable in her own skin. Tossing tresses of long fair hair over her shoulder, she looked expectantly at the counsellor.

'Please sit down.' Maggie motioned to an easy chair beside a coffee table. 'Thank you for coming today Alice, we have about an hour, which should be plenty of time to get to know each other and for you to decide how you would like things to progress.' Maggie paused before briefly outlining the confidentiality clause which covered their sessions and the exceptions to it. Alice seemed comfortable with this information so Maggie asked if she would like to begin by telling her why she had come.

'I'm in a mess.' Alice said bluntly, which was certainly not how she appeared but then clients rarely wore their problems on a label around their necks. Maggie nodded.

'My Dad died four weeks ago, I don't live at home now of course, I have a little flat in town but I've been surprised by the strength of my emotions. He hadn't been ill at all, it was a heart attack whilst at work and as he was only fifty nine it came as quite a shock.' The young woman's head dropped at this point and there was a moment or two of silence. After the pause Maggie asked,

'Would you like to tell me how you're feeling now?'

Alice looked up to meet the counsellor's eyes.

'I'm just so glad he's dead.' The words were almost whispered through gritted teeth and Alice's blue eyes looked suddenly very cold and sad.

'We never had a particularly good relationship, in fact I moved out as soon as I began to earn a living. Now that he's dead I feel a huge sense of relief but surely that's not normal is it? I've never thought of myself as a heartless person, but my reaction to Dad's death makes me wonder. What do you think Maggie?'

'What I think doesn't really matter but your feelings are certainly not an indication of being heartless in any way. Everyone reacts differently to the death of someone close and our emotions are generally more to do with the relationship we had when that person was alive. Do you think it would be helpful to explore the relationship you had with your father? It might bring a measure of understanding as to why you feel this way.'

'Well I'm happy to try anything. My head's been swimming with all kinds of thoughts and memories and I can't seem to get past these awful feelings. I'm usually such an organized person, in practical ways as well as in my thinking but this has completely thrown me and I don't like it. Is this the sort of thing a counsellor does, help me to sort my thoughts out?'

'Absolutely. Our thoughts and feelings are obviously connected and it's often good to step back and take stock. You sound like you want to spring clean your internal filing system, is that about right?'

'Oh yes, that's it exactly! I'll probably bore you to tears but I think I'll burst if I don't sort myself out somehow. Can we do this then? I liked what you said about confidentiality, so is it okay to tell you everything?'

'Yes, of course. Do you know where you want to start?'

'The funeral I think, that's when I realised my feelings were so strong and negative, it's probably as good as any place to begin.'

The small room was warm and comfortable. It was generally quiet too and the only noise in the background was the pattering of heavy rain on the flat roof outside. It seemed an appropriate backdrop to Alice Greenwood's story as the young woman took a deep breath, shuffled back in the chair and began to tell Maggie all about her father's funeral.

Chapter 4

Standing at the sink in the tiny kitchen peeling potatoes, Alice deliberately dug the knife deep into the skin, wastefully taking off huge chunks of peel, with a smile at the memory of a time when she was about twelve years old and doing this very same task. She never minded helping with the household chores but if her father was in the house Alice could never seem to get anything right. That particular day her uncle and aunt had dropped by and she was hurrying the potatoes in order to join them in the lounge. Uncle Stan was her mother's brother and Alice was very fond of him. Finishing the chore and dashing through to see their visitors, she passed her father on the way. No sooner had Alice settled on the sofa to enjoy the visit than Ronald Greenwood returned to the lounge, carrying the dustbin liner with the potato peelings inside.

'Just look at these!' Grabbing a handful of peelings, he waved them in the air for all to see. 'This is what passes for peeling, there's hardly any potato left. Thinks I'm made of money she does, you've no idea what I have to put up with!'

Alice had been so embarrassed her face burned with shame. Ronald however seemed to enjoy the discomfort he was causing until Uncle Stan spoke up in the girl's defence.

'Well why don't you try deep frying them Ronald? They're all the rage in posh hotels you know and there wouldn't be any waste then.'

The words had been spoken in jest but Ronald had been the one to blush then and with his temper diffused, he returned the peelings to the dustbin.

The memory now brought a wry smile, a typical unpleasant incident had been averted by Uncle Stan's joke, he'd been her advocate and she loved him all the more for it. These days Alice almost deliberately took off too much potato when peeling them, a little act of defiance, something to remind herself that she was now in control of the little things in life and could waste half the potatoes if so inclined. Having spent an hour in the company of Maggie that morning, many such issues had been brought back to mind, some resurfacing from very early years and the growing realization as Alice became older, that her father simply did not seem to like her. Of course she had many friends who didn't get along with their parents either, particularly during those difficult teenage years but Alice always felt the poor relationship with her father was somehow more than simply the normal growing up squabbles. At times she was certain that he simply disliked her; that something about her very existence displeased him and at times Ronald even seemed reluctant to be in the same room as Alice. This left the distinct impression that she had done something wrong, why else would a father struggle to be civil to his own child? Perhaps Maggie was right and delving back in time might reveal a clue as to why Ronald acted in such a way, not that anything could be altered now but Alice didn't want to carry this awful feeling of hatred and guilt anymore and was eager to try anything which would help to get rid of it.

Alice's mother was coming to lunch that day, a rare occasion in the past but something both women recognized could now become a frequent part of their relationship if they both desired. Caroline Greenwood was still in mourning but at the same time her husband's death had brought a sense of freedom, certainly in regard to how often she was able to see Alice. Ronald had been a reasonably good husband but had never been cut out to be a father, a facet of his personality which Caroline tried to make up for but which often left her feeling like a referee or an arbiter at best. That role was now no longer necessary and Caroline was aware that perhaps the relationship between herself and Alice could now be more uninhibited, but in fairness to Ron she may find herself defending his memory.

'How are you doing Mum?' Alice greeted Caroline with an affectionate embrace, well aware that it was only a month since Ronald's death.

'Oh, you know, a day at a time love and you?'

'Okay thanks.' Alice turned to make for the kitchen, avoiding any further scrutiny. 'It's only a cottage pie I'm afraid but I bought a couple of cakes from the bakery for afters.'

'That sounds fine, it's such a treat to have a meal cooked for me but it's my turn next, you've not been home since the funeral.'

'I know and I'm sorry. Things have been so busy at work... but that's no excuse and I will be round this week, promise.' Smiling, Alice began to serve the meal which they ate at the tiny kitchen table.

Caroline's eyes scanned the small flat where they sat before taking a deep breath and saying what was on her mind.

'You know you could move back home now if you wanted? There's more than enough room and it seems silly paying rent on this place when you have other options.'

Alice was taken aback at the sudden suggestion. She had paid rent since leaving home at eighteen which meant that there was no money left over to save up for a deposit on a house of her own. This had never particularly bothered her as getting away from home had been worth the exorbitant rent she shelled out every month. It was undoubtedly a sensible offer but would it work? At thirty one did she really want to move back in with her mother? True the flat was small, one bedroom, a broom cupboard of a bathroom and an L shaped lounge with a tiny kitchen but it was a ground floor flat and Alice had the luxury of a small square courtyard garden, a sun trap when the weather was fine and a place to fill with colourful blooms in pots and troughs throughout the summer.

'It seems a little too soon to be making decisions like that Mum. Wouldn't you rather move to a smaller place yourself? It's a long time since I've lived with anyone, I'm probably too set in my ways now.'

The reply was about what Caroline had expected but the idea had been planted and hopefully Alice would consider it as she longed to make up for the difficulties her daughter had experienced in childhood, none of which were of the child's making at all.

'Well, think about it love and we'll discuss it another time eh?'

Alice nodded and the matter was dropped.

****

Malcolm returned to work on Tuesday morning still undecided as to whether to continue at the Town Hall or not but common sense told him not to make any decisions without allowing the time and space needed to think them through carefully. Jenny had already given notice at the school where she worked part time as a dinner supervisor but would work out the month to give them time to find a replacement. Malcolm hoped she wouldn't go in and tell everyone about their win, she was obviously finding it difficult to contain her excitement.

Jenny didn't really want to work out the notice period but also didn't want to let them down. The head teacher had been genuinely sorry when they spoke on the phone the day before to say she needed time off for personal reasons and would also like to tender her resignation. She would miss the children and the other staff but there was so much they could do now and spending more time with their own grandchildren was an appealing thought. There were holidays to take and work would simply get in the way, hopefully Malcolm would eventually see it that way too. His reaction to their win had been quite puzzling really, almost as if he didn't want the money. As Jenny pondered their good luck, something she had not stopped doing since Saturday, the phone rang, catching her just before she left for work.

'Mrs Grainger?' A female voice enquired.

'Yes?'

'My name is Penny Jones, I'm a reporter at the 'Argos Local', the free paper for the area?'

'Yes, I know it.'

'I'd like to congratulate you and your family on your recent win, you must be delighted!'

Jenny wondered how on earth this young woman knew, it was only Tuesday and they hadn't told many people themselves.

'Thank you but how did you find out?'

'Oh, I'm sorry, is it a secret? I'm a friend of your son's wife, Angie. We were at school together and I happened to see her out with Matthew celebrating last night. I thought perhaps you would like to share your good news with our readers? Everyone loves a good story, such a change from all that constant bad news and as our paper's only a local readership I hoped you would let me do a piece on your lottery win?'

Jenny didn't know what to say. This girl was good, making it sound as if everyone would be so pleased but Malcolm might not like it.

'I'm afraid you've caught me at a bad time Penny, I was just on my way out to work. Could you ring again later, this evening perhaps, when my husband will be home?'

'Certainly Mrs Grainger, I'd be delighted to! So, you're still going to work are you, and your husband?'

'Well nothing's been decided yet, I must go now though.'

'I'll speak to you later then, goodbye and thank you so much for talking to me.'

Jenny was trembling. So the news was out, Angie can't have known they didn't want publicity, or that Malcolm didn't anyway. She'd let him talk to the reporter later, he could make the decision for them.

'Why on earth did Angie have to tell a perfect stranger our business?' Malcolm wasn't pleased to hear about the reporter's phone call.

'She wouldn't mean any harm by it. Matthew probably never thought to tell her to keep it quiet. Anyway, she was an old school friend not a stranger, a nice girl; you can speak to her this evening and decide what to say.'

'I will and I'm going to ring the kids too and ask them to keep quiet about it all.' He went off to make the calls and Jenny went into the kitchen to begin their evening meal wondering why he was so determined not to share their good news. Sometimes she couldn't understand her husband at all.

Malcolm did take the evening phone call from the local reporter and could see how his wife had been cajoled into speaking to her; she was certainly good at her job. To Jenny's surprise he agreed to answer a few questions over the phone and for a photographer to call round the following evening.

'You can be in the photo and the kids if they like, but I'll pass on that one,' he told Jen afterwards. 'Penny already has the details and was going to run a story with or without our input so I thought it better to answer the questions and at least the facts will be right.' Malcolm didn't seem overjoyed at the prospect but was appeased by the fact that it was only a local rag with a small circulation. Jenny kissed him and he smiled, his reactions to this win were certainly enigmatic but his pleasure at her delight and the children's excitement seemed genuine. Family had always come first and last for Malcolm Grainger.

Chapter 5

'And I found sixteen toothbrushes in the tumble drier!' Helen Price didn't know whether to laugh or cry when relating this latest incident. Maggie too hardly knew how to react. If it wasn't so sad it would be quite funny but in reality it was another indication of her father's worsening condition.

'Well what did Dad say about it?' Maggie was trying to understand behaviour which was completely illogical.

'He just grinned at me and patted me on the bottom!'

'Oh Mum!' Maggie had to laugh then picturing her father's actions, simultaneously both hilarious and distressing.

'Mrs McKay at the village shop had wondered why he always bought a toothbrush when he went for his paper but she's never liked to ask your Dad or me, silly woman!'

'She would think it none of her business Mum but sixteen is a bit odd and why would he put them in the tumble drier?'

'Search me. I'm obviously going to have to watch him even more than I already do but the thing is what if he does something dangerous, like trying to light the oven? It's a worry Maggie, it really is.'

'Perhaps it's time to get some help in Mum. You'll make yourself ill if you take on all the responsibility and then what'll happen to Dad?'

'You're right I know but the thought of someone else in my home doesn't sit very easily with me and I don't know how your father would take to a stranger fussing about him.'

It wasn't an easy conversation and one which highlighted to Maggie how useless her own position was to offer any practical help. She relayed the details of the call to Peter later that evening.

'You know that if you want Helen and George to come and live with us that would be fine by me don't you?'

'Oh Peter that's so kind of you and I do appreciate it, but it wouldn't be fair on you.' Peter's health was a constant concern to Maggie. He suffered from Multiple Sclerosis although 'suffer' was not a word they would use to describe it. He kept remarkably well, largely due to the prescription a couple of years ago of a new drug, Gilenya, which seemed to suit him and had almost eradicated the symptoms of the illness to an extent where they lived mainly without thinking about it at all. It was only at times like this that the illness was brought to the forefront of their minds. Peter knew his limitations and lived accordingly with Maggie on hand to remind him to take care if she felt a gentle nudge was needed. She too had thought about the option of having her parents to live with them but the stress this would place on Peter, who worked mainly from home, made the idea untenable and another solution would have to be found.

'I honestly don't think Mum would go along with that anyway, you know how independent she is.'

'Well what about some kind of compromise? Perhaps suggesting they move back to Fenbridge where we'll be on hand to help out when necessary?'

'I had been wondering about that myself and really, if it's going to happen a move would be better sooner rather than later before Dad becomes any worse. It's such an insidious disease, taking away dignity and even changing personalities. At least there's still much of the old George left in him for now, let's hope we can keep that for as long as possible. I'll ring Mum again and make the suggestion then we'll have to look at the options for housing for them.' Before Maggie had chance to do that another possibility occurred to her which she shared with Peter.

'I remember having a client, over a year ago now, whose grandmother was in some kind of sheltered housing. The girl was really impressed with the facility, it was individual bungalows built around a central garden with a warden on site to check up on residents and help when necessary. It's at the other side of town which would be ideal. I'll ask around at work and make some enquiries as to waiting lists and such like. Mum and Dad could still have their independence but have support on hand if needed and they'd be much closer to us of course.'

'Sounds perfect, but first of all ring Helen and sow the seed then we'll take it from there.' Peter liked the idea and hoped his mother in law would too.'

The next morning at work Maggie asked Sue if she knew the name of the sheltered housing complex in Fenbridge. Sue was aware of her friend's concern over her parents and was keen to help if possible.

'I think I know the one you mean but there are others too which the district nurses visit regularly. Leave it with me and I'll catch one of them later and find out for you.'
Maggie thanked her friend. Sue worked on the reception desk in the same health centre where she was based and therefore saw all the nurses coming and going so was well placed to ask around. Sure enough at coffee time Sue knocked on Maggie's door and entered waving a piece of paper in her hand.

'Mission accomplished!' She grinned, handing over three addresses gathered from the nurses.

'I think the one you had in mind is the top one on the list and although they're all quite good that one certainly gets the best recommendations. They probably have websites you could look at to find phone numbers and arrange visits and if you want company I'd happily visit them with you.'

'Sue you are an absolute angel, thank you and I'll probably take you up on that offer. Peter would come but I know he'll only say 'well if you think its okay, it's fine by me.' He does that every time we're looking for something new for the house!'

'Yeah, Alan's a bit like that too. Just shout when you've made some appointments, you know when I'm free.'

Helen had been more receptive to her daughter's idea than Maggie expected, yet another indication of just how worried she was about her husband. The more they had talked about it, the more convinced they both became that it was a good idea so Maggie would make some calls to arrange viewings after her next client.

****

The article appeared in the Friday edition of 'Argos Local' less than a week after the Grainger's life had been turned upside down by their lottery win. It wasn't quite front page but featured on page four under the unoriginal headline 'Eight million pound lottery win for local family.' Underneath was a photograph of Jenny and the children looking rather stiff and posed holding champagne glasses which were actually filled with apple juice and grinning unnaturally at the camera.

'Oh goodness, look at my hair, I must make an appointment to get it styled' was Jenny's first reaction. Malcolm was relieved that they had got the facts right and not printed their address which he had insisted on but rather disappointed that they had printed the amount of the win. He hoped that the matter of publicity would be dropped and they could carry on with their lives with some degree of normality. The money was now sitting in their bank account having been transferred as promised earlier in the week. During his lunch break Malcolm intended to visit the bank and transfer a million pounds into each of their children's accounts. An appointment the following week with a financial advisor had been set up by the lottery company which seemed somewhat early to Jenny, she was still thinking of new ways to spend the money, investing it seemed a tad boring. The lounge was presently cluttered with exotic travel brochures and estate agent leaflets of houses which, Jenny said were only pipe dreams and they didn't have to move unless they both agreed. Her husband however could read between the lines and although saying little on the subject was not entirely against moving house, he was simply anxious that their lives didn't change too much too soon, after all they had always been happy with things the way they were. The following day, Saturday, there was to be another celebration meal, this time with friends as well as family. It seemed as if they had eaten out every day that week and Malcolm longed for a simple meal of egg and chips. On Sunday he would visit his father again and a wave of sadness washed over him as he reflected on the fact that all this new found money could not change his dad's circumstances, there were so many things which money could not buy.

Bill Grainger was still very much aware of current affairs outside of his own small room. He had his little portable television turned on for the news bulletins at least twice a day and although conversations were very one sided, he was always keen to hear local news from those who cared for him. On Friday morning a member of staff had connected the local newspaper article to his patient and brought in a copy of 'Argos Local' which he read out loud with obvious envy. Each word brought a chill to Bill's limp body as his mind raced with the possible ramifications of his son being in the public eye. By the time Malcolm arrived to visit that afternoon, he had mentally lived every possible scenario, none of them good, which could befall his family. His eyes told his son that he knew about the article in the paper and the first words Malcolm spoke to his father were,

'So you've heard about the publicity then?'
A slow blink confirmed it and Malcolm pulled a chair up closer to the bedside, trying to sound optimistic.

'Never mind Dad, it was so long ago, ancient history really and the 'Argos' is just a local paper, it would never reach Liverpool and even if it did, who would connect the name to us now? People have moved on, forgotten, so don't worry now will you?'
Bill tried to smile but as usual only half his face would respond. His son took out the Telegraph, already folded at the crossword page and began to read the clues to his father. Neither man really had the heart to finish the puzzle and very soon Bill began asking about the family. *'Jenny?'* He typed and Malcolm smiled as he related some of his wife's shopping expeditions and described the new spring in her step and some of the more outrageous ideas of how they could use the money. Not all these ideas were selfish though and he laughingly told of her plans to donate money to all the local animal shelters, joking that there were going to be several cats and dogs that would be better looked after than himself if Jenny had her way. Then there were the orphanages overseas that she'd been looking at on the internet. He was delighted and proud that she wanted to use the money for such projects but rather alarmed when she suggested visiting some of these places to see the needs firsthand. It was all very altruistic but Malcolm had never taken to foreign food and even the heat of a British summer was becoming too much for him these days.

She'll settle down' Bill typed and his son smiled in agreement.

'I know Dad and I also know that all this money won't really change my Jen, she's always been one to put others before herself.' As it neared time to say goodbye to his father, Bill became almost agitated and again began to type on his electronic pad. *'Never chance to talk.'*

'Talk about what Dad, the past?'

'Yes, Mum'

'I know. There's so much I don't remember but my memories of Mum are good ones and you always emphasized the positive when I was growing up, that's all I needed to know.'

'My boxes'

'The ones in the attic, what about them?'

'Diaries.'

'I haven't opened those boxes since your stroke. I'm keeping them for when you get better.'

Bill gave his lop sided smile to his only child and typed again,

'Read them.'

'Okay, I'll have a look when I get home but you get some rest now, Sunday afternoons were made for dozing and I've kept you talking far too long.' Squeezing his father's hand, Malcolm left the room and began the journey home wondering why his dad would want him to read those old diaries. He and Jenny had packed them away with various other personal items and stored them in their loft where they remained as a emblem of hope that one day Bill might be able to pick up the threads of a normal life and would need his belongings again.

Chapter 6

Monday mornings were always frantic in the 'Liverpool Mercury' office and that particular dismal, foggy one was no different to any other. Frank Stokes cleared his inbox of the weekend's emails, at least half of them being consigned to the spam folder, and then began the regular trawl of the dozens of local presses, which, very occasionally, proffered some undiscovered gem of a news item. Mostly Frank doubted the wisdom of this task but his editor was adamant that it be done and there was no one on staff who would argue the point with him, least of all Frank, who was the newest recruit to the newsroom. His employment at the 'Mercury' was a temporary situation, a three month trial wrangled only by pulling in several favours owed by ex-colleagues. His previous post at a more prestigious newspaper had come to an abrupt end when he messed up an important assignment, missing the deadline completely and winging the actual content of the report entrusted to him. Frank's brain had then been befuddled by alcohol, the demon drink which he had vowed so often to eradicate from his life. Not only had it cost him his job but his wife and family too, leaving him on the long hard road of proving his worth once again to those who mattered. Thirty two days sober and counting, but the decline in his circumstances was a hard one to swallow and the hard work needed to restore his position was not an appealing thought, he much preferred short cuts to the longer paths in life.

Frank had allotted two hours to this task, two boring hours which needed the assistance of several cups of coffee to keep his mind focussed. All the good stuff was picked up by the nationals and unless it had a local theme was of little interest to his editor who constantly banged on about human interest stories, extremely good news or devastatingly bad, he didn't care which as long as his reporters could make good copy out of it. Already on his fourth cup of coffee, Frank was tiring fast when his eyes rested on a name which sounded familiar, Malcolm Grainger. Not an uncommon name, true, but the age was about right and if it was the Malcolm Grainger he remembered then there could be a story in this. Eight point two million, the reporter whistled, what he could do with that amount of money made his mind burst into life. He wondered what that kind of cash looked like, what it felt like to handle such a sum and an idea began to germinate in his coffee-wired brain. Rather than share the news item he'd discovered, Frank decided to do some investigation of his own and googled the name into his computer. In less than half an hour he had most of the information he needed and now all that was to be done was to square some time out of the office with his supervisor. It grieved him that a woman and one younger than him too, should be supervising an experienced journalist like himself but he had to admit that she was good at her job and would probably rise to the top some day, a good enough reason to keep her on-side. His charm paid off and Kirsty authorized three days out of office with a warning that if he wanted to claim any expenses connected to this 'mystery story' he had better make it something good. It was 11.00 am, Frank had time to return to his flat, do a little more digging on the internet and hopefully by mid afternoon be on the road to Fenbridge.

****

Alice Greenwood kept her promise to visit her mother at home and share a meal. She hadn't been to the house since the funeral when it was filled with neighbours, eating the buffet and talking about her Dad as if he had been some kind of saint. She had been surprised at how many people attended the funeral as they didn't have a huge family so the mourners were mostly friends and work colleagues. The eulogy too had made Ronald Greenwood sound like an exemplary human being. Alice wondered if everyone was elevated to such high stature after death but she was probably biased, more biased than she wanted to be in fact, such mean thoughts were unlike her but she couldn't feel the same sense of loss which her mother obviously did. The house now seemed quiet and empty yet there was still a sense of Ronald's presence there, at least in Alice's mind. Caroline had switched on a few lamps to disperse the early evening gloom and the rooms were comfortably warm but Alice could not feel at home here. True she hadn't lived there for a dozen years or more and visits were only of sufficient frequency to keep the peace yet she had somehow expected to feel differently today and it simply wasn't happening. She loved her mother dearly but the wedge between them was somehow still tangible when Alice had expected it to have disappeared when Ronald died. Still it was early days for them both and she made the effort to be sociable, determined to work on those negative feelings and somehow rebuild a relationship with her mother.

'You always could make great pastry Mum that was delicious, mine's like leather, I obviously need more practice.' They cleared the dishes away and carried their mugs of tea into the lounge.

'Have you been getting out and about at all?' Alice was concerned that Caroline should begin to build some kind of new life for herself.

'Oh, the odd bit of shopping and I met a couple of friends for coffee over the weekend.'

'That's good, you need to make the effort.'

Caroline smiled wistfully,

'I miss your Dad.' The words were solemn then she completely surprised her daughter by asking, 'Don't you?' Alice was stunned, what a provocative question, surely her mother knew better than that.

'Well you can't say we had the closest of relationships can you? Even from being very young I always felt I was a nuisance to Dad, that he somehow didn't want me around.'

'That's not strictly true. Dad did try his best you know.'

'Try his best, what was there to try Mum, I was his daughter!' The anger was rising, 'Surely he should have loved me for who I was? I wasn't the most difficult of children but he couldn't wait to get rid of me, you know that as well as I do!'

'You don't understand, it was difficult for him.'

'Why? I know he had a hard time in the navy but surely he could appreciate his family after all the trouble he saw? Anyway, he left the service after the Falklands didn't he? He wasn't the only one to be traumatized and it was over thirty years ago!'

'Yes but settling back into civilian life wasn't easy, you were just a tiny baby and he wasn't used to children.'

'Not many new parents are. Couldn't he have tried a bit harder? You always did defend him Mum but why? He was the adult, I was the child but I don't remember any genuine affection from him ever. My only memories are all of being in the wrong, not doing the right thing whether at school or at home. Would it have been too much to ask of my own father to have found something in me that he could be proud of? And now that he's dead I'm feeling guilty again, I've even started seeing a counsellor at the surgery. He's still making me feel as if I've done something wrong!'

Angry tears were spilling over, words had been said which couldn't be taken back and Alice both regretted and was glad to have spoken them. A few moments of silence seemed to cool the room. Caroline was pale and thoughtful but neither woman knew what to say next. Eventually Caroline spoke in measured even tones,

'Perhaps there is something you should know. Your Dad tried with you he really did and I don't want you to remember him with such negative feelings as you so obviously do, he wasn't a bad man at all. Maybe I should have told you before but again it wouldn't have been fair on your Dad...'

'There you go again, defending him Mum! What about me, what is it that I should know?'

'When... your Dad came back from the Falklands I was already nearly three months pregnant with you.'

'So what?'

'He'd been on a tour of duty for four months Alice. You weren't his baby.' Caroline was still ashen and if she hadn't already been seated would most likely have collapsed. They had been the hardest words she'd ever had to say to anyone. Over the years she'd often considered telling Alice, thinking she had a right to know or that it would help her daughter to understand Ronald's position but courage had failed, until now. Somehow it had become vital that Alice's memory of the man she had called father was not one of a bully or a bad man. Caroline owed that much to Ronald at least. The silence seemed an eternity with both women unable to think of the right words to say. Eventually Alice broke into the quietness.

'So, are you saying you had an affair while Dad was away fighting in the Falklands conflict?' The words sounded accusing; understandably so and Caroline hardly knew how to answer. She was used to defending her husband... but not herself.

'I wouldn't actually describe it as an affair, no.'

'Just a one night stand then? That's perfect!' Alice stood up, grabbed her coat from the back of the chair and ran out of the front door, slamming it as hard as she could as if that simple act would make her feel better. It did not.

Chapter 7

The attic was predictably dusty. No one had been up there since last Christmas when the decorations had been retrieved for their annual appearance. Malcolm wasn't one for hoarding things and apart from the Christmas tree and assorted ornaments, it housed only the boxes containing his father's personal belongings. It seemed intrusive opening them now. They had been sealed a couple of months after Bill's stroke when it became obvious that he would not be returning to his little rented house at least for some time. When they cleared the house out most of the furniture was given away and only personal items like books and photographs were kept, among which were half a dozen leather bound diaries. Malcolm remembered seeing his Dad writing regularly in these books with his neat script, a fountain pen being his choice of implement. Bill had been the town librarian in his working life, a fitting occupation for a man who so loved the written word to read and to write. His job had included purchasing new stock and his wife often remarked that he had read almost all of the books he bought on the library's behalf. Memories seemed to come to life from the dust as Mal opened the first couple of boxes, ancient photographs from his grandparents' day lay yellowing in an album barely held together by its crumbling spine. Other images were encased in ornate frames, dated pictures recording his boyhood which stopped abruptly after his eighth birthday. It all came flooding back to mind and tears stung his eyes at the inevitable recollections. A tinted photograph of his mother, Mary, made him gasp momentarily as she smiled up at him, carefree and beautiful, the image of her that he liked to hold on to. Gently placing the photo back on top of the others he moved on to the next box, finding there what he was looking for yet not really wanting to find. Reluctantly he took the diaries downstairs and after wiping away the dust from the cracked leather covers, opened the first one.

June 1st 1967

What a sad and strange summer this is turning out to be, I can't believe the doctor is right about Mary. She looks her usual self, a little tired perhaps but then caring for her mother as well as Malcolm and I must be taking its toll... but cancer, no, surely not, please God no! Perhaps I just don't want to believe, don't want to imagine life without my beloved wife. The day we learned this news was the worst day of my life so far, yet somewhere inside of me I have to acknowledge that it is only a portent of an inevitably worse day to come. Cancer, such an ugly word synonymous with death, my beloved Mary has ovarian cancer and will not be with us much longer. Such a hateful, insidious type of cancer which has remained undetected until now it is too late to treat. Typically Mary had ignored any early symptoms, brushing them away as simply feeling 'under the weather'. She has such a beautiful nature and is one of life's givers, never a taker, never one to focus on herself. Embracing the role of wife and mother, she has always lavished her love and attention, (which to my shame I often took for granted,) on me and our son. When her own mother took ill, Mary waited on her too, a caring daughter for whom nothing was too much trouble. Even when Joan became bed ridden, Mary insisted on her living with us, caring for her every need with only an hour's help each day from a woman who comes to help bathe Joan, a task too difficult for one, especially when the patient can offer no help herself. For over a year we have watched Joan's condition deteriorate. Bed sores and ulcers becoming a constant source of pain, resulting eventually in the amputation of her left leg, a low point for us all. But Mary remained cheerful, lifting her mother's mood and somehow managing to care for Malcolm and I without either of us feeling in the slightest way neglected. She is the heart and soul of our family, the very life blood which keeps us happy and content, her love is an almost tangible presence throughout our home. How will I ever manage without her?

For Mary, the diagnosis typically focussed her thoughts on her family rather than herself. She began to prepare us and we talked late into every night about a future I did not want to contemplate, a future which did not include my wife. She made plans and I could see the agony in her eyes as she talked about our son growing up without a mother; he was not yet eight years old and still in need of maternal love and support.

'Don't be afraid to hug and kiss him.' She instructed, adding with a smile, 'Just not in front of his friends!' But it's a seemingly impossible task to be both mother and father to our child, I feel so utterly inadequate. And then when the doctor broke the news that we had only three months left at the most, I nearly crumbled. Mary however has continued her planning and instruction, now deciding that Malcolm and I should, for some reason, move right away from Liverpool.

'A fresh start in a smaller town,' she says, 'Away from all the memories.' For myself I don't want to consider any kind of life without her, yet she remains so strong, willing that strength into me for Malcolm's sake. So now I'm writing these feeble words in the hope that expressing my feelings on paper will bring some degree of release from the utter helplessness and overwhelming sadness which is at present my constant companion. Mary's positivity should inspire me but I lack her strength and selflessness. Each day is one step nearer to our parting; is it possible to prepare for such an event?

Malcolm, reading about his own history from the perspective of his father and to some degree his mother too, was near to tears. Naturally he too had memories but they were sketchy and jumbled and not the sort of thing Malcolm had ever wanted to think about. It was clear that if he continued to read his father's diaries many of those partial memories would be completed. Did he want this? Obviously reading the content of these dusty tomes was his father's wish so perhaps the right thing to do was to trust this man who had never let him down in the past. He turned the page.

June 10th 1967
What a change in such a few days. Mary, my determined, strong wife, is obviously suffering but stubbornly refuses to slow down. She has lost weight which she could ill afford and her face is so pale and drawn but as always there is not a word of complaint and all thoughts are of those whom she loves. Joan is at a low point too, knowing that your only child will not outlive you must be hard to bear, it's unnatural, so very wrong. I worry about what will happen to the old lady when Mary's strength fails... which is beginning already. As usual Mary tells me not to worry, that things will work out in the end, but how can they? And I am so weak when I should be the strong one, how pathetic to be feeling sorry for myself when Mary is so ill yet so positive! She speaks confidently as if truly believing that we will all survive without her and even hinting at a plan which is forming in her mind, something she says she must do soon while she has the strength...

The doorbell rang, bringing Malcolm back to the present day. He had been in the attic far too long and Jenny would wonder what on earth he was doing. Climbing down the ladders and brushing the dust from his clothing, Malcolm found Jenny in the kitchen, happily chatting to their neighbour, a woman who had suddenly begun to desire their company far more than ever before. He was however reassured that Jenny wasn't taken in by this woman's fawning when his wife turned towards him and winked with a rather mischievous look on her face. He grinned and left them to their chatter while he went to catch the news on the television.

****

Frank booked into a cheap B & B, the only requirement, other than the price, was that it had internet connection, like most journalists he was lost without this link to the wider world. Tonight he would take a look around Fenbridge which shouldn't take long as it appeared to be a fairly quiet little town, hardly comparable to Liverpool, which of course would be why Malcolm Grainger's father had chosen to move here. As predicted, an hour walking the town centre streets was all that was needed to get the measure of the place after which Frank found a cafe and ordered a full all-day breakfast with a mug of tea. The greasy bacon and runny egg were welcome but not healthy, the tea washed them down nicely then he paid the bill and returned to the B & B to plan the way forward on this little mission. Before leaving home Frank had printed off several old newspaper articles from the summer of 1967, although how he would use them was yet to be decided. The first priority was to find out where Malcolm Grainger lived which shouldn't be much of a problem as he was bound to be on the electoral roll and surely there were not too many men with the same name in such a small town. Ten minutes later he had all the information he needed. It amazed Frank that in these days of data protection, just a few clicks of the computer mouse could reveal so much about a person. He discounted Wikipedia which wanted to lead him on the trail of a Zimbabwean cricketer of the same name and found that there were two Malcolm Graingers listed in Fenbridge. This presented no confusion at all as the age range placed one candidate in the twenty five to thirty five age bracket and the second between fifty five and sixty five. Bingo, he had found his man; Grainger was the same age as Frank. The site, as well as revealing the address, also gave information about court judgements, other residents of the same address and even the price they had paid for their property. Sadly there were no court judgements recorded for Malcolm Grainger which could have been the icing on Frank's cake, but the other occupant was listed as Jennifer Grainger, further confirmation that this was the right man as Jenny had been featured in the 'Argos Local' interview which began Frank's quest, or what he now liked to think of as his treasure hunt. With the information to hand and nothing more to do that evening, the immediate temptation was to wander across to the pub opposite and have a drink or two but Frank held fast to the sobriety achieved of late and besides, he needed to keep a clear head. He was planning on the hoof but would try to get some sleep and figure out the best way to make contact in the morning. Sleep didn't come easily. Counting sheep never worked for Frank so he tried his own version and eventually nodded off counting fifty pound notes.

Chapter 8

Maggie's room offered a temporary oasis from Alice's confused and agitated state of mind. Since the visit to her mother's, which had ended so badly, she had relived their conversation over and over again, trying to make sense of this shocking revelation. In some ways the discovery did make sense. It explained Ronald's lack of affection but raised even more questions about who her father really was and if Ronald, (Alice could no longer think of him as a father) could not accept her, why had he remained married to Caroline? Alice blurted out this recent development to Maggie, hardly stopping to draw breath and now sat back in the chair and took in the surroundings. The room was warm and tidy, no clutter on any of the surfaces and a fresh lemon scent freshened the air. Alice thought it reflected the counsellor's own life although she knew virtually nothing about the woman but somehow the atmosphere drew her in, it seemed to represent what she wished her own world could be, neat, calm and uncomplicated. Some chance of that now, Alice almost wished her mother had not told her.

'This must have come as quite a shock?' Maggie spoke quietly. Alice met her eyes and nodded solemnly.

'It has. I don't know why Mum told me. Ronald's dead now so what purpose does it serve? If anything it's given me an understanding of why he treated me so badly but on the other hand it's changed my perception of Mum. Why do that now?'

'It's almost impossible to understand people's motives for the things they do when we don't know the full circumstances.'

'But Mum could have kept quiet! I was beginning to think that we could build a closer relationship now that Ronald's dead but any chance of that is ruined now. All these years I've struggled to understand why the man I thought of as my Dad didn't like me and now I've found out it was her fault, not his.'

'I can understand why you feel this way Alice. Perhaps you need to talk to your mother again particularly as you've both had some time and space to think things over. Could doing that help the way you're feeling?'

'At the moment I don't want to see her but I know I can't avoid the issue forever. I'll think about it. I suppose I did leave rather abruptly so there may be more I need to hear. Heaven forbid that there are any more skeletons in the cupboard!'

'Last week you began by telling me all about the funeral and how you were feeling about Ronald's death. A new issue seems to have come into the equation now. Do you think looking back to your childhood and your relationship with your mother could help to make sense of this?' It sounded logical to Alice and something which certainly wouldn't be particularly taxing or upsetting, so, taking a deep breath she began to recall childhood memories relating to her mother. Concentrating on the good times relaxed Alice and a faint smile played on her lips at the memory of some of those happy occasions which had been undoubtedly of her mother's making. The picture building up was one of more good times than bad and it became obvious that it had been Caroline Greenwood's effort and energies which had instigated these. To a great extent, Caroline had been a shield from her husband's shortcomings as a parent. Whatever the circumstances of Alice's conception, her mother appeared to have done everything possible for the girl whilst having to deal with her husband's negativity.

'Maggie, have you deliberately led me down this path?' Alice's puzzled face searched for an answer.

'What do you mean?'

'Well, the more I think and talk about my childhood the more I can see what a positive role Mum played. Was that your intention?'

'No Alice, please don't think that. I wouldn't try to engineer that kind of scenario. My reason for asking if you wanted to go down that line of thought was as an attempt to help you remember your past as it really was. If your mother is coming out of this in a better light, that's your own conclusion, drawn from the memories stored in your mind. I wouldn't try to influence your thoughts or feelings in any way whatsoever. Last week it seemed to help to look at your relationship with your father and I hope applying the same principle with your mother has also helped today, has it?'

'I think so. Perhaps I was too hard on Mum but I'm curious as to why she's told me all this now. Maybe it's another attempt to show Ronald in a more positive light, goodness knows she's played referee for nearly all of their married life. It does of course bring up other issues, like who my father really is. I've even begun to look at men of around the same age, wondering if they could be my biological dad, silly isn't it?'

'Not at all; it's a huge shock to find out that you are not biologically who you thought you were but it doesn't change the person you are today. Yes, we inherit genes from our birth parents but upbringing has much to do with the finished product too and the experiences of your childhood play a significant part as well. You are still Alice and always will be. Again, if you need to know more, your mother will be the best starting point. I hope that looking at the positive parenting she's provided over the years has helped to take away some of the hurt and anger you initially felt? A calm dialogue is always more productive than one conducted in anger.'

'You're right, I didn't give Mum a chance to explain I was so mad. Perhaps a gentle approach will be better, it must have taken some courage to admit what she did and I didn't see it like that at the time.'

'We're all so much wiser after the event but from the little I've learned about your mum, it sounds as if it's worth trying again don't you think?'

'Absolutely.' Alice appeared thoughtful and Maggie, who was learning more about the girl's background wondered about her client's life in the present.

'We've done some looking back at relationships but what about the present Alice, is there someone in your life who you're close to and you could possibly confide in?'

'There are a few good friends who I see socially from time to time but if you're asking about boyfriends then no, there's no one special. I've dated a few times in the past but find it difficult to trust any potential boyfriends. I always visualise my future as a spinster, an old maid, but at least I'll only have myself to please.'

This was exactly what Maggie had expected. Alice's role model of marriage was a flawed one and it was understandable that she wasn't going to find relationships with the opposite sex easy to sustain.

'And are you happy with that version of your future?' She ventured.

'I don't know really. I haven't reached thirty one without being attracted to men but I always get scared off too easily. My mind races ahead to a scene of domesticity which makes me panic, that's when I usually end the relationship, before it can get in any way serious.'

'Are you assuming that this 'scene of domesticity' will turn out like your parents marriage?'

'Yes, that's certainly how it appears in my mind.'

'Don't you know any couples who have happy marriages?'

'Well, some that appear happy, but who can tell? Many people saw Mum's marriage as a happy one but there were huge cracks in it. To be honest, I'd like to believe in 'happy ever after' romances but that probably only exist in novels.'

'So are you saying you don't think romantic love exists or that it's just not for you?'

'Probably both. Gosh that sounds so cynical doesn't it? I simply can't see myself in the role of the happy little wife, peacekeeper, domestic servant and all that.'

'Is that the way you view your mother's marriage or marriage in general?' Maggie was pushing Alice a little, trying gently to nudge her into thinking about herself and what the future could be rather than living a life which has been coloured by the perception of her mother's life. Alice sighed,

'Do you know Maggie, this is all so confusing. Having previously thought to know my own mind, now I'm not so sure. As soon as I could afford to I moved away from home. I have a job I love but actually when pushed to think seriously about it I have no goals or ambitions for the future. That makes me a bit pathetic don't you think?'

'Absolutely not; you're thinking these things through now, here with me. Very often it takes an event such as this to make us take stock in life. Perhaps Ronald's death and your relationship with your mother is the catalyst which has made you explore your own feelings and beliefs. You've embarked on a journey in a way and hopefully you'll discover who Alice really is along the way.'

****

'It's over there on the right.' Sue pointed to a pair of ornate wrought iron gates standing open. They had the name 'The Lawns' interweaved in the design and a rather pretty clock set above an archway through which they drove. A tree lined drive led into to a square lawned garden edged with flower beds on one side and car parking spaces on the other. Maggie drove slowly to a parking bay, adhering to the five mile an hour speed limit and they both got out of the car to take in the surroundings. It was late October but the flower beds were still a mass of colour with roses and winter pansies neatly planted in the well turned soil. Recent rain had caused some of the petals to drop and an elderly man, whom Sue was convinced could be a great Father Christmas, was picking them up from the ground. He smiled and nodded, touching an imaginary cap as they approached to ask directions to the office.

'You'll find the warden in the end bungalow. It's not so much an office as her home and the car's there so I think you'll find Audrey's in.' He resumed picking up the fallen petals as Maggie and Sue made their way to the warden's home.

'Makes it sound like a prison doesn't it, 'warden'

'It does but she seemed very nice on the phone and should be in, I made an appointment.'

Audrey answered the door immediately having seen the visitors arrive. From the position of the bungalow there would probably be very little that this lady would miss.

'Come in, come in!' Audrey invited with a welcoming smile. Maggie introduced herself and Sue before taking the seats they were offered. The bungalow was immaculate with magnolia walls, a large bay window and rather chintzy furnishings, the most comfortable looking chair already occupied by a large, sleeping ginger tom cat. The visitors tried not to stare but they were both dying to look around, Maggie already had a good feeling about the place and was ready with questions about its running, rents and most importantly, availability. Audrey seemed to sense their interest and sat opposite them, hands palms upwards in a gesture of openness.

'Okay, shoot.' She said which made Sue laugh out loud, so incongruous were the words with the appearance of this rather prim lady. Audrey had more than her fair share of middle aged spread and her grey perm was tightly compacted on a rather large head. Her eyebrows had been plucked to extinction, replaced by arched pencil lines which gave her an almost startled look. It was hard to determine Audrey's age but Sue would have guessed late fifties or even early sixties. Maggie began to ask questions, receiving ready answers and all the relevant information they needed. The complex had been built with money bequeathed from a local benefactor after the First World War. It was run by a committee who set the rents, approved new residents using a scale of points awarded as to each applicant's circumstances and kept the fabric of the buildings in good repair. The last point was obvious to them both from what they had already seen but Maggie still had one or two questions relating to the upkeep of each bungalow.

'Are the residents responsible for the decoration of their own home?'

'Generally, yes. When a bungalow becomes available the new resident is encouraged to decorate before moving in. If the bungalow is in a poor condition we can commission decoration, at least to a certain standard, and the incomers can add to this as they wish. I think the best thing we can do is to have a look around and I'll answer any questions as they arise.' Audrey invited them to see her own bungalow first.

'It's quite typical,' she explained, 'and then we can go and see number sixteen which is the only unoccupied home at present.' The cosy lounge with its wide bay window was the largest room off a small square hallway. A compact kitchen, a shower room and a double bedroom were all that was left to see. It was certainly small in comparison to Helen and George's present home but practical and as all the bungalows were set around the garden Maggie could imagine her dad enjoying the views from the window or even pottering in the garden as seemed to be encouraged. Audrey led the way to number sixteen and Maggie whispered to Sue,

'It's lovely, what do you think?'

'Yes, I like it, think I'll put my name down while I'm here!'

Maggie nudged her friend then asked Audrey,

'It's a lovely setting and I can see it must be very popular. Is there a long waiting list?'

'I wouldn't say long and as I explained we use a points system to allocate the homes. From what you tell me of your parent's circumstances they would be certainly be eligible but the committee has the final say, I can't predict their decisions.'

Number sixteen was slightly larger than Audrey's.

'This is one of our doubles' she explained. 'The same design with slightly larger rooms and hallways which many residents use as a dining area.'

Maggie could see how this would work and liked the feel of the whole place. It would certainly mean downsizing but that would also mean less work for her mother and more time for Helen to give to George. It was also on a bus route into the town centre and only about fifteen minutes drive from Maggie's own home.

'I'm certainly impressed Audrey and I'm sure Mum and Dad will be too. Can I make an application on their behalf of do they need to come in person?'

'I can give you the forms to fill in now if you like and you can come again when it's convenient for your parents too.' The warden beamed at the visitors, proud of her domain and Maggie felt sure they had found the right place. She and Sue left with the application forms, promising to be in touch to arrange another look around in the not too distant future.

'Well, I think that's certainly spoiled any chances of liking another place, it's perfect, I only hope they'll have a bungalow available soon.' Maggie could envisage her parents living there and it would be such a relief to have them nearby.

'I rather think they'll have a high turnover of residents, after all most of them don't move in until they're over seventy, life expectancy isn't too long then is it?'

'Oh Sue, don't say that, it sounds like I'm wishing ill on some poor soul!'

'Hmm.' Sue smiled.

When Maggie returned to work she made a quick call to her mother to tell her about the visit.

'Hi Mum, how's everything going?'

Rather than the usual chirpy answer Helen normally gave, she burst into tears, leaving Maggie feeling helpless and horrified. Things must be bad for her mother to lose her composure like that. After a few minutes, Helen quietened and began to apologise.

'I'm so sorry love, it's just a particularly bad day. Your Dad didn't sleep well and he's been like a bear with a sore head all day. He's frustrated of course when he can't remember what it is he wanted to say and he even threw a book on the floor and stormed out into the garden which is so unlike him.'

'Oh Mum, I wish I was there with you. Look, is Dad around, can I talk to him?'

'He's still in the garden but I'll call him if you think it will do any good.'

Maggie listened as the door opened and Helen called her husband.

'Hello?' George sounded agitated.

'Hi Dad, I was hoping you and Mum would come down for a few days, stay with us as a little break for you both, what do you think?'

'Who is this?' again his voice was brusque.

'It's Maggie, your daughter.' She was close to tears herself by this time.

'No, my daughter lives in Yorkshire, you can't speak to her now, she's not here.' He passed the phone back to Helen and the slam of the kitchen door could be heard over the line.

'Pack a bag Mum for both of you.' Maggie instructed, 'Peter and I will be coming up this evening to bring you down here for a few days.'

There was no protest from Helen Price, only a barely perceptible sigh of relief.

Chapter 9

Frank Stokes had not slept well at all. The mattress was lumpy with a distinct smell of something he didn't wish to think about and the room was like an icebox. Added to that, a multitude of thoughts were keeping his brain active, resulting in a bad night all round. Breakfast did nothing to improve his mood, overcooked eggs and fried bread was the offering, with weak, barely warm coffee. It was tempting to approach Malcolm Grainger immediately, prolonging this trip to Fenbridge was far from an appealing thought, but he would proceed with caution and so, twenty minutes later Frank was sitting opposite the Grainger's house ostensibly reading the local paper but actually waiting to see his quarry. It was early, not yet eight o'clock, which Frank hoped would be early enough to see the Graingers leaving for work, assuming they were still both working as the article in the paper had suggested. The streets were wet from the overnight rain and a grey sky indicated more was on the way. Suddenly the door opened and a woman, obviously Jenny Grainger, stepped out and walked quickly down the road. Frank grinned, this could be his chance. Malcolm would be alone, what a stroke of luck, he would approach him now, strike while the iron's hot and all that. Perhaps he could complete his mission and be out of this dull little town today after all.

The doorbell chimed some ridiculously happy tune and heavy footsteps began clumping down the stairs. Malcolm opened the door and looked enquiringly at his visitor. Neither man spoke for an instance until Malcolm asked,

'Can I help?'

Frank smirked as he looked at his old classmate.

'Well I suppose you've aged pretty well all things considered.'

'I'm sorry, do I know you?'

'Frank Stokes, Liverpool Road Infants?' He had the nerve to offer his hand to a rather shocked looking Malcolm. 'Well, aren't you going to ask me in so we can reminisce about old times then?'

Malcolm stood back as this unexpected visitor almost pushed his way through the open door. Nausea enveloped Malcolm, with a mixture of fear and apprehension as he closed the door quietly before following Frank into the lounge. Someone from his past resurfacing at this particular point in time was surely not good news.

'Nice place, things must be going well for you pal?'

'I don't think we were ever pals. Perhaps you could get to the point and just tell me why you're here?' Although asking the words, Malcolm knew the answer. His mind was hauling him back in time until he could see himself cowering in the playground as the class bully stood over him demanding his dinner money. Looking into the face of the man before him now, it was easy to recognise that same bully with the same smug expression. The memories fast forwarded to a later incident, probably the last time he saw the boy Frank Stokes, when the intimidation had escalated and Stokes was actually kicking Malcolm, showering him with verbal and physical blows,

'Your mother's going to hang, did you know? Hanged until she's dead and good riddance too!' The words were delivered in a childish sing-song voice and even now were embedded somewhere in the depths of his mind, struggling to the fore like a haunting, recurring nightmare which won't release its icy grip. Frank had seated himself on the sofa with an arm stretched along the back tapping his fingers as if he hadn't a care in the world.

'Not even an offer of coffee for an old friend?'

'Like I said, we were never friends so just get to the point will you. I'm assuming this isn't simply a social call?'

'You always were the bright one and yes, you're right, we have a little business to attend to.' Stokes expression made Malcolm want to punch him but instead he simply nodded, recognising that the class bully had not changed in the least, only these days the stakes were much more than just a child's dinner money.

'So, you've graduated to blackmail have you?' he asked, sitting down himself in fear that his trembling legs wouldn't support him.

'That's such a dirty word Malcolm. Shall we just call it a financial arrangement; after all you've got more than enough money for your needs. Look upon it as sharing your wealth, it sounds so much more altruistic and I can assure you I'm a very worthy cause!'

'And if I refuse?'

Stokes stood up and deliberately made a show of walking to the window where Jenny displayed the cherished family photographs. Picking up a silver framed photo of Matthew, Kate and their families he asked,

'Do they know about your past?'

'Actually they do.' Malcolm lied and felt his face flush as Frank laughed out loud.

'I don't believe you. Such a happy little family, are these your children and grandchildren? Do you think they'll understand the word matricide? That granny and great granny was a murderer? No, they don't know do they? But even if they did I'm sure the local newspaper would be interested. Human interest stories are always in demand and a lottery winner with a secret past is quite a scoop, believe me.'

'That's your version, not mine.'

'Ah but it's the truth isn't it? Murder is murder no matter what fancy name you think up for it. I happen to have the facts right here.' He pulled a crumpled envelope from his raincoat pocket, unfolded it and withdrew copies of the old newspaper cuttings. Malcolm stared in horror. He had never seen these before, Bill Grainger had been careful to keep any newspapers out of the house but Malcolm could remember their home being besieged by reporters. His Dad had closed all the curtains and refused to answer the door; they had stayed inside, the three of them, for three whole days until the reporters gave up and eventually left. Dad had made it into some kind of game for Malcolm but he remembered being bored by not being allowed outside. Even footie in the back yard was banned in case some enterprising photographer scaled the back gate. It had been a confusing and frightening experience for a seven year old boy but there was worse to come.

'I think you'd better leave!' Malcolm stood up and moved towards the door.

'So soon? We've hardly had time to catch up on the good old days, well maybe bad old days for you. Now, don't be so hasty and I'll tell you what happens next. I'm going to leave those cuttings with you, you might learn a thing or two yourself and I'll come back in a couple of days, about the same time?'

Malcolm was torn. The very thought of blackmail abhorred him but to let Jenny and the children find out about this was frightening too. He needed time so he remained silent as he opened the door for Stokes to leave.

'We'll speak soon then?' the unwelcome visitor said, whistling happily as he walked up the garden path.

Malcolm retreated into the house and slumped onto the sofa. His legs were weak, he felt sick and his whole body was shaking. Stokes had only been inside for about fifteen minutes but it was enough to throw Malcolm's world into complete turmoil. He put his head back and closed his eyes; why hadn't he ever told Jenny about the past? The answer was obvious of course, he was a coward. It had been easier to pretend it had never happened, after all it wasn't the sort of thing which came up in polite conversation, 'Oh by the way, did you know that my mother killed my grandmother?' Bill had never spoken of their past and Malcolm had taken his lead, the easy way as always. Avoid unpleasantness, avoid confrontation, don't rock the boat...he was so good at that, but now it seemed as if the boat was being rocked from outside the family and he hadn't a clue what to do about it. Making towards the kitchen to put the kettle on, he remembered work. He couldn't possibly go now; he would have to ring in sick, which was perfectly true he felt sick to his stomach and was shaking all over. After making the call he poured boiling water onto his tea bag and stirred the mug thinking that was exactly what Jenny would do in an emergency, make a cup of tea! For the first time Malcolm really wished they had not won the lottery. Life had been so uncomplicated, mundane and peaceful. They had enough to get by and were happy too, why on earth he had even bought a ticket now escaped him, he should have thought about what winning would really mean. It occurred to him that he hadn't even asked Stokes how much he wanted to keep silent but it was immaterial. The thought of paying a blackmailer was totally abhorrent but then so was the alternative. For a brief moment Malcolm considered visiting his father but knew in his heart that the old man wasn't strong enough to take such a shock. Bill Grainger had spent years protecting his son, now it was Malcolm's turn to protect his father. For once he would have to face things himself, there were forty eight hours in which to make a decision and he would use the time wisely. Seeking peace and solitude, Malcolm pulled down the loft ladders and went up to continue reading his father's journal.

June 18th 1967
Mary seems but a shadow of her former self. She appears to take up less space in this world every day and I can see the time when she will leave us altogether coming far too quickly. I feel so useless with no idea of how we will cope without her.

June 20th 1967
Why did I not see it coming! I must be blind as well as stupid! Mary had hinted at a 'plan' yet I remained so ignorant. Joan had reached out to embrace both myself and Malcolm last night with tears in her eyes which I assumed to be from the stress of the life we were living. Now I realise that she was saying goodbye! When had they hatched this plot, for they had obviously colluded in this? I found Mary sitting beside Joan early this morning. It appeared that Joan had died several hours earlier. I called the doctor's surgery before persuading Mary to come downstairs. Even then I didn't suspect the truth and assumed my mother-in-law had passed away naturally. It was only when the doctor arrived and began to ask questions that I realised something was not quite right. Yes, he told us, Joan was elderly and in pain but he was surprised by her death, apparently her heart was strong and she had been responding well to the morphine tablets. As he hadn't seen Joan for several days he said there would have to be a post mortem examination. Mary sobbed quietly when the doctor left as I held her close, the only way I knew to comfort her. Malcolm was in school, unaware as yet that his grandmother had died.

Mary then told me everything. When she had been diagnosed with cancer and realised how little time there was left, her thoughts turned to her mother as well as to Malcolm and me. She confided her fears to Joan, fears as to how we would all cope without her and that was when Joan asked Mary to do one last thing for her. They began to reduce the number of morphine tablets which Joan took each day, secreting the excess away until the time was right. Mary had begun to believe that the estimation of three months more to live was overly optimistic so together they chose the time while there was still strength to do it. How could I have been so blind not to have seen what was happening! I don't even know how I feel about it. Horrified? Stunned? Shocked? Yes, perhaps all of these and more. Mary is so quiet, so sad. I can see her grief, she loved her mother dearly but was it right to have helped her to take her own life, if indeed this was what it was? So many questions, so many emotions, I almost envy Joan that she is out of it all now, at peace...

Malcolm laid the diary down, remembering so well the day his grandmother died although he didn't find out until after school, by which time her body had been removed and his parents were making an effort to carry on normally. Mary was in the kitchen making tea and his father took him into the lounge to break the news. Mal remembered running upstairs to his grandmother's room hoping it wasn't true and that he might find her there smiling at him as was always the case. But the bed was empty with the sheets and the pretty flowered eiderdown gone too. An open window made the room feel cold even though it was a hot, balmy day. He remembered his anguish and the hot tears streaming down his face, his much loved grandmother had gone and Malcolm felt so alone, but more than that, he was frightened for the future. It was the first time the boy had faced the reality of death and it brought an uncertainty to life which he had never experienced before. If one constant could depart from his life so suddenly, anything could happen and Malcolm's childhood was changed forever.

Chapter 10

Before leaving work Maggie phoned Peter to explain what she had done. Peter was in his office, a large room at the end of the sprawling bungalow, sorting out the numerous cupboards and shelves which held the tools of his trade as an architect and also the artist's materials for his more recent hobby of painting. The office was lit by two large windows, one full length, matching the windows in the lounge and the other a skylight window which afforded extra light to work and paint by. The largest proportion of the space was occupied by a rack and pinioned drawing board which nestled at an angle on a long desk. Ample wide shelving held the rolls of drafting film and cupboards housed technical drawing equipment and the more recent acquisitions of oil paint, watercolour pencils, various canvases and brushes. On an easel beneath the skylight window, Peter's work in progress was displayed, a watercolour painting of the view from their house. He found painting to be relaxing and a pleasant way to fill the free time reducing his working hours had provided. Art had always been a favourite lesson at school but apart from sketching the occasional landscape or portrait, he had never seriously indulged his hobby. Maggie encouraged this interest and praised his talent, although perhaps through rose tinted glasses. It was no problem to break off the task and make the necessary journey to Scotland and within fifteen minutes of Maggie arriving home they had set off. During the drive periods of reflective silence were broken as Maggie remembered things she wanted to relate from the telephone conversation earlier.

'Dad didn't recognise my voice.'

'I know love, it's just part of the illness, he'll most probably know you when we arrive.'

'I certainly hope so. I don't think I've fully understood what Mum's been going through, she sounded worn out.'

'Well, you did the right thing by insisting they come to us. Not much further now. Thank goodness they didn't retire to the Outer Hebrides. Tell me more about this housing complex. Do you think it could be the right one?'

'Yes, it seems perfect, a little small if anything so they'd certainly have to downsize but that's not a bad thing really. The only problem could be availability, there's one bungalow free at the moment but I think it might have already been allocated. I've got the application forms which I was going to fill in myself but now Mum can do them and hopefully we'll be able to have another look around altogether.'

Helen Price certainly looked tired and Maggie was sure she had lost weight. As mother and daughter greeted each other Peter detected a few tears welling up in both women. George was in the bathroom.

'He's been in there ages, supposedly packing his shaving gear. I'll tell him you're here.' Helen went to knock on the bathroom door as Peter began to load the car with their luggage. Maggie, needing to do something practical, went into the kitchen to check the fridge only to find that her ever organised mother had already removed anything perishable and packed it into a cool bag to take with them. George Price's voice could be heard coming from the bathroom and Maggie braced herself for what might happen when he saw her.

'Maggie! What are you doing here?' He was smiling and she breathed a huge sigh of relief. Helen reminded her husband,

'I told you George, we're going for a little holiday to Maggie and Peter's, they've come to pick us up.'

'Oh, you needn't have come all this way, I could have driven!'

Mother and daughter exchanged a knowing glance, George hadn't driven for most of the last year, the car was firmly locked away in the garage and Helen had hidden the key. Maggie hugged him, holding on for several seconds in an effort to comfort herself as well as him.

'All packed up!' Peter appeared at the kitchen door, smiling. 'Are these to go as well?' He nodded towards the cool bag and a couple of carriers on the table.

'Yes, thanks. It's just the perishables from the fridge and a few cakes and scones I had in the freezer.'

'Mum, you don't need to bring those; we do have food at home you know.' But Helen did need to contribute in some small way simply to retain her sense of normality and a degree of being in charge of a situation which was rapidly developing into one over which she had no control at all.

Within minutes they were off, the cottage locked up and prepared for an indefinite period of absence. Maggie sensed the sadness in her mother's face which was echoed in her own heart. Alzheimer's was such a cruel disease, taking a person away piece by piece and the extent or outcome was impossible to predict.

It was dark when they arrived in Fenbridge but their house was warm and comforting as they entered, with Ben adding his own enthusiastic welcome to their visitors. Maggie hadn't taken the time to prepare the guest room before they left and Peter suggested that she and Helen might like to make up the bed while he made coffee and kept an eye on George. The dog was in his element, fussing around George's feet, tail wagging in complete little circles as his back was scratched just where he liked. Peter smiled, Ben would be good for his father in law and Tara too when in the right mood. When the coffee was ready and he had buttered some of the scones he'd found in one of the carrier bags, Peter called Maggie. They settled in the lounge, an almost tangible tension hanging over them all, the immediate future was an unknown quantity and they knew that they would have to live one day at a time.

'These scones are lovely Helen but I can warm some soup if you'd like something else?'

'No thanks, we had a sandwich just before you came. Have some yourselves though.'

Maggie shook her head, although they hadn't eaten since lunchtime she had no appetite. Peter contented himself with another scone. George ate in silence with one hand resting on Ben who had jumped up beside him on the sofa, correctly sensing that no one would stop him taking such liberties that evening. It was eleven o'clock when Helen and George retired for the night, leaving Maggie and Peter to talk quietly about the day's events. The room was lit only by a single lamp and they drew back the curtains to view the night sky from the French window. The scene was inky black with stars like sharp little diamonds suspended in mid air, a sign of a heavy frost to come overnight.

'You know, if we didn't have the darkness we wouldn't see the stars.' Peter whispered wanting to give Maggie something to hold on to. Wrapping his arm around his wife's shoulders, he drew her close, sensing the concern for her parents. He gently kissed her hair and she lifted her face to his, responding with a long, gentle kiss.' They stood for several minutes in silence, arms entwined, before Maggie spoke.

'At least I'll be able to take them to see 'The Lawns' for themselves. If they like it I don't think I'll go to see the other options. This one has a great reputation and the location couldn't be better. I know it's not what they had planned for their retirement but I can see them living there, hopefully quite happily.'

'It'll be a huge change but Fenbridge is their home town and they know it so well. We'll be able to keep an eye on them too, that's the important thing, there'll be no more long distance driving if they live closer.' Peter added, hoping that things would work out for them all.

'I'll ring the warden in the morning to fix up another visit. Right now I'm ready for bed it's been a long day.'

The next morning Maggie came into the kitchen to find Helen already in the throes of making breakfast.

'You don't have to do this Mum.' She protested.

'I know, but I want to, I need to keep occupied.'

'Well, how about visiting 'The Lawns' today? I told you a little about it but you really need to see for yourself. Peter said he could bring you and Dad to the surgery at lunch time and we could go together to see what you think.'

'Sounds good to me. Your Dad's in the shower now but he'll go along with that I'm sure.'

'Did you get any sleep last night?'

'Surprisingly yes; I think knowing that you and Peter were on hand helped me to settle and your Dad went out like a light, must be the change of scenery.'

'Good!' Maggie helped herself to the hot buttered toast then sat at the table.

'I've got the application forms here. I was going to put your names down for you just to save time but I'll leave them for you to look at and fill in. The sooner you're on the waiting list the better and it's not a definite commitment so it doesn't tie you in. The bungalows are awarded on a points system of eligibility and hopefully the committee will look favourably on your application. We need to make some solid arrangements for you both Mum.'

'I know and I'm so grateful for your help. Being here is such an enormous relief and to have you sharing the burden is wonderful. If we could get settled quickly I think it would be far better for your Dad and easier on you too.'

'You don't have to worry about us, we want to help. I'll be more at ease and much happier too when you're living in Fenbridge.'

Helen planted a kiss on her daughter's forehead. 'Leave those forms with me and I'll have a look at them before we come to meet you. I'm sure Peter will be able to help if I get stuck. Is he working from home today?'

'Yes, all week in fact. He's cut down on his hours lately, not because the MS is any worse but in an effort to take life more easily and he wants to help with Dad too you know.'

Helen smiled; suddenly the future was looking more positive than it had done for several months.

****

Alice had rung Caroline to suggest meeting at the weekend for coffee. Somehow she felt a neutral venue would be appropriate although she didn't know why. Too many memories at her mother's home perhaps, or the fear of losing her temper again if they were at her flat? Caroline readily agreed and the following Saturday morning found them seated opposite each other in a quiet corner of a coffee shop on the High Street. The day had a real autumnal feel to it and Alice shivered as she wrapped her hands around the hot latte, unsure of what to say.

'I owe you an apology Mum; my behaviour last time we met was completely out of order, I shouldn't have stormed off like that.'

'You'd had a shock love, it was as much my fault as yours. Perhaps I shouldn't have told you but I hoped it would explain why your Dad, sorry, Ronald, felt as he did.'

'Well maybe I can understand that better now but it's raised all kinds of other questions for me. Do you know who my real father is?'

Caroline hesitated before giving a reply,

'Yes' her voice was low and sadness clouded her face.

'Well, are you going to tell me?'

'I really don't think it would do any good now. He doesn't know about you and I'd rather keep it that way.'

'But what about me, don't I have a right to know? What if there was a medical emergency and I needed a kidney or something?'

Caroline lowered her head with a slight shake.

'Okay, I know that's a bit far-fetched but surely it would help me to understand if you told me more about it?'

'Please Alice, I need you to trust me on this matter, it wouldn't benefit you in the least to know who he is. Haven't I always done what's best for you in the past? Can we just drop this subject and talk about something happier?'

Alice felt again that familiar sense of frustration and a degree of anger. It was perhaps as well that they were meeting in a public place. Looking at the hopeful expression on Caroline's face however softened her mood. The good times from childhood, so recently recounted to Maggie, flashed across her mind and she knew that for the present at least, she would have to trust Caroline's judgement.

'Alright Mum, I'll try to forget about it for now. I've actually been talking it over with Maggie, the counsellor at the surgery I told you about? She's been really helpful and it's probably because of her that I'm here today. I'll not pester you anymore on the subject but I would ask if you could give some serious thought to it and maybe next time we meet at least have a reason for why you think I shouldn't know who he is, can we leave it at that?'

'I won't change my mind love, so can I ask you to do something too? Simply consider trusting me on this?'

Stalemate. Disappointment clouded Alice's face but if she was asking her mother to reconsider then it seemed reasonable that she too should consider all aspects before they next met. The subject was closed, at least for that day and Caroline began to ask about work and how things were going in general. Alice mentally clung to those good times she had spoken to Maggie about which helped in keeping calm and seeing other facets of her mother's personality instead of dwelling on their one major disagreement. An hour went by and the two women managed to avoid talking about the past other than in general terms. Walking home later, Alice was glad to have made the effort to remain calm. Their relationship was too precious to ruin, surely they could find a way to resolve the issue even if it meant compromise on both sides. Her thoughts moved on to anticipate the next session with Maggie. Alice was feeling proud for remaining cool and rational and was sure that her counsellor would be pleased too.

Chapter 11

The attic had become Malcolm's place of solace. It was warm and quiet, housing amongst other things his father's few remaining possessions, in particular the diaries. Frank Stokes visit had shocked Malcolm to the core, sending him scurrying back to those diaries as if the past could bring the answers he needed for the future. Over the years his grandmother's death had often come to mind and the part his mother had played in it but it was perhaps only now, through reading the record of those dark days that Malcolm began to form some understanding of the entirety of the event. His memories were vague so he turned again to the diary, seeking clarity whilst knowing it could only bring pain.

... but what about us, Mary, Malcolm, myself? How will we survive if the truth comes out which it surely must when the post mortem is done?

Mary seemed to have spent all her tears and began to move about the house like a ghost, attempting to maintain a degree of normality and busying herself in the kitchen. She had shared the facts, who knows if she would have remained silent if there was not to be an inquest? I think she may have taken it to the grave but it was not to be that simple for her, for any of us. For myself, I now have to break the news to Malcolm. The boy has been so close to Joan, so loving and caring that I know he will be distressed. I need to be strong for him and for Mary but where on earth can I find such strength?

June 27th 1967
It is now a full week since Joan died, the worst week of my life and surely of my wife and son too. The police came in the early morning for Mary, three uniformed officers and one detective. They cautioned and arrested her on a charge of unlawful killing. I could hardly

believe it when they put handcuffs on her bony wrists, were they afraid this shadow of a woman was going to escape? She looked so frail, almost skin and bone now with an unhealthy sallow skin but she tried to smile as they took her. Malcolm had heard the doorbell and came downstairs, sobbing as he watched his mother being led away. How can you explain such events to a child? But I was all he had left; there was no indication of how long Mary would be gone and I was completely ignorant of such matters. The detective advised me to employ the services of a solicitor, a task which must be done as soon as possible for Mary's sake. Surely they would let her come home; it was obvious how ill she was. Taking Malcolm with me, I made my way to the only firm of solicitors I knew in Liverpool, 'Jenkins, Smith and Wilson', who had handled Joan's will. They were very kind and efficient, a receptionist finding a drink and biscuits for Malcolm while I spoke with Mr. Jenkins, a thin wiry man with a long face and pointed chin, who advised me to be truthful and so I began to relate every detail I could recall.

The solicitor sat silent and solemn behind a huge oak desk, elbows spaced on the leather top, hands clasped and forefingers steepled. Although nodding encouragingly Mr Jenkins did not interrupt and allowed me to finish my story, after which he stood and walked around to my side of the desk, put his hand on my shoulder and squeezed gently. I saw empathy in his eyes as he returned to be seated again, pulled a note pad towards him and began to ask questions. When these were answered as best as I could I asked some of my own, anxious to know what would happen to Mary and in particular whether the police would allow her home. The answers were on the whole reassuring; he was almost certain that Mary would be allowed home on bail due to the circumstances of the charges and her own illness but there was no time to waste. He would go to the police station immediately and advised me to take Malcolm home to wait for news. It was not quite midday when we set off home but the day had already seemed endless, with still more hours stretching out before me into an unknown destiny.

It was almost an impossible task to console Malcolm. He asked questions for which I had no answers and I tried to be as truthful as *possible, urging patience which I could barely find myself. At four in the afternoon the doorbell chimed for the second time that day and my heart leapt. Surely it could only be good news? It was; Mr Jenkins stood with Mary, all but propping her up as he helped her over the doorstep. The relief I felt soon turned to apprehension as I asked about the charges, bail and the dozens of other things which were swimming through my mind. Mr. Jenkins was patient and informative and talked us through the process which would follow. Mary was bailed to report to the police station every day with instructions not to leave the city. It was such a relief for us all. We could truthfully tell Malcolm that his mother would not be taken away in such a manner again.*

I thought we could spare our son the details of the 'crime' but bad news travels fast. The very next day he came home from school at midday, face streaked with dirt and tears, trousers ripped at the knee and several bruises on his arms and legs. Through the sobbing he told us of the bullying and taunts which had occurred and we comforted him as best as we could. I decided to keep him at home until things settled down, without actually knowing if the situation would improve at all but I couldn't let my son suffer at the hands of school bullies. Whatever is to become of us?

Bill Grainger had broken the news of Joan's death as gently as possible but it was still a major blow to the young Malcolm, a blow he remembered all too well. For a few days, life continued as normal although a heavy sadness hung over them all and he could sense the anxiety on the faces of both parents without fully understanding the complexities of the situation. Today, he could vaguely remember the police taking away his mother and a trip into the city with his father to see a man in a dusty old office but the first intimation that his grandmother had not died an entirely natural death came cruelly in the school playground at the hands of Frank Stokes. Malcolm remembered the blows, physical and emotional. Stokes repeating over and over that his mother was a murderer and others blindly joining in the accusations! Malcolm had run home from school even though it was only lunch time, and had never returned there again. He'd never seen Frank again either until he turned up on the doorstep like a menacing shadow from a recurring nightmare, the nightmare Malcolm had thought to be behind him.

The sound of the front door opening jolted Malcolm back to the present, looking at the clock he realised it was long past lunch time, Jenny was home and certainly not expecting him to be there.

'Hi Jen,' he tried to steady his voice as he descended from the attic.

'What on earth are you doing home... and in the attic again?'

He kissed her on the cheek; it was time for some serious talking.

'Let me make you some tea and then there's something I need to tell you.'

Jenny's brow furrowed at this comment, her husband was never a great one for talking and this sounded rather ominous.

'Is everything okay, with the kids I mean?'

'Yes, everyone's fine, there's just something I need to tell you about, something I should have told you years ago.'

Jenny was pale, the tea beside her had gone cold and she looked into Malcolm's eyes trying to take in the story he had just recounted.

'Your mother was actually charged with murdering your grandmother?' Why on earth had he never told her this before?

'Yes, that's right.'

'And you didn't tell me... because?'

'It's not something I'm particularly proud of Jen. You might not have wanted to marry me if you'd known. It's this Stokes chap turning up out of the blue, trying to blackmail us...'

Jenny's eyes flashed as she stood suddenly, knocking the tea to the floor and grabbing her coat and bag before slamming the front door behind her. Malcolm watched her storm down the garden path before cleaning up the cold tea. Perhaps he shouldn't have told her, just paid Frank Stokes to go away and leave them all in peace, but it was too late now. Jenny knew his worst secret, that the mother he rarely talked about had killed his grandmother. Why hadn't she stayed so they could talk rationally about it? Where had she gone and would she come back soon? Malcolm felt worse than ever and really wished he had never bought that winning lottery ticket.

****

'You were right Maggie, its lovely!' It was the first genuine smile they had seen on Helen's lips for a long time. The four of them met with Audrey at lunchtime, who had repeated the tour of her own bungalow and number sixteen and now Helen was walking George around the garden. George had stopped beside a rose bush, frowning as he examined its leaves.

'It's very kind of you to show us round again so soon. My mother's completed the forms. Can I leave them with you?'

'Yes, certainly dear; has she explained their situation fully? I'm sorry to ask but the more information the committee has the easier it is to prioritise allocations.'

'I think it's all in there but you can see for yourself that although Dad is physically fit he's becoming confused. They need to be back in Fenbridge where we can support them, and their home in Scotland is too big for them now, particularly the garden.'

'Well the fact that they originally come from Fenbridge is in their favour, we get so many applicants who've never lived here before but wish to retire here. That's not what the original bequest stated; the complex is to benefit local residents which of course your parents have been. The proximity of your own home will also be taken into account as we like to work with family members as our residents get older.'

Maggie had the feeling that Audrey was in their corner and that George and Helen would be made very welcome at The Lawns.

'Number sixteen Audrey, is it already allocated?' It would be wonderful if they could get a place so soon but, Maggie realised, number sixteen was probably already spoken for.

'Yes, I'm afraid it is and we never know when our homes will become available, as I'm sure you understand, but the committee meets at the end of next week so I'll be sure to bring up your application. If you'd like to ring me after Friday I may be able to give some indication of where you are on the waiting list.'

'Thank you, you've been very kind, I'll do that. Now we had better take Dad home before he rolls his sleeves up and finds something to do in your gardens.'

Audrey laughed and saw the visitors off. George seemed quite taken with the place although as expected he thought the roses needed spraying and would have been very happy to do the job there and then. It was good to see him so content which was of course reflected in the demeanour of both his wife and daughter.

Chapter 12

On returning to work after a rather hurried lunch, a message was waiting for Maggie from a Mrs Jenny Grainger who wished to see her as soon as possible. The message on the post-it note also contained a mobile phone number. The name seemed familiar but she couldn't place it but was sure it wasn't a past client self referring again. There was time before the next appointment to call and Mrs Grainger answered on the second ring.

'Hi, this is Maggie Sayer I believe you've been trying to get hold of me?'

'Oh yes, I hoped it would be you, thank you for ringing so promptly. I want to make an appointment to see you and I wondered how to go about it?'

'Referrals generally come through the GP Mrs Grainger unless you want to be seen as a private client?'

'Yes, a private client, that's right, how soon can I see you?'

This lady sounded eager. Maggie currently only had GP referrals on her list, she, like Peter, had cut down on working hours of late but the caller sounded pretty insistent.

'Can I send you some details about the kind of service I offer with the scale of fees so you can consider it first?' Maggie liked to ensure private clients knew the terms before committing themselves to counselling.

'No, thank you but I'd rather start straight away. The money's not an issue I just need someone to talk things through with. Could you see me soon?'

Something in the woman's voice held a sense of urgency which Maggie couldn't refuse and she began flicking through the desk diary

'I have a free morning this Friday if that's of any use?'

'That would be wonderful, can you visit me at home?'

'Of course, if you give me the address I can be there at 9.30?'

'Thirty four Acacia Avenue and 9.30 is perfect, thank you so much Ms Sayer.'

Maggie wrote the address down. She had kept Friday free with the intention of spending time with her parents but that would still be possible after the visit to Mrs Grainger. She could also finish early that afternoon as the only other client booked in the diary was Alice Greenwood in a few minutes time.

****

Alice looked immaculate as ever, long blonde hair swept up and neatly secured with an ornate clip, slim fitting black trousers complimented by a red chunky sweater and the look finished off with black knee high boots. Her expression gave nothing away as the two women settled in the easy chairs beside the coffee table.

'What kind of week have you had Alice?' Maggie began.

'Okay in some respects, frustrating in others.'

'Do you want to tell me about it?'

'Yes,' she nodded thoughtfully. 'I arranged to meet Mum for coffee last Saturday and thought it might be best to meet at a neutral place so we met at 'The Coffee Pot' on the High Street for an hour. The first thing I did was apologise. I'd been feeling so bad about storming off last time we met but Mum was fine about it. I got the impression she's wondering if it had been a wise move to have told me that Ronald wasn't my biological father. It's a bit like Pandora's Box, isn't it, but she did tell me and yet now won't answer my questions.'

'Did you ask specific questions?'

'Absolutely, like, who is my real Dad? But she still wouldn't say, maintaining that it would do absolutely no good if I knew and that he doesn't know about me and that's the way she wants it to stay.'

'And is that a good enough answer for you?'

'No! I think I have a right to know and did ask if she'd rethink the decision but she countered that by asking me to think about trusting her on the issue. So we reached an impasse. It's really frustrating Maggie, having never been the most patient of souls I want to know and it's driving me crazy!'

'Obviously it's difficult when you know your mother has the information you want. It could simply be that the timing isn't right. Your mother is a grieving widow and possibly feels unable to face another major upset so soon. The loss will still be very raw but given time, she may come round to your way of thinking.'

'She seems pretty determined not to at the moment and as I said I'm not very good at waiting.' Alice attempted a smile, the issue was certainly tying her up in knots and not being in control of this aspect of her life was infuriating. Maggie smiled.

'I have a cat,' she began to tell Alice. 'Tara came to live with me a few years ago when her owners moved and couldn't take her with them. Tara was already a regular visitor to my home, not from any affection for me but simply to tease my dog, Ben. The cat would spend many happy hours just sitting on the garden wall, aloof as cats can be and her very presence annoyed Ben until he would literally chase his tail in circles, which did no good at all. Eventually she became part of our family which is all beside the point because what I'm trying to say is that I believe we can learn a great deal from cats. Tara lives in the moment. If her needs are met on a daily basis, she's happy. While there's enough to eat and drink for the day and a warm place to curl up and sleep, that's all she needs.

Cats don't worry about tomorrow, only today and I often think we can learn much from their attitude to life. We can't change the past no matter how much we'd like to and we can't predict the future either. Of course I'm aware that our needs and emotions are much more complex than a cat's but perhaps they've got the right idea, certainly about living in the moment. We all expend so much energy worrying about things we cannot change from the past or anticipating the worst for the future and we miss out on the happiness we could have in the present, today. Tara also takes us as she finds us. I'm the provider of food and a lap to curl up on when she's in the mood and my dog is a sometimes reluctant playmate and an alternative warm spot to sleep beside. She doesn't judge us for what we've done in the past or worry what we'll do tomorrow and she's as content as a cat can possibly be.

'Sorry Alice, that's quite a little monologue isn't it? I'm not trying to belittle your problems but perhaps thinking about Tara's philosophy of life we can all learn something. Life comes in bite sized chunks; a week; a day; an hour. It's those chunks which are all we have to control. We can't control other people's lives either. They make their own decisions and will go on making them, just as we do. Do you think that breaking down your life into manageable chunks could perhaps help?'

Alice took a deep breath and smiled.

'Thank you, I needed to hear that. I'm in danger of wasting the present by obsessing about the past, my past and Mum's. You're quite right though, I can't change it nor force the issue with Mum either. Having asked her to consider my position and in light of her response I think I'll have to be content for the moment and get off my high horse. Whatever happened in the past is done and can never be changed. I'll simply have to accept that.'

'You're still being hard on yourself here Alice. Your mind processes each new thought and idea but you need to give yourself time. It's not easy to say, 'I'll have to accept it' and do it. Process things a little slower; relax instead of trying to solve everything immediately.' Maggie smiled, Alice was keen to learn and understand but was putting pressure on herself to do the right thing and to do it quickly.

'A little pampering is good for the soul too you know. Spoil yourself occasionally, a long, lazy bath with a few drops of lavender oil, a bar of your favourite chocolate and a glass of wine. Encourage yourself to relax. It might sound a little mad but it does help and to quote a TV advert, which I'm really rather tired of seeing, *you're worth it!*'

Alice left in a happier frame of mind and after tidying a few things away Maggie too left for home with thoughts of her parents at the forefront of her mind. It was such a relief to have them close by but living together permanently was not a viable option. Oh, Peter wouldn't object, he was very easy going and genuinely fond of Helen and George but Helen was an independent woman and although able to adapt when necessary, Maggie knew she would be much happier when they were in their own home. The Lawns seemed to be the ideal solution but in reality would they get a place anytime soon? It would be difficult for them to go back to their home in Scotland unless there was a marked improvement in George's health which realistically was not going to happen. Perhaps they should look at some of the other options available. Maybe she had been short sighted in pinning all her hopes on The Lawns? Pulling into the driveway at home Maggie was suddenly struck by the thought that she was doing exactly what she had spent an hour warning Alice not to do, mentally crossing bridges, worrying about tomorrow and all those other stress inducing things over which she had no control. Perhaps she needed to pay a little more attention to the Tara philosophy of life.

Chapter 13

Jenny barely spoke to Malcolm on returning home and as he didn't ask where she had been, the information was not volunteered. A cool atmosphere prevailed throughout the evening until Jenny disappeared upstairs at around 9pm announcing she was having an early night. The atmosphere was equally strained in the morning.

'Are you going to work?' Jenny asked.

'Yes, perhaps we can talk when I come home? I know this has been a shock but we need to discuss what we're going to do.'

'You mean about this blackmailer?'

'Yes', Malcolm looked sheepish, 'He'll be back again tomorrow, we have to decide what to do.'

'Oh, so I am to be involved now am I?' The sarcasm didn't go unnoticed.

'Look, I'm really very sorry that I didn't tell you about my mother before. It was wrong, I can see that now... but can we move on or at least talk about it? Jen, please, I want you to be with me on this love; we've always been a good team together haven't we?' No reply was forthcoming so Malcolm silently gathered his things for work and left without the customary goodbye kiss from Jenny. Throughout their marriage they had experienced very few serious disagreements and always managed to talk through their problems but now Malcolm wondered if he'd ruined that closeness altogether, a blow he would find hard to bear. Jenny's anger was understandable and he regretted not having told the truth before but his motives had been the right ones, surely she would see that eventually?

Jenny's anger hadn't cooled and she banged about in the kitchen, cleaning an already spotless oven and sweeping the floor of imaginary crumbs. When there were no more tasks to complete she slumped at the kitchen table with a mug of tea, rested her head in her hands and sighed. Malcolm's attitude to their win and the resulting publicity was beginning to make sense now. If only he had explained she would never have agreed to speak to the paper but Malcolm wasn't one for cosy heart to hearts, the strong silent type she had always joked but perhaps not so strong now? The lottery win had brought such excitement and delight, their children's futures were looking so much more positive, there was security for their own old age and money to enjoy some of the good things in life but now this was completely overshadowed by something as distasteful and ugly as blackmail. Reaching for one of the holiday brochures from the growing pile on the dresser, Jenny flicked through it thoughtfully. Images of ecstatic families enjoying the luxurious resorts filled every page; images she had assumed could be them in the not too distant future. They had almost agreed on which hotel to stay in and the family were getting together the next day to finalise their travel plans. But the blackmailer was coming the following day too and Jenny needed to decide how they were going to handle the situation. Malcolm would need her help with this, he was right; they had always been a good team.

The following morning Frank Stokes was sitting in his car in the same spot as two days previously with the feeling of déjà vu bringing a smile to his thin lips. His mood was buoyant from anticipating the payoff he was about to receive and he was all but wringing his hands like Scrooge. The first inclination had been to ask for a million pounds which he viewed at as a mere percentage of the winnings, a nice, tidy round figure, but he had revised this thinking and decided to ask for only seven hundred and fifty thousand. Grainger would surely be more likely to agree to a sum under a million. A frisson of excitement ran through Stokes' body as he watched Jenny Grainger leave the house, exactly the same time as before, obviously a creature of habit. As she turned the corner out of sight, Stokes leapt out of the car and headed to the front door of number thirty four Acacia Avenue. This was it, the big pay day, Frank had to consciously stop himself from smiling and attempted a dark menacing look; he wanted Grainger to be afraid. It took a long time for Malcolm to reach the door and when he did it was with a demeanour which reflected the anguish he had been going through. Stokes, unmoved, pushed past him and in seconds was seated in the living room.

'Hmm, you look done in, not been getting your eight hours pal?' He thought this funny, Malcolm did not. 'So now that you've had time to reflect on my proposition let's get down to business.' He allowed himself a smug smile but before there was chance to say more they heard a key turn in the lock and Jenny appeared in the doorway.

'Aren't you going to introduce me Malcolm?' Jenny sounded brisk and business like and stood as tall as her five foot two would allow, looking directly into the stranger's eyes. Stokes recovered his composure well and when there was no response from Malcolm, moved forward with an outstretched hand, 'Frank Stokes, I'm an old school friend of your husbands.' Ignoring the hand, Jenny announced,

'I know exactly who you are and friend doesn't come into it! You're the despicable low life who's trying to blackmail us.'

Stokes turned to look at Malcolm who shrugged, leaving his wife to continue.

'There's nothing about my husband or his family that I don't already know so I suggest you leave now and never return otherwise I'm calling the police!'

Stokes laughed,

'Oh Malcolm, hiding behind your wife's skirt are you? It appears that you've forgotten what I said; if you don't pay me, the national papers will. Quite a story it'll make, lottery winner - the son of a murderer. Do you think your children and grandchildren will enjoy reading all about it in the papers?'

Jenny had moved to stand beside Malcolm in a gesture of solidarity and continued as spokesman,

'Do whatever you wish, but you'll not get a penny out of us, I'd rather burn the money than let you get your hands on it!' The sharp words threw Stokes momentarily. The couple before him were in accord and had obviously discussed this.

'Okay then, this is your last chance. Twenty five thousand, cash, and I'll disappear forever, if not I'll be selling the story to the nationals.' The words were followed by a silence broken only by the ticking of the clock on the mantel piece. Stokes no longer felt in control of the situation. Malcolm walked calmly to the front door and opened it.

'Fine, have it your way but you'll regret this, I promise!' Stokes retreated up the drive, this time without the smug smile.

'Have we done the right thing?' Malcolm looked searchingly at Jenny.

'We'll soon know if we haven't but I don't think he'll go to the papers, it's a bluff. Surely they've got bigger stories to report on than the history of a lottery winner. I hope that Frank Stokes gets laughed out of their offices, if he ever gets that far.'

'Thanks love, you've been great sending him packing like that. At least he knows that we present a united front.'

'We'll have to see about that and I did it as much for the kids as for you. I can't pretend I'm not disappointed in you Mal, I didn't think we had any secrets.'

Frank Stokes was seething. The plan had been perfect in its simplicity, foolproof he'd thought and in his mind it was a certainty that he would come away with something for his efforts. He'd even lowered the figure again which was quite generous of him really. Now he was out of pocket and with that crumby B & B to pay for, not to mention the petrol. And what was he going to do about returning to work? He'd hoped to have enough cash to forget about the poxy job and begin to write that novel he'd been going to get around to for years. He certainly hadn't expected to be sent away with a flea in his ear, and by Grainger's wife too. No, this wouldn't be the end of it; he would make them wish they'd paid. Climbing into the car Stokes thumped the dashboard in frustration, an action which resulted in bruised knuckles rather than easing the growing dark mood into which he was descending. He'd pick up his few belongings and head back to Liverpool. The drive home would give him time to think up plan B, the Graingers were not going to get off the hook that easily. It was still early and he could be back in Liverpool by lunchtime if he really wanted to but the anger in his head was giving him a headache. Perhaps a cool beer would help calm his nerves, just one and then he'd be on the way home to work out what to do next. Letting go of such a golden opportunity simply wasn't an option, he'd make Malcolm Grainger regret sending him away. Frank pulled up outside the B & B then walked over the road to the grimy looking pub which was just opening up for business.

****

Working as a lab technician in the local hospital's pathology department was Alice's idea of a dream job. Strange though it seemed to some, it had sufficient variety and challenge to make it interesting and the opportunity to learn new things almost daily. Friends ribbed her about having to work with samples of blood and other unsavoury bodily fluids but the samples were miniscule and she wasn't troubled by such gruesome thoughts, purely looking at it as science. In the eight years of working there she had secured two promotions and was currently one of two supervisors in the lab heading up a team of six. In the adjoining lab there were five more technicians and another supervisor, Joel. Although Alice had worked at the hospital longer than Joel, he had seniority due to his degree and previous experience elsewhere but this had never been a problem to her and in general it was a great place to work. When Joel first arrived, he had caused quite a stir amongst the girls due to his Nordic good looks, blonde hair worn just a shade too long causing him to frequently flick it from his face, baby blue eyes and a tall, muscular build. Joel however seemed genuinely unaware of the effect his presence had on the opposite sex. Alice had to agree with these female colleagues that he was certainly good looking but otherwise she was impervious to such physical charms. On the day following her last visit to Maggie she had been deep in thought about the future and what she really wanted out of life. To be honest, life was at times dull with any interest and excitement generated solely through working where she did. Home life was presently frustrating due to her mother's continued refusal to reveal the name of her biological father. Peculiarly, for someone who dealt with biology every day and had previous involvement with genetics from a spell working in the infertility section of the lab, the issue of paternity was important to Alice. To anyone else in a similar situation she would have said he was just a sperm donor but when it was her own genetic makeup, it suddenly took on greater relevance. Lost in thought she failed to notice Joel approaching.

'The key Alice?' his voice broke into her reverie.

'What? Oh sorry, what did you say?'

'Can I have the key for the storage room? Are you okay, you seem very quiet today?'

'Yes, I'm fine thanks.' She fished the key from her white coat pocket. 'Sorry, I should have put it back in the key box, I forgot.'

'That's okay, no harm done. I was wondering, I have a couple of tickets for the theatre and I er...wondered if you'd like to come with me? It's a musical show, a mash-up of songs from musical theatre, if you like that sort of thing?' Joel had actually gone quite red to Alice's surprise.

'Yes, I love musical theatre, thank you, I'd enjoy that.' Joel told her the date, which was in four days time and left with a smile on his face. Alice went to write it in her diary wondering why on earth she had accepted such an offer. The last thing she needed at this time was the complication of a 'date', particularly with a colleague.

Chapter 14

Maggie arrived at the neat semi detached house two minutes before the appointed time. It was a vaguely familiar area, an attractive tree lined avenue with sturdy red brick pre-war houses, each with a small forecourt and a larger garden at the rear. Two neatly manicured box trees stood at either side of the blue gloss door like sentinels and a trumpet voluntary announced her arrival on pressing the doorbell. A small framed lady, probably early fifties, answered the door, wide brown eyes scrutinising the visitor. Maggie thought her face was familiar but couldn't quite place her. Perhaps she was a patient at the surgery.

'Hi, I'm Maggie Sayer, Mrs Grainger is it?'

'Yes, please come in.' Jenny stepped aside for Maggie to enter. The inside of the house was as pristine as the outside, everything clean and tidy, magnolia walls in the hall and lounge with the heady scent of lilies from a huge bouquet on the hearth.

'Can I take your coat?' Jenny asked before motioning to a sofa for the visitor to sit down. When both were seated Maggie began to outline the verbal contract which she explained to each new client. The element of confidentiality was stressed and the exceptions to it which would be in the case of a client stating they were intending to harm themselves, someone else, or disclosing information regarding a child at risk. With the business side taken care of, Maggie asked if Jenny would like to begin by telling her why she felt the need to see a counsellor. Jenny was happy to do so and began the story with the most original opening line Maggie had ever heard.

'Well, we've actually just won eight point two million pounds on the lottery, which is wonderful but it seems to have brought with it its own peculiar set of problems.'

Now Maggie could place this new client. Her picture had been in the local paper a few weeks ago. It wasn't very often that Fenbridge had a lottery winner, certainly one with such a huge amount. She nodded encouragingly for Jenny to continue.

'At first it was a dream come true. You know how everyone talks about what they would do if they won millions, well, we actually did but things have been quite bizarre since, which is probably my fault... You wouldn't believe the begging letters we've had, parents pleading for cash to take their sick children abroad for treatment, men telling us they're dying and their families will be left penniless, even people who say they run animal shelters and the bailiffs are after them and they've no money to feed the animals. People are so cunning and I'm afraid I've become rather sceptical of such letters, almost expecting them to be lies. To be fair, the lottery people warned us about this sort of thing.' Jenny paused for a moment, reflecting on recent experiences and Maggie took the opportunity to ask,

'Why do you say it's probably your fault?'

'Well, I agreed to do an interview with the local paper which with hindsight was maybe a stupid thing to do. Mal, my husband, was against it but I was so happy, living on a cloud and naively expecting everyone to be pleased for us. Actually many of them are but it's been a real eye opener how others react. We've got neighbours who would hardly give us the time of day before suddenly acting like our best friends. I don't think I'm a gullible person but you do start to wonder. Some of our real friends though have gone the other way, almost cutting us off in case we think they're after our money. It's quite surreal and turns your whole world upside down. Then there are the hate letters, they're the worst of all. Strangers who don't know us from Adam say the most appalling things, telling us we don't deserve the money and they hope it kills us! I simply can't understand the motive for such behaviour. And I'm amazed at how easily they can find out our address.'

'So is this why you felt counselling could help?'

'Yes, partly, but something else has happened more recently which prompted me to call you. Malcolm has told me things about his past, things that he's never mentioned before. I always knew his mother died when he was very young but it seems that before her death she helped her own mother to commit suicide.'

'Do you know why he's told you this now?' Maggie's question took Jenny by surprise having expected some expression of shock at the event rather than a simple enquiry as to why Malcolm had disclosed this now.

'Oh yes, someone's been trying to blackmail him.' Jenny Grainger looked down at her hands clasped in her lap and continued. 'If I'm honest Maggie, I don't care about the blackmail, what really upsets me is that the man I have loved for thirty years had this secret from his past and didn't trust me enough to tell me.' Her expression was pained and a few moments of silence hung between the women until Maggie spoke again.

'How do you feel now Jenny, right at this moment?'

'Hmm... a little sad when I think about it, and angry; confused, disappointed, in fact I'm beginning to wish we'd never won the lottery. In no way did I expect it to bring anything other than good into our lives.' There was another reflective silence.

'There seem to be two issues here,' Maggie tried to sum up, 'The blackmail and your husband's revelations, although obviously they're connected. Have you and Malcolm discussed either of them?'

'I haven't given him much chance to talk about it if I'm honest. I sort of blanked him out after he told me.' On reflection Jenny now felt she had been rather unfair to Malcolm, perhaps in an attempt to make him suffer for not having told her before, which now seemed somewhat childish.

'The blackmailer was almost the easy part, he turned up again yesterday demanding money and we told him to leave and do his worst. He's threatened to go to the papers but in all honesty I don't care, we'll be telling the children now anyway and they're the ones who really matter.'

'Have you considered going to the police? They can be very sensitive in these situations.'

'I'd happily do that but I'm not sure about Mal. He's worried about the implications for his Dad. Bill's health isn't good at all and I don't think he could survive any kind of scandal.'

Maggie understood the dilemma and how this news had shattered Jenny's trust and confidence in her husband but as for doing any work with Jenny on the issues it seemed almost too soon. The situation was still very much a shifting one and there had been little time for Jenny to have processed any kind of feelings on the matter.

'You appear to have had a solid marriage until now; do you think you could talk openly with your husband? At present you seem to be in a place which is changing constantly so it may be a good idea to let things settle for a few more days and then perhaps we can meet in a week or so?'

'Yes, that sounds reasonable. I have to admit that I don't exactly know what I expected from counselling, I just wanted to talk to someone rather than bottle it all up.'

'Well you've got that right, bottling things up is never a good idea.' Maggie began explaining the different methods of counselling, in particular the person centred approach which she felt would be the most appropriate for Jenny and also the possibility of seeing her and her husband together. After an hour, the women parted, agreeing a time for their next meeting. Maggie left for home and Jenny began to clean an already spotless house in an effort to distract from the intrusive thoughts on which she did not wish to dwell.

****

When Maggie arrived home, looking forward to spending the rest of the day with her parents, it was to some excellent news. Helen wore a huge grin and as she made coffee, explained what had happened.

'I had a telephone call from Audrey at 'The Lawns'. Apparently the couple who were due to move into number sixteen have decided to relocate nearer to their family and have dropped out. The next ones on the list have a property to sell and don't want to move yet. Audrey said the committee were happy to offer us the place as our situation is classed as high priority and we can take the option immediately, which suits them too.'
Maggie was delighted, having worried that a place may not become available for several months this was an answer to prayer.

Peter and George took their coffee to the lounge to watch the news on the television and Maggie sat opposite Helen whose face reflected relief at this welcome news.

'You've been so good in having us stay here but being able to move permanently is wonderful. It's strange but I never thought we'd return to Fenbridge when we left. Scotland was our dream retirement home with the only negative being that we were leaving you here alone.'

'I know that Mum, it was the right decision for you at the time and you've made some very happy memories from those years in the cottage. And I wasn't alone for long was I, before Peter came along? We could never have anticipated this happening to Dad but when you're settled in I'm sure he'll be happy. He knows Fenbridge so well, it's not like starting somewhere new again is it?'

'That's true, his mind is more often in the past these days so perhaps he'll improve when he's living back here. And although I've loved the Scottish countryside, Yorkshire is equally as beautiful and in many ways has the same wild, rugged appeal, not to mention the damp weather! We'll have to work out the practicalities of the move and put the cottage on the market.'

'Don't worry about that, there's no reason to hurry and Peter and I will help as much as we can. Alan's very practical too and often has time on his hands, I'll mention it to Sue, I'm sure he'd be happy to help. I wonder if I rang Audrey now we could go back for another look, then we could take measurements for curtains and things. I remember number sixteen as being quite well decorated but I wasn't looking at it for you so I'd like to go again.'

'Oh yes, me too. Shall I make the call while you finish your coffee?'

Maggie smiled and nodded, it was so good to see Helen more relaxed than she'd been for months. There was no reason why the move couldn't be arranged quickly and easily, it was quite an exciting prospect and one Maggie would enjoy helping with.

Chapter 15

July 20th

The reporters thankfully left us alone after the expected 'three day wonder' period. The police officially charged Mary with murder; she had never denied helping her mother to take the tablets which they had saved in sufficient quantity to end her life. The authorities were not interested in the fact that it had been at Joan's request and initially there were discussions with Mr. Jenkins about a lesser charge of manslaughter or assisted suicide. They soon realised however that it was purely academic as it became clear that Mary had not long to go before her own death. Whether out of compassion or the simple futility of the situation, the police did not pursue the case and so in our last few weeks we were left alone to manage as best as we could.

One night, from the turn of the staircase I stood in the shadows and listened to Mary talking to our son. I could picture her in my mind, stroking his forehead, kissing his hair and breathing in as much of him as she could to remember for eternity. Her words were soft and kind, expressing love and regret that she would have to leave him. There were silences and muffled sobs as our boy tried to be brave. It broke my heart to listen but I was frozen to the spot, torn between running in to join my family and giving way to my own stifled tears. Malcolm was being forced to understand things that no seven year old should have to grapple with. His years of innocent childhood had been snatched from him and I will be the only one left to love and protect him. I feel so inadequate, so small and weak; if only I could have the same strength that Mary has.

July 25th

Mary is at peace. It is barely a month since we buried Joan, a month of agony and despair and now I have lost the love of my life too. If it were not for Malcolm I think I would have crumbled but I have to go on for his sake. My life feels as if it is over but his is just beginning and he must have the opportunity to live it well. During *those last few weeks Mary became so frail in body but her spirit was strong, a spirit she willed into me attempting to empower me, instructing and encouraging... but I am slow to learn. Yet now her words come back to me in the dark silent hours, those instructions for our future without her, those wise words which I now cling to in my despair and sorrow.*

August 19th
Malcolm has not returned to school since that awful day he was bullied. I kept him at home with me and I gave up my job at the local library. In the days immediately after Mary's death I found solace in activity. I spruced the house up with fresh paint, Malcolm being my willing apprentice and then together we tidied the neglected garden before putting the house up for sale. Mary had suggested places where we might move to and there was comfort in knowing we were doing her bidding, so our next task was to seek out a new home. We settled on Fenbridge which was at the top of Mary's list. The town was large enough for me to find employment but small enough to provide a friendly atmosphere in which to raise our son. Mary had always loved the Yorkshire countryside with its rugged moors, hills and dales. I knew that I would feel close to her there and hoped that the peaceful surroundings would be a healing balm for my son and me.

September 5th
The house sold quickly and we have found the perfect little home to rent in Fenbridge, a two-up two-down terraced house with open fields at the back and only a five minute walk to the local school. Malcolm has been so brave, I sometimes catch him looking at me with that same concerned expression his mother had and I know that in spite of everything which has happened I am blessed to have my son. It is still not long since we lost Mary and there are times when my heart aches at the almost unbearable loss and grief which

attempts to swallow me up but I look at my boy and see his mother's gentle eyes smiling back at me and I know we will survive.

Malcolm had an uncomfortable sense of intruding on his father's privacy reading the diaries and needed to remind himself that Bill had wanted him to see them. The words brought back bitter sweet memories, but this written record somehow gave him strength. Through the pages he gained an insight into the remarkable love his parents had for each other and felt proud to be the child of two such extraordinary people. In reading, he also had to face, perhaps for the first time, his own feelings on his mother's actions. Frank Stokes assumed that Malcolm would be ashamed of the past and of his mother, but the more Malcolm thought about it, the more the opposite became true and a sense of pride that his mother had the courage to do what she thought was right was swelling in his heart. In those days, assisted suicide was almost unheard of although it most probably still happened. The debate was so much more in the open today with sympathies on both sides. Would Mary have been called a murderer today or perhaps a mercy killer? Whatever, Malcolm's memories were of a loving, caring and patient mother who showed strength and courage in her actions; how could he be ashamed of such qualities, how could anyone judge her actions if they had not been there, never walked in his mother's shoes?

The sound of activity downstairs reminded Malcolm that his family were assembling and this was the time to tell them of past secrets. Had he done such a good a job at being a father as Bill had with him? Perhaps today he would discover the answer to that question. He picked up the diaries and clasping them gently, almost reverently, carried them carefully down the attic steps and went to join the others. Matthew and his wife, Angie had just arrived, beaming faces unable to disguise the happiness they felt at this time. Angie was wearing a new three quarter length leather jacket which Kate was admiring when Malcolm walked into the centre of his family he felt almost traitorous knowing he was about to shatter the buoyant mood. Kate and Mike had already flicked through the travel brochures, revelling in the thought that they could afford to choose whichever package they desired without having to look at the prices. Jenny was doing her best to act normally and nodded towards her husband as if to tell him to get straight on with the bad news. She was right, the sooner they knew, the better.

'Before we get carried away with holiday plans I've got something to tell you.' Malcolm was standing anxiously by the window, still clutching the diaries. Jenny caught his eye and smiled before patting the seat next to her, a simple gesture which gave her husband all the strength he needed. As he sat down, she took his hand and Malcolm knew then that he could take on the world.

He began by telling his captive audience that their parents had been approached by an old acquaintance who was attempting to blackmail them. Questions were immediately fired back from puzzled faces as to what on earth anyone would have to blackmail them about. Patiently Malcolm began to explain the circumstances of his mother's and grandmother's deaths and the resulting murder charge. Matthew and Kate looked at their parents in disbelief.

'Did you know about this Mum?' Matthew was always the first to speak on any occasion.

'Not until the other day.' Jenny's voice was heavy with emotion, hearing the account from her husband's lips had affected her more than she expected.

'But why didn't you tell us Dad? Why didn't you even tell Mum?'

'I really can't give you an answer Matt. There are so many reasons. I suppose initially I was ashamed of my past and worried that it might colour the way your mother saw me. Then, not having told her at the beginning, it became almost impossible later on. I've pushed it to the back of my mind for so long that it never seemed appropriate to just come out and tell you all.'

'And I suppose you never would have if this blackmailer hadn't turned up? So what's going to happen now, will he go to the papers like he said?' Matthew's anger was rising, life had been so good of late and now his Dad was spoiling it all.

'I don't know son. I can't see it being of great interest to the nationals so I'm just hoping we'll not hear from this man again.'

'Oh that's just great! So what, we live in fear of being the centre of attention because our grandmother was a murderer?' The words were harsh, bitter.

'Matthew! Don't speak to your father like that and don't call your grandmother a murderer, you didn't even know her!' Jenny was shocked at the way he had taken the news, she hadn't known what to expect but it certainly wasn't this.

'Come on Angie, we're going.' Matthew stood up and took his wife by the hand, leaving before anything else was said. Jenny made to go after him.

'No, leave him; he's got to work it through for himself. It's been a shock to him, to you all.' Malcolm then looked at his daughter. Kate's face was pale as were her knuckles where she was grasping her husband's hand.

'I'm sorry love, I should have told you all before, I can see that now.'

Kate stood up, went over to her father and put her arms round his neck.

'No Dad. I know you well enough to realise that whatever you did or didn't do, you thought it was for the best. Matt will come round, he's shocked but he'll see sense eventually. My goodness, now I know why you asked us not to bring the children!'

Malcolm was close to tears. At least Kate wasn't angry with him. She always was one to think things over before acting or speaking her mind, rather like himself. Matthew had his mother's more fiery temperament.

Jenny picked up the scattered brochures from where they had fallen on the floor.

'I don't suppose anyone wants to look at these now? Another time perhaps?'

Kate smiled,

'Yes, another time. Mike and I will go now, give you time to yourselves and we'll talk later.' Kate hugged both parents before leaving, a very welcome act of love.

'What are those?' Jenny asked when the children had left. Malcolm still had the diaries beside him; he'd been touching them as a kind of talisman, as if he could draw strength from their proximity.

'Dad's old diaries, he told me to read them. I thought you might like to read them too, I'm sure he wouldn't mind and they'll probably tell you much more than I can and in a more coherent way too.'

Jenny was touched that he wanted to share them with her.

'Okay' she said, 'But not today, another time perhaps; I feel worn out now don't you?'

Malcolm nodded. It was only mid afternoon but the family meeting had drained them both of any energy and the subject was dropped by mutual and unspoken consent although they both knew that the past would continue to affect their future, at least for the time being.

Chapter 16

Frank Stokes was livid. He had worked the phone almost solidly for two hours, ringing old contacts and trying to call in a few favours which were owed to him but there was barely a glimmer of interest. He'd spent the evening before writing up his copy, the 'big' story which was going to make his name but the reality was it was only a scoop in his mind.

'So what's interesting about that?' An old colleague had asked bluntly. 'The mercy killing debate is old hat.'

'Well it's the angle it's written from, the piece will be great, you know I can do it!' But the piece was rather pedestrian and Frank was reluctantly beginning to see that for himself.

'A couple of hundred and a by-line; take it or leave it.' It was the best offer he'd had but Frank would rather refuse than settle so cheaply. He put the phone down with a grunt, opened the fridge and took out the last of the six pack he'd bought the day before. There was nothing else in the fridge except a tub of cheap margarine, shopping had not been high on his list of priorities but the beer would take the edge off his hunger. Next he fired up the laptop and played around with a few headlines, 'LOTTERY WIN FOR MURDERER'S FAMILY' not catchy enough. 'EIGHT MILLION FOR SON OF MURDERER' no, it needed punch; he must be losing his touch. 'THE WAGES OF SIN IS EIGHT MILLION' a possibility, distorting a quote was always good. Yes, he decided to go with that and began tweaking the piece again. As a last resort he would run it by his supervisor, Kirsty, that afternoon. She was already pushing him for the 'mystery' story which he'd taken time off to pursue. The only trouble was there would be no payment as such from the Mercury, he was salaried staff after all. At least she might be interested in the 'local born lad' angle. After another hour, Frank had had enough. He emailed the piece to Kirsty then decided to drop in at the pub on his way to the office. Hard work deserved a little reward, surely?

The pub was quiet, still Frank hadn't been in for weeks himself and it looked even more run down than he remembered. It smelled musty and damp, with about as much ambience as a dentist's waiting room. The beer was warm but welcome and the first pint was downed in one go, the second he took to a table by the window. Stokes idly ran his finger around the top of the glass studying the frothy amber liquid while replaying the last few days in his head, days which he had hoped would change his luck but in reality had left him angry and frustrated. Life certainly sucks when blokes like Malcolm Grainger, the son of a common murderer, could win eight million. Where was the justice in that? And he had been such a pathetic little wimp at school and even now was hiding behind his wife's skirt, letting her do the talking! What kind of a man does that? Frank got up wearily and went to the bar for another pint, deciding to make this the last. Kirsty would have had chance to read the article by now, he'd better get into the office to discuss the finer details although he thought it was pretty good as it stood.

'And this is what you needed time off for?' Kirsty was furious. 'Don't even think about putting a claim in for expenses Frank. This piece could have been written by a rookie without even leaving the office! No quotes, no up to date dirt on the subject. Whatever you were doing in the back of beyond certainly wasn't any kind of quality work was it? This might get into page six if you tighten it up a lot but the so called 'story' isn't worth much more than five hundred words... and have you been drinking, I thought you were on the wagon Frank? This doesn't bode well for the case to keep you on you know. Now, cut it down, tighten it up and do it as quickly as you can, you've already wasted enough time chasing ghosts!'

Frank didn't trust himself to say anything in his own defence. If this uppity kid didn't recognise a good story when she saw one then she wasn't worth arguing with. He sauntered over to his desk and switched on the computer. With an angry flourish he deleted the first three paragraphs, two from the middle section and put minimum effort into tying the story back together and re-working the ending. He emailed the new copy to Kirsty's computer, grabbed his jacket from the back of the chair and stormed out of the office. Even a rundown pub seemed more welcoming than the Mercury office and half an hour later Stokes found himself back in the seat by the window, drowning his sorrows and trying to think how he could make Malcolm Grainger pay for ruining his big chance to make something of himself. His thoughts were interrupted by his mobile phone ringing, it was Kirsty. For a moment Frank considered not answering but maybe her mood had mellowed if she'd read the edited version of the story. Three minutes later he was wishing he hadn't answered.

'Is this supposed to be the improved article or are you trying to be funny?' She didn't sound a happy bunny.

'I cut the word count down, isn't that what you wanted?' Frank was curt, rude almost.

'You're drunk! I thought you'd stopped drinking.'

'Oh, so you're my mother too now are you?' He didn't care anymore.

'Actually I'm your boss, or I was. You're fired Stokes, I'll get HR to send your P45 and any pay due to date, not that you've earned it.'

'Since when were you in charge of hiring and firing?'

'You forget, your contract is temporary and conditional. I have the discretion to keep you on or terminate the contract as I see fit. Read the small print Frank, goodbye!' The phone went silent. Frank gulped down the dregs of his pint and went to get a refill. His mind was clouded by beer and anger. The beer was a welcome soporific, the anger wasn't and it was all Malcolm Grainger's fault.

****

'You can move in as soon as you like.' Audrey smiled at Helen Price, enjoying the feeling of making someone's day.

'Oh thank you, that's wonderful. I'd like to take the bungalow on and perhaps do a little decorating first if that's okay?'

'No problem at all. Shall we say from next Monday? I'm afraid you'll have to begin paying the rent from then, it will be officially yours when you get the keys.'

'Yes, of course, that's fine. I don't quite know when we'll actually move in but I'll be spending time here every day so I should be able to keep you up to date.' Helen thanked Audrey once again and after glancing round what was to be their new home one more time, followed the warden out of number sixteen and joined her family in Peter's car.

'Everything okay?' Maggie asked.

'Fine, everything's just perfect.' Helen had decided which rooms needed a coat of paint to freshen them up and had mentally arranged the furniture she wanted to bring with them back to Fenbridge. There wouldn't be space for all their things of course but downsizing wasn't always a bad thing and there was room for enough of their possessions to meet their needs.

'Shall we call at B&Q on the way home to pick up some colour charts?' Peter offered.

'Oh could we, if it's not out of your way? I know the place is already in good order but putting a coat of paint on the rooms will freshen it up, make it feel like ours, you know?'

'Well, it's no problem at all. There's time for a look round too if you like, perhaps get some ideas?'

'Yes, that would be great wouldn't it George? Do you fancy a look round B&Q?'

'Has it got a garden centre?'

'It has but we won't have much to do in the way of gardening love. The grounds are tended for us, just think, no more grass to cut.' Helen tried to put a positive spin on their move.

'Well if you miss gardening George, you can always come and do ours. We only have a little patch of lawn but it grows far too quickly for my liking.' Peter too wanted George to feel comfortable about moving back to Fenbridge.

After collecting numerous colour charts Maggie suggested stopping for coffee on the way home.

'It's going to be wonderful having you close by, we can have trips out for coffee on a regular basis.' The sentiment was genuine but Helen was keen that she and George shouldn't take over their daughter's life.

'I've been doing some thinking,' she said, 'About our cottage in Scotland. We don't actually have to sell it as the rent on the new place isn't a problem. I thought we could keep it in the family, as a holiday home perhaps? It's your inheritance Maggie and we could put it in your name, it would save a lot of hassle in years to come.'

'Mum, that's not necessary! If you want to keep it as a holiday home then please do, but there's no need to put it in my name.'

'Just think about it love, talk to Peter before you decide. It would actually make life easier for us but I wouldn't want it to be a burden on you. I did think you could even rent it out as a holiday let if you wanted? It's a beautiful area, quite stunning all the year round but I know I've just sprung this on you so have a think, there's no hurry.' Helen had certainly given them something to contemplate and Maggie's mind had already sprung into action. It would be good for Helen and George to go back for holidays too and they could all go together so Maggie could help with her father. It was close enough for weekend visits too; maybe her mother's idea wasn't such a bad one.

****

It was not going to be an easy decision, that was apparent as soon as Alice walked into the first pen. Four cats vied for attention, a silver tabby, a petite pure white queen with huge green eyes and two black cats, identical except for a small white mark on the chest of one. The tabby was the pushy one, jumping into her arms before she even had chance to sit on the bench.

'All right, I know you want a fuss.' She tickled the cat's ears, exactly the right move to elicit a gentle purring sound. The three others waited patiently by her feet, six bright eyes pleading for attention. Reaching down to stroke the others, Alice was rewarded by a playful nip from the tabby cat on her knee, he had claimed this visitor as his own exclusive property.

'Goodness how do people decide, I could take them all home!'

Pauline, the owner of the rescue centre and full time cat slave replied candidly,

'That's what I was banking on! No, seriously the cat usually does the choosing and most of them have mastered the art of pleading even if it's only with a simple look. Remember this is only the first pen, there are eleven more and then the sheds for the kittens and the isolation unit for our new arrivals.'

'I honestly don't think I should look any further, what can you tell me about this tabby?'

'Well, he's been here about two months which is surprising really as he's such a friendly boy. He was found on the outskirts of town in quite a bad way, dehydrated and with an injury to his back leg. As you can see he's fully recovered now, eating us out of house and home and none the worse for the ordeal. Obviously he wasn't micro chipped or we would have located his owners and the vet thinks he's probably four or five years old. Most of the cats have already been neutered but if you choose a new arrival we'll still get that done for you together with a full health check and inoculations.'

'Hmm, the age is about right, I don't think I want a kitten as I work full time so an older cat would probably suit my lifestyle better. Does this one have a name?'

'Wallace.' Pauline smiled as she watched him making his pitch. Alice tried to put Wallace back on the floor but he dug his claws into her trousers, clinging on pitifully.

'As you can see, he's very friendly!'
Managing to extricate herself she picked up one of the black cats.

'They're brothers and I'd really like them to be re-homed together. Perhaps they're a bit young for you, only about eighteen months so it's probably unwise to leave them alone for long periods.'

'I wouldn't mind taking two, they'd be company for each other when I'm out.' The little white cat had curled up on Alice's feet. 'What's this one called?' she asked.

'Unoriginally, Snowball, she's been with us for nearly a year now. I think she gets overlooked as she's so quiet and a bit older than the others, about five or maybe six but very healthy and friendly. Snowball would certainly be a gentle pet and perhaps less demanding than Wallace.'

Snowball was a bundle of soft white fur. Her coat was longer than Wallace with little whorls and cow licks all over giving the impression that she'd just come out of the tumble drier. She was petite with spindly legs which hardly looked strong enough to support her body, small though she was.

'Do you think they would settle together if I took them both?'

'Why yes, they've always shared the pen so I don't think there'd be any problem at all.'

'Right, I'd like to take them both please. What happens next?'

'Well, first of all I shall resist the urge to give you a big hug for your generosity! I do like to come out for a home visit first if that's okay with you? Although I'm sure from what you've told me everything will be fine but it's our policy to visit beforehand.'

'That's no problem Pauline, it's a very sensible policy and I'm happy to go along with that.'

'The next thing is to take them to our vet for a health check and to update their inoculations. They've both been neutered so that's not a problem. Could we arrange the visit for this weekend, Saturday perhaps and then I can bring them to stay on Sunday?'

'Great, that will give me time to get some things together. You will advise me about food and so forth, I've never had a cat before.'

'Of course although I think you're going to be a natural. I can show you what food they're used to before you go and I'll bring a few days' supply on Sunday. If you have any problems I'm always on the end of a phone and am happy to help. I like to keep in contact with as many of the cats as I can. It's so rewarding to know they're going on well.'

The decision was made and as Alice drove home Pauline and the sanctuary filled her thoughts. She was obviously a very special person to devote her life to rescuing needy cats. Of course the idea for a pet had come from Maggie and the story of Tara but she wondered why she had never considered having a pet before. For the first time in weeks Alice's mind was occupied with thoughts other than the situation with her mother and she realised she was quite excited at the prospect of having not one, but two feline companions. She decided to do a detour to the retail park where a pet superstore would still be open. It would be fun choosing a few things, a couple of baskets perhaps, litter trays and toys. Alice couldn't wait for the weekend.

Chapter 17

'I haven't seen mother this week.' Alice told Maggie the following Tuesday. 'Not deliberately but mainly because it's been such a busy week, for which I blame you entirely.'

Maggie's eyes widened, mystified as to what her client could mean.

'I am now officially a cat herder or a fur mummy, whatever you like to call it. I have not one, but two cats!'

'Really?' Both women were smiling. 'Come on then tell me about it?'

Alice briefly related the visit to Pauline's cat shelter and the swift decision to adopt two cats. The newcomers had obviously made a difference to Alice's mood, she was certainly more upbeat than usual.

'I'm so pleased for you Alice, but that's not why I told you about Tara.'

'I know but it started me thinking and perhaps I've been alone too long. It's only been three days but they've taken over my life, in the best possible way of course. I've probably had only myself to think about for too long and it's good to have the cats to care for. You should see them Maggie, they're so sweet. I thought Wallace was going to be the dominant one, he's big and boisterous and knows how to get his own way but then along comes little Snowball in her quiet manner with an almost silent 'meow' and he's a pushover! It's amazing to see them snuggled up together, I'm utterly captivated by them.'

The conversation eventually moved on to more serious matters, in particular Alice's continued frustration at her mother's refusal to reveal the identity of her father but Maggie was amazed at what a difference the two cats had made to Alice's life. Reflecting on this later brought to mind the changes she had noticed in her own pet dog,

Ben. Since Helen and George had moved in, Ben had made a point of being close to George whenever possible. He rested his chin on George's knee or curled up at his feet, affectionate actions which had previously been bestowed on Maggie or Peter. The more she thought about this, the more it seemed that some animals have a natural instinct to know when and where their affection is needed. Ben's presence was a calming influence on her father and a bond seemed to be developing between the two. It was generally recognised that owning pets could be therapeutic but there seemed to be more than one facet to this.

'And we call them dumb animals.' Maggie thought.

****

Kate Burton had been shocked by the things her father had revealed a few days ago. It was fair to say that her Dad was never one to talk about his past but then he wasn't a great talker at the best of times. She had known that he was still a young boy when his mother had died and assumed that he had very few memories to talk about. How wrong this had been and how terrible for Dad and Granddad to have been through such an ordeal. Kate had been furious with her brother and as soon as possible she rang him up to tell him so. Matthew had always been a bit of a hot-head but there was no excuse for treating their father in such a way. Having made these feelings known she knew it was best to leave Matt alone to think over the incident, he usually saw sense in the end. Kate had met with Jenny afterwards who had shared her own disappointment that Malcolm hadn't shared his past. The revelation had left Jenny with a feeling of insecurity as previously she would have sworn that they had absolutely no secrets from each other. Now she didn't know what to think and although loyalty to her husband prevailed as mother and daughter talked, Kate could tell it had shaken Jenny more that she admitted. Kate's mind was spinning with all these thoughts as she juggled Daisy on her hip, rummaging through her bag to find some change to pay for the eggs she'd just bought. Life was certainly a roller coaster at the moment with these surprise revelations and the lottery win, where would it all end she wondered. When she carried Daisy out of the supermarket it had begun to rain. Pulling the giggling child's hood up she dashed to the car. Kate had been so preoccupied with these thoughts that she had failed to notice the rather shabby looking man who was taking much more than a passing interest in both mother and daughter.

****

Alice was already regretting accepting the invitation to the theatre with Joel. Having witnessed firsthand the kind of marriage Caroline had endured she had never felt the desire to form a long term relationship, or even a short term one come to think about it. Perhaps if her mother had been faithful to Ronald things could have been different but that was one of those things which would never be known. You only get one chance at this life, Alice thought, and sadly you can't press re-wind to try again. That was one of the reasons she had previously avoided romantic relationships. How could you know who to trust? Wasn't it a huge gamble committing your life to another person? No, marriage was not for Alice who had realised a long time ago that hers was to be a single life, apart from the recently acquired cats who were already firmly rooted in her affections. By remaining single there would never be someone else to acquiesce to and Alice had always wanted to be her own woman, to please herself as to how she lived without having to answer to a man for every action and decision. Hopefully Joel realised that this was only a platonic thing. He had two tickets and presumably asked her to accompany him rather than waste one of them. With hindsight maybe she should have arranged for them to meet in the theatre bar, it wouldn't have seemed so much like a 'date' then but it was too late to change the arrangement, Joel would be arriving in less than half an hour. Alice scanned the wardrobe wondering what to wear. Not having many choices for such an occasion should have made it easier but it didn't. What did people wear for the theatre these days? It was such a long time since she had been; casual or smart? Well, it was only Fenbridge Civic Theatre, not London's West End so she eventually settled on semi-smart. A calf length skirt with high boots and a soft light blue jersey top were hopefully the right combination. She didn't want Joel to think she had made a huge effort with her appearance, yet again, it was important to look right for the occasion. But, Alice thought, what was the occasion, a date or a couple of friends sharing an evening out together?

'Stop it Alice!' The words were directed to her reflection in the bedroom mirror. 'You always have to over-think things. Just let it go and enjoy the evening for what it is.' She finished brushing her long blonde hair which was loose tonight rather than pinned up as it always was for work. Joel was bang on time and also looked different from when he was at work but then they all wore the same boring white lab coats, individuality was nonexistent in the working environment. Alice felt slightly awkward as Joel complimented her appearance, it sounded remarkably like the beginning of a date rather than the friendship thing she was hoping for but she thanked him graciously and they set off in his black

Peugeot 308 convertible, a step up from the battered ten year old Mini which Alice drove, when it deemed to start.

The show was brilliant and had the effect of relaxing both Alice and Joel as they were drawn into the music, performed excellently by only a small but exceptionally versatile cast. During the interval they ordered wine at the bar and chatted easily about the first half and the music they had enjoyed.

'It amazes me how they can alter the whole feel of the stage with only a few simple props and clever lighting.' Alice commented. 'They've achieved exactly the right atmosphere and mood for each song with such fluid, subtle changes.'

'You seemed to be almost singing along with most of the songs, do you have a favourite?'

'Oh gosh, I wasn't singing aloud was I? I love them all really but the music from Les Miserable's is what really moves me. I saw the London show with a friend one weekend ages ago and was hooked immediately. I didn't know the story then and wished I had so I bought the CD and read up on it afterwards. To hear those songs again now I have some idea of the story behind them makes them even more powerful, I love them!'

'Well, I'm glad you came and that you're enjoying yourself.' Joel smiled and reached across the table, covering her hand with his own. Alice was taken completely by surprise and immediately snatched her hand away as if she'd been scalded.

'Sorry...' Joel looked hurt and a little confused, 'I didn't mean to offend you.'

Alice immediately felt stupid, it was hardly the most intimate of gestures.

'Shouldn't we be getting back in now, I think they've rung the first bell?'

Joel drunk the last of his wine and stood to leave, arm outstretched to allow Alice to go first and being careful not to make physical contact. The second half of the show was every bit as good as the first. Andrew Lloyd Webber compositions featured largely in this section and Alice found herself lost in the evocative music from shows including 'Phantom of the Opera' 'Aspects of Love' and 'Evita'. When the final encore was over and the curtain fell, her thoughts returned to reality. Turning to look at Joel whose handsome face still reflected some of the earlier confusion, Alice attempted to make up for her previous reaction by smiling warmly and thanking him for the invitation.

'It's been a lovely evening Joel, I've really enjoyed it, thank you so much.' Joel smiled too but his eyes still reflected a degree of confusion, obviously unsure of where he stood. On the way home their conversation focussed solely on the performance and content of the show and when Joel left her an awkward goodbye was said and he made no attempt to touch her again.

Walking into the darkness of the flat Alice was pleased and comforted by the presence of her two cats. Wallace jumped down from the sofa. Stretching his front paws before padding over to rub against her legs. Snowball opened one eye, yawned then dropped her chin onto her front legs again to resume the interrupted sleep. Somehow their presence lifted Alice's mood. The theatre had been an excellent mid-week interlude in what was normally a rather mundane life but Alice was left with a strange feeling of melancholy. Opening the back door to let the cats out she then filled a glass of water, picked up an apple from the fruit bowl and settled down on the sofa. She would give the cats half an hour or so before calling them in for the night, strangely in need of their company. Reflecting on the evening brought mixed emotions to mind. The music had been incredible and for that Alice was glad to have seen the performance but Joel was a different matter. Undeniably good company and a very attractive companion, she felt somehow that she had handled the evening badly. With hindsight it may have been better to have laid down some ground rules before accepting the invitation but she could hardly have given Joel a list of conditions. It was only natural that he had thought of the evening as a date and truthfully part of Alice knew this too. Had she been unfair to Joel? Perhaps so, and she would apologise tomorrow at work. Another question which gnawed at the back of her mind was whether she wanted to go out with him again? Wasn't she the one intent on a single life and wouldn't seeing a man confuse the issue, especially if he had romantic inclinations? Yet the thought of seeing Joel outside of work really appealed; his company was enjoyable, he possessed a gentle personality, was amusing and even witty at times. But had she ruined it by recoiling from his touch? It had hardly been taking liberties, Joel had only reached for her hand. That simple touch however seemed to pierce the protective bubble Alice had built around herself. The persona presented to the world of being a happily single young woman had been challenged by that one gentle touch. Was she really so happy being alone?

An urgent mewing at the door broke into her thoughts and rising to let her new housemates in, Alice decided to call it a day and go to bed. Wallace and Snowball followed on to the tiny bedroom, claiming their space on the duvet. Patting their heads, she wondered if these two would really be all the company necessary for a happy future.

Chapter 18

At four o'clock on a rather dismal Wednesday afternoon Maggie was about to leave for home. The nights were drawing in and she preferred to make the journey in the last of the daylight if at all possible. As she shrugged into her coat there was a gentle tap on the door and Sue came in.

'Oh, are you leaving already?'

'That was the plan, why, will you miss me?'

'As if! Actually there's a lady in reception who wants to talk to you. I don't think she's one of your clients and hasn't got an appointment but does seem rather agitated, what do you want me to do?'

'I'm okay for a few minutes, ask her to come in will you Sue?' Maggie looked at the time and sighed, hung her coat back on the peg and moved towards the door to meet this unexpected visitor. It was difficult to guess the lady's age, the style of dress was that of a woman in her sixties but her face suggested a much younger age even with the anxious expression. Maggie smiled a greeting and invited her inside.

'Sue tells me you want to talk to me. Do you want to arrange counselling?'

'No, well I don't think so. My name is Caroline Greenwood and you're currently seeing my daughter, Alice?'

Maggie nodded. 'Well it's lovely to meet you Caroline but if I was seeing your daughter there would be no way I could discuss it with you I'm afraid.'

'Yes, I realise that but I'm not here to ask about Alice, I just want to tell you something.'

'Please Caroline,' Maggie broke in, 'This is really not appropriate. While I'm sure you have your daughter's best interests at heart, I really can't have this conversation with you.'

Caroline Greenwood ignored Maggie's gentle protestations and launched into what she had come to say.

'I love Alice, of course and I know she's furious with me at the moment because I can't tell her who her father is... It's because I was raped Ms Sayer, Alice is the product of rape.' Caroline searched Maggie's face for a reaction before continuing. 'So you see, I'd much rather my daughter believed that I was unfaithful to her Dad, Ronald that is, than learn the truth. No one should be faced with that kind of knowledge and I'll never tell Alice the truth, it could be devastating.' An unhappy silence lingered between the women. The trouble with words is that once they are spoken they can't be unspoken. Eventually Caroline spoke again. 'Ronald knew about the rape. He was serving in the Falklands at the time and I didn't tell him until he came home by which time I was well into the pregnancy. He wanted me to have an abortion but I was almost three months by then and I'd come to terms with it and simply looked upon the baby as my child, however it had been conceived. I suppose I'd already bonded, I'd had plenty of time to think of nothing else whilst Ronald was away. It was so much harder for him of course, knowing the circumstances. He felt that the child would be a constant reminder of the rape and I think there was a degree of guilt in that, irrational guilt of course, but he had been away and unable to protect me. Throughout the pregnancy Ronald tried to persuade me to give the baby up for adoption but I couldn't do that. Perhaps I should have because in the end he was proved right. He could never look at Alice without thinking of her origins, she was a permanent reminder. I'd hoped of course that he would change his mind, fall in love with the baby as I did, but he never did, he couldn't bear to look upon what to him was simply another man's child and one conceived in violence at that. He stayed with me, even though there were constant accusations of choosing Alice over him but Ronald provided for us both yet never could find it in his heart to care for her in any way.'

Maggie looked with compassion at this distraught lady.

'Caroline, I can understand what brought you here this afternoon and I admire your bravery and resolve. This isn't however information which will help me in my work with Alice. Naturally I will never disclose this but I still cannot enter into any kind of dialogue with you about the issue. It does however seem that you might benefit by talking to someone yourself. What you're carrying around is a very complex and difficult burden. Obviously I couldn't offer to counsel you myself, as that would present a conflict of interest, but I have a colleague who may be able to help, he's very understanding and works from this practise too. If this is something you'd like to consider you can make an appointment through your GP.' Maggie felt terrible dismissing this lady in such a manner but it would be totally unethical to enter into any further dialogue on the issue. Caroline had shared this disturbing secret and it was to be hoped she would consider counselling for her own well being. Maggie stood and placed her hand gently on the other woman's shoulder.

'You've been remarkably courageous in coming here today and I'm truly sorry that I can't be of help to you.'

Caroline nodded sadly. 'I suppose I knew it was futile but thought it might help you to understand Alice a little better and you could perhaps persuade her to forget about her parentage?' Even as she spoke, the realisation that Maggie couldn't possibly do what she was asking was apparent. Perhaps it had been a mistake to come after all.

'I'm so sorry Caroline but I won't be able to use this information in any way. Counselling is about finding your own answers and I never try to influence my clients, they have their own lives to live and my opinions simply don't enter into it at all. This must be so disappointing for you but there really is nothing I can do, except to urge you to consider counselling for yourself, will you think about it?'

Caroline smiled weakly and stood to leave, offering only a brief word of thanks before walking quietly out of the office, wondering why it had been so important to tell Alice's counsellor the truth. Whether it was to protect her own integrity or in some indirect way to ask Maggie to intercede on her behalf, she was unsure but the visit had been fruitless. Although perhaps having told someone the truth after all this time was a good thing and even though there was no positive outcome from going to the health centre, in a small way Caroline did feel some degree of relief.

Maggie reached again for her coat, mulling over what a terrible secret Caroline had carried throughout the years and now she too must keep that same secret and somehow not allow the knowledge of it to colour the sessions with Alice. Half an hour after the first attempt to leave, Maggie switched off the office light and headed for home.

****

Joyce Patterson was Maggie's supervisor with whom she met every couple of weeks. Their relationship spanned over a decade and had taken them beyond the counsellor/supervisor roles to that of good friends although they rarely met between the supervision visits. Walking into Joyce's house felt like entering another world, one of peace and tranquillity. The older woman's calm personality and even temperament overflowed into her home making these regular visits a pleasure. Maggie could always rely upon Joyce's wisdom, which had been invaluable on many occasions. When the coffee was brewed and the two were seated in the warmth and brightness of the conservatory, nursing the hot drinks to warm them against the worsening weather outside, Maggie began to talk about Caroline's visit the previous day.

'Alice is quite a complex character who appears to be in control and very capable but is eaten up inside by the strength of these feelings which she can't explain. Sometimes she flits from one idea to another without processing the thoughts and feelings. Everything I suggest or mention is latched on to it as if this is the new idea which will be the answer to all her problems. I have my work cut out just keeping the focus on one thing at a time. In a way, I can't see where this is going, Alice sprints off at a tangent and I can barely keep up with her. Do you know, I used my cat as a kind of illustration about living in the moment and on her next visit she told me she'd acquired two cats! And now after meeting her mother I feel my job's going to be even more difficult. I have information which I shouldn't have and which is impossible to forget.'

'If you feel compromised in this situation it would be entirely understandable for you to refer this girl to a colleague.' Joyce smiled at Maggie's instantaneous frown. 'But of course you don't want to do that do you?'

'No, although we haven't been meeting for very long there's a relationship developing and I'd like to stick with it. Yes, it'll be a challenge but I'll simply have to box the information from her mother and continue as if I had never met Caroline. I did suggest that she might like to see someone too; Can you imagine the suffering such a burden must have been over the years? It's understandable that she doesn't want her daughter to know, how such information would affect Alice is almost impossible to judge.'

'Hmm, this is a difficult one. If the daughter knew the circumstances surrounding her birth it could go a long way to understanding why the man whom she thought of as father behaved like he did. And it could also strengthen the relationship between mother and daughter which sounds rather tenuous. On the other hand, if she knew about the rape, it could have far reaching effects on the girl's own mental health. There are solid arguments for both sides. The daughter is judging the mother on information which is inaccurate and incomplete but if the mother doesn't tell the truth, this can never be resolved. How often people are quick to judge others when they don't know all the facts; we should walk in a person's shoes before we make any judgement of their actions.' Joyce was rather thoughtful.

'How about you Joyce, would you want to know the truth if you were Alice?'

'Good heavens, what a question! Knowing you were conceived in such a violent way would naturally have its own psychological impact. As to whether it's preferable to know, I have absolutely no idea at all, do you?'

'No, I don't think I do. Having always believed that honesty is the best policy, this is one of those cases which challenge such a belief. My only hope is that mother and daughter can build some kind of relationship and move on from here. It would be tragic if this clouded their future as it has clouded their past.'

'And you Maggie will have to remain the silent pig in the middle, I don't envy you.'

Maggie rolled her eyes, taking a sip of coffee and mulling over the problem before changing the topic.

'I have a new private client too, a lady who has won over eight million pounds on the lottery. Close your mouth Joyce it's not a good look! Apart from the expected begging letters, someone from her husband's past is actually trying to blackmail them. My client has found out that his mother was accused of murder when he was just a child and this has only come to light because of the blackmail attempt. Apparently his mother was suffering from a terminal illness and helped her own invalid mother to commit suicide. There seem to be judgement issues here too although my client's more upset that her husband had never told her about it rather than the actual event.'

'I suppose it would be called mercy killing today, a difficult issue at the best of times. I hope they're not going to pay the blackmailer?'

'I don't think so, as you say this was probably a big thing at the time but now it's almost a daily occurrence. Yet you're right, mercy killing is another tricky issue and again almost impossible to form an opinion about when you've never been in such a situation.

As always, sharing the difficult issues which clients' presented made Maggie feel so much lighter. These confidential conversations between counsellor and supervisor were pivotal to her own well being and often gave another unbiased opinion, a fresh look from a different angle which invariably proved that two heads were better than one.

Chapter 19

Frank Stokes plugged the phone into his laptop and opened the photographs he had taken that morning. They looked pretty good, he'd managed to get reasonably close without being spotted, but then no one took notice of people holding mobile phones any more, everyone seemed to be obsessed with them and devoted more attention to their phones than to other people. A little bit of cropping on one would make it perfect and the other one was a dream with the baby looking directly at him and smiling as if she knew her picture was being taken. He hit the print button and watched the photos come slowly out of the ancient printer he had borrowed from the lady who ran the B & B, two copies of each. He wasn't particularly pleased to be back in Fenbridge so soon but now that he was unemployed he needed to find an alternative way to make some money. Malcolm Grainger was the reason for his downfall so it seemed only fair that he should be Frank's new source of income, he could certainly afford it. Frank opened another can from the six pack he'd bought earlier, his third one so far, and downed it in one go. Looking at the photographs brought a smile to his face. Yes, they were good, the woman was certainly a looker, nice body, petite like her mother and a pretty face too, Grainger was a lucky man, a family and money, some people had it all. He placed the photographs carefully in the bottom of his case and shoved it back under the bed until he decided what to do with them. Having followed the young woman home he now had her address too, another day of planning and observation and he would be in a position to decide the best way to proceed. But now it was time to make another telephone call, thinking up his next move was actually proving to be quite enjoyable, and hopefully if the moves were right it would be profitable too.

****

Jenny answered the phone. 'Hello?'
No reply; she looked at the caller display, 'number withheld'. Replacing the receiver she said to Malcolm,
'That's the fourth one of those calls today, 'number withheld', someone trying to sell something I suppose.'
Malcolm smiled, pleased that his wife seemed to have got over their recent problems. They hadn't really talked about it in any depth but at least she was speaking to him and the cogs of their life seemed to be turning reasonably well again. Maybe things were a little cooler than usual but admittedly it had been a huge shock and he'd always found it best to let Jenny take time to mull things over after any kind of altercation. He was confident that she would bring the subject up in her own good time. So much had happened since the lottery win; they had both given up their jobs now, Jenny was delighted to have done so whereas he had a few reservations but was eventually persuaded that the freedom it would bring was worth it. They shared a desire to travel and see more of the world while they were still young enough to enjoy it and work commitments obviously presented an obstacle in doing so. Jenny had a fancy for cruising and as some of the cruise liners seemed to stop at very exotic destinations they both felt it would be a good way of seeing more of the world in a leisurely fashion. There was also the much talked about family holiday to Florida which had been put on hold since the evening Malcolm had told his children about his past life in Liverpool. Kate understood but Matthew hadn't been in touch since, although he knew their son had spoken to Jenny on the phone a couple of times. Hopefully, like his mother, Matthew would come

round in his own time and they could finalise the plans for Disney World which even Malcolm was looking forward to.

'Want some tea love?' Jenny asked.

'Please.'

The telephone rang again and Jenny picked it up on her way to the kitchen. Looking puzzled she turned to face Malcolm and switched the loudspeaker function on. They were both silent as they listened to the unmistakable sound of a clock ticking. After a few seconds she replaced the receiver, shaking her head as she said,

'Sounded like an office somewhere do you think?'

'I don't know, was the number withheld again?'

'Yes, probably another cold caller, they're becoming quite a nuisance.' Jenny continued to the kitchen only slightly perplexed but there were no more calls and after watching a repeat of 'Morse' they made their way to bed. Malcolm lay awake for a while listening to his wife's gentle breathing. She had fallen asleep almost as soon as her head hit the pillow whilst Malcolm was thinking over the diary entries his Dad had made after his Mother died. He could only imagine how painful it must have been for Bill, being widowed so early was bad enough but to have the stigma of his beloved wife's reputation sullied by the press must have been intolerable. The grieving would also have been put on hold as the young Bill Grainger concentrated on finding a new home in a different area. Malcolm could barely remember that brief period of time between his mother dying and moving to Fenbridge, the events must have been close together as they were certainly simultaneous in his memory. There wasn't much more to read of the diaries, he'd finish them tomorrow and pass them on to Jenny, surely she couldn't fail to be touched by her father-in-laws own words and hopefully gain an understanding as to why Malcolm had never talked about that period of his life. Feeling slightly more positive, he draped his arm around his slumbering wife before also drifting off to sleep.

The phone sounded louder than usual in the quiet stillness of night. Malcolm and Jenny both woke instantly and Malcolm reached for the receiver, panic rising within him at the lateness of the hour and anticipation of bad news.

'Hello?' There was no reply.

'Who is this?' he asked but the only response was the ticking of a clock which seemed to echo round the bedroom as he passed the receiver to Jenny. She listened only for a moment then slammed the phone down, annoyance replacing earlier concern.

'It's two o'clock in the morning, is this someone's idea of a joke?' As she spoke the words another idea sprang to mind and she grabbed her husband's arm. 'It's that Frank Stokes, that's who it'll be! He said we hadn't heard the last of him.'

'Surely not, what good would making silly phone calls do him?'

'I don't know but I'd lay odds on it being him.'

'Look it could be anyone, kids playing pranks or something, let's not jump to conclusions.'

'Kids, at this time of night? No, it's him, I'm certain.'

'Well there's nothing we can do about it now, get some sleep and we'll discuss it tomorrow.' They settled down but sleep didn't come easily to either of them. An hour later when they had just begun to doze it happened again. The phone ringing, the clock ticking, the unsettling feeling which would probably deprive them of any more sleep that night. Jenny went to the kitchen to make cocoa and Malcolm went to the bathroom then followed her downstairs.

'We should go to the police.' Jenny said.

'Maybe not, they're only phone calls, he hasn't threatened us, assuming that it is Stokes, so what can the police do?'

She gave her husband a wry look and asked,

'Is that the real reason or are you afraid your secret will come out again.'

Malcolm's heart sank; is this the way it was going to be, would she bring this up every time something went wrong? His reply was slow in coming, his words measured,

'If you're right it's only because I worry about Dad and you and the kids. I remember what it was like being the centre of such awful publicity and I don't want it to happen to any of you.' He placed his half empty cup on the table and walked sadly back upstairs to bed.

****

On Friday evening Maggie and Peter were taking her parents to Scotland to begin sorting things out ready for their move. Helen had got the keys to their new home the previous Monday and with help from Sue's husband Alan, the walls in all the rooms were painted in fresh pastel colours. She had also ordered new carpeting throughout which was due to be laid the following week, when a new sofa and twin beds would also be arriving.

'Alan's been wonderful, he's quick and efficient and such great company. Your Dad and I seemed to laugh the whole time he was there.'

'Yes, he's great and always so willing. Being a policeman does have its advantages and having rest days in a block is certainly one of them. Mind you Sue keeps him busy when he's at home, he probably enjoyed being at yours for a change.'

George was sitting in the front passenger seat while Peter drove and the women were in the back.

'How long a drive is it Chris?' George's words stunned the other three; Chris was Maggie's first husband who had died more than fifteen years ago. Helen placed her hand gently on his shoulder and leaned forward.

'This is Peter not Chris, you're getting confused love.'

'Well where's Chris then?'

'Chris died a long time ago Dad, don't you remember?' They were sad words for Maggie to have to speak.

'Then why didn't someone tell me?' George was beginning to sound agitated. Peter switched on the radio,

'Shall we have some music, radio two George?'

'Yes, that'll be good, how much longer then?'

'About another forty minutes I should think, if the traffic stays light.'

Helen shook her head sadly; this was another reminder of George's state of mind. Peter had done well to distract him it wouldn't have been easy for him to be mistaken for Chris. Maggie squeezed her mother's hand grateful for the music filling the car instead of what could have been an embarrassing silence.

The cottage was cold with a damp, unlived in feeling pervading the atmosphere. The first job was to turn the thermostat up and light the gas fire in the lounge. Helen felt quite emotional entering the house which had been their home for so many happy years but as was her way she immersed herself in busyness to distract such thoughts, unpacking the few provisions and overnight bag they had brought. Three weeks ago when they had left quite suddenly, Helen had no idea of what their future held. Within that relatively short time they had found a new home back in Fenbridge, an unanticipated move but one which she strongly felt was the right thing to do in the circumstances. They needed the support that Maggie and Peter could offer; she would look forward not back telling herself that there were still good memories to be made and happy times still to come.

It was Friday evening and there was little time to do much more than make a hot drink and unpack the few things they had brought for the kitchen before retiring for the night. An early start would enable them to get through the necessary jobs and two days would probably see the task completed.

George and Helen slept surprisingly well.

'That bed's moulded to my shape.' George proclaimed at breakfast.

'Yes, but it's time for a new one for our new home.' His wife told him.

'Why do we need a new home? What's wrong with this one?'

Helen sighed, they had had this conversation at least once a day since finding the bungalow at The Lawns. Maggie answered the question and also the one that Helen had asked a few days ago about this cottage she so loved.

'We really want you and Mum to be near to us Dad. You're both getting older and we can be on hand to help if you need it. But we'll keep this place for a holiday home shall we, then you can come and stay whenever you like?' Maggie and Peter had discussed the unexpected proposition from Helen and decided that it made sense. Her parents still had an emotional attachment to what had been their dream retirement cottage so keeping it would enable them to come whenever they wanted. Peter and Maggie both loved the area too and would enjoy being able to get away for occasional weekends. As for Helen's idea of renting it out, that perhaps would prove difficult with practical complications which they could presently do without. They would however be able to let friends use it, Sue, Alan and Rose would be delighted at such an offer. Helen was smiling, delighted at the decision. They could discuss transferring it into Maggie's name at a later date, she was just glad that they were in agreement to keep the cottage on. Without their input Helen would never manage the upkeep of two homes. She mouthed a silent 'thank you' to Maggie before turning her attention to the tasks of the day.

'I have lists.' She announced and Peter rolled his eyes. Helen's lists were famous in the family and she possessed several notebooks which were frequently used for 'to do' lists. The first list was of furniture they would be taking. This was a surprisingly short list, but as she explained, they were downsizing, they had new beds and a sofa on order, their present suite was far too big, and with all the fitted wardrobes in the new place they could leave most of the furniture in situ. Now that it was decided to keep the cottage it made sense to leave several pieces of furniture and Helen would adjust the kitchen list in order to leave enough equipment for visitors. After explaining all this she smiled at the other three and said,

'Let the work commence!'

Chapter 20

Monday morning found Maggie returning to Acacia Avenue, unsure exactly what Jenny Grainger needed from their time together. As was often the case listening was the main priority and in many cases Maggie found that simply reflecting a client's words gave them another perspective on their situation.

'Come in, please.' Jenny greeted her warmly. 'Shall we sit in the conservatory, it gets the morning sun and is quite warm at this time of day?' It was a small conservatory but as promised, warm and bright, a relaxing place for them to talk.

'What kind of week have you had?' Maggie began.

'Strange really but more low points that high I'm afraid.'

'Would you like to tell me about it?'

'Well, things between Mal and I are a little better but still cool if not so frosty. I honestly don't know what to think about his revelations which have certainly made me see him in a different light and Bill too when I think about it. We haven't really discussed the subject yet but I know I'm going to have to address it soon. Malcolm has some diaries that his dad wrote years ago which he wants me to read. It seems a tad intrusive reading someone's diaries but apparently it was at Bill's request and Mal thinks they might help me to understand it better too.'

To Maggie, Jenny's words brought to mind her recent conversation with Joyce about not judging a person unless you've walked in their shoes.

'Perhaps they might bring a fresh insight into exactly what your husband's family went through?'

'Yes, they probably will. What Mal's mother did keeps going round in my mind. I honestly don't know how she could take her own mother's life. It's not something I could do, at least I don't think so but perhaps you never know unless you're faced with the same situation? Still, the hardest part for me to accept is that Mal never told me any of it. I always thought we were so close and knew everything about each other...' Jenny turned to gaze from the window, thoughtfully studying the wintry garden scene. Leaves that had so recently been vibrant and crisp with autumn reds, gold and orange, lay shrivelling on the damp grass; the scene felt appropriate for her mood.

'If Malcolm's father had never talked about these events could it be that Malcolm took his lead from that? We're all made up of our life experiences and our values are often absorbed from our parents. Could these introjected values have caused your husband to remain silent?' Maggie broke the reflective mood.

'I suppose so, he's always been very close to his Dad, understandably so and you're right, Bill has never discussed their past, almost as if their lives only began when they moved to Fenbridge. I've assumed that it was too painful to talk about his wife so have never intruded on those memories and men don't generally talk about emotional matters do they? But I can't get over the hurt that Malcolm's kept such a huge secret from me and I need to know why. Is it because he doesn't trust me, in which case our marriage hasn't been all that I've thought it was.'

'I wouldn't read too much into that, as you've said, men don't find it as easy to talk as women do and it's not just you he hasn't told. Malcolm doesn't seem to have been able to share it with anyone. It's still very early and very raw for both of you. Yes, you need answers but perhaps offering you the diaries is an attempt to give you the information you need when Malcolm may feel unable to verbalise all that happened in his childhood.'

'I never really looked upon it that way. So could he have been in denial, is that what you would call it?' Jenny was once again focussed.

'Perhaps it's not so much in denial as 'boxing' the issue. He's obviously aware that it happened and some of the facts are in the open, his mother's death at such an early age for example, but the details which are painful and confusing can get pushed into the sub-conscious mind, put in a box almost and never addressed. Very often an event in later life can bring these issues to the fore, in this case the blackmail attempt, and it can be quite traumatic.'

'Oh Maggie, I've been looking at it purely from my point of view and not even thinking about what Mal suffered, and is suffering now... how utterly selfish!'

'No, don't berate yourself Jenny. Your reactions have been perfectly natural and as I keep saying it's very early days. Your understanding of the situation is changing all the time as will Malcolm's too. Perhaps reading the diaries will not only help you to understand but give you a focal point to discuss the issue together?'

'Yes, you're right, I'll read them and then hopefully we can talk about it. I think that Malcolm needs to talk to a counsellor more than I do. Could you see him as well?'

'Not unless I saw you together if you both wanted that, or I would happily recommend a colleague if he decides it's the right thing to do.'

Jenny was silent again, organising her thoughts. 'We've been getting some phone calls too which I think could be this blackmailer.'

'Is he making more demands?'

'No, it's just silence or the ticking of a clock. It might not be him but I rather suspect it is and he's trying to spook us in some way. We had them throughout the night too and eventually unplugged the phone.'

'Have you told the police?'

'No, we can't be sure it's him and if it is, Mal has the same problem with the whole story becoming public. I think this blackmailer's just a pathetic little man who's miffed at not getting his own way and now he's trying to frighten us.'

'And does it frighten you Jenny?'

'Actually, no; it makes me angry. He's obviously a bully who's used to getting his own way and I'm not going to give in to that sort of man.'

'You will be careful though won't you? If there's anything else suspicious happens it might be time to consider going to the police.' Maggie left it at that, her role was not to give advice but in cases where there is possible risk she felt the need to urge caution. Jenny wanted to talk about her son next. Matthew was still angry with his father and she was feeling like a referee, a situation which saddened her immensely.

'We've always been such a close family and now when we should be enjoying our good fortune Matt chooses to fall out with Malcolm.'

During the rest of their time together, Jenny focussed on telling Maggie about her children and grandchildren, speaking with obvious pride. There did however seem to be an underlying concern that the lottery win could have a negative effect on their relationships; it had already unearthed a long held secret and it was to be hoped that there would be no more repercussions on the Grainger family.

Jenny felt happier for talking to Maggie, it was such a luxury to have a whole hour to offload problems in such a way. Everyone should have a counsellor she thought. Feeling surprisingly upbeat Jenny decided to ring Matthew and ask if they could meet for lunch. Malcolm had gone to visit Bill and wouldn't be back until mid afternoon so perhaps time alone with her son would prove fruitful in reconciling him and his father. Matthew agreed in spite of guessing the ulterior motive so she set off to walk to town, a thirty minute walk which would be good exercise to offset some of the weight she'd been gaining from eating out so much.

A sense of pride filled Jenny's heart as she watched Matthew enter the cafe and search the customers for his mother. He was well over six feet tall, broad shouldered and handsome and Jenny loved him to bits, as she did all her family but it was a rare treat to have him all to herself. Naturally the first question was an enquiry about Angie, Tom and Becky and Matthew was happy to report that all was well with his wife and children.

'I know they've been looking forward to Disney World, are you still keen to go?' She knew where this topic would lead and so did Matthew, who grinned,

'You're so transparent Mum, is the holiday to become a carrot on a stick for me to make up with Dad?'

'No of course not, it's just that we had almost settled all the details that night and then you got all huffy and left.'

'It was a shock, how did you take it when he told you?'

'Pretty much the same I suppose.' She admitted. 'But I'm doing my best to get over it.'

'And so am I. I'll come round later to apologise, I don't like these atmospheres any more than you do. Will that make you happy?'

'You know it will, thanks love. Dad not having an easy time at the moment and I'm only just beginning to understand what all this has done to him. Like a typical man he's tried to ignore what happened all those years ago but it's been dragged up again by that nasty Frank whatever his name is and it must be upsetting to be forced to re-live it all again.' Jenny went on to tell him about the mysterious phone calls. Matt suggested they go ex-directory or get rid of the landline altogether.

'A mobile number's much harder for people to get and you can get a new iphone now, you can certainly afford it.'

'Sounds sensible, but I don't want anything too complicated and you'll have to show me how to work it, you know what I'm like.'

'Of course I will but if there are any more phone calls or anything else you will go to the police won't you?'

'I'd have to persuade your Dad first. He's still worried that involving the police will bring the past out in the open again and is worried about the effect on your Granddad as well as us.'

'Does he really think anyone would be interested these days? There are loads of people who favour assisted suicide and I think I could easily be included among them.'

'Matt, surely not!'

'Well why not? If I was in some kind of vegetative state, like Granddad, I'd want someone to pull the plug for me. They wouldn't be doing me any favours by keeping me going with no quality of life.'

Jenny was shocked to hear her son's opinions but had to admit that it was a subject she had never previously thought much about.

'Yes, I think I might feel like that myself, but to actually get someone else involved is a different matter. They'd be breaking the law and would have to be held accountable which I suppose is what happened with your Grandmother Mary.'

'But if you were in a position where you needed someone to physically help you to die what would you do then?'

'Oh Matt, do we have to talk about this, it's so depressing.'

'Of course it is but I think it probably happens more often than we know. Even doctors can't agree on the issue but I bet there are many who help terminally ill patients to end their suffering. One day it'll be legal I'm sure.'

'That would be terrible, what about when the patient can't communicate? Will the doctor or the family decide for them?'

'Perhaps you're right Mum, let's change the subject, this one's always going to be controversial. It wasn't actually the fact of what Mary did that upset me, and I shouldn't have said she was a murderer, but it was Dad keeping it from us all this time.'

'I know love, that's just how I felt and I'm trying to be more understanding. Thanks for agreeing to come and see Dad, he needs our support at the moment.'

'I'll pop round tonight and bring Angie and the kids. Perhaps we can sort this holiday out then too.' Matthew grinned at his mother who was smiling once again.

Malcolm arrived home to an empty house, made a cup of coffee and took the opportunity to retrieve his father's diaries from the drawer in the sideboard which had become their new home. There wasn't much left to read, obviously Bill had needed to write down his thoughts during that dark period but it appeared that for some reason the need abated and he abandoned the entries, which were at best spasmodic. Turning to the back of the last book Malcolm began to read.

September 20th
Malcolm loves his new school which is such a relief. His enthusiasm has increased almost daily and although only into his third week, the difference in him is amazing. The first day was understandably difficult, a new school in a new town and having so recently lost his mother, but he put on a brave face and even attempted a smile to reassure me! While he lives, Mary will always be with me and I thank God for him. But I can take no credit, Mary had prepared

him well and her strength endures in his young life. She would be as proud as I am; he is the one ray of hope in my life at present, the one reason to keep going.

Our new home is taking shape, nothing like it would have been had Mary been here but we are comfortable and I'm learning to cook if it can be called such. I have an interview tomorrow at the library and am hopeful of getting a position there soon. Malcolm will be able to come there after school and do his homework while he waits for me, I do so hope things work out, surely it's time for our fortunes to change?

This entry was almost the last, another the following week confirmed that Bill had been successful in securing the post of senior librarian and then the diary entries ceased, hopefully having served their purpose in getting Bill Grainger through the most dreadful time of his life. Malcolm could remember those early days in Fenbridge. He did go to the library every evening after school, walking home with his Dad when work was over and talking over their respective days. Memories of those years were patchy but he did recall his father's conversation being centred very much in the present and the future. There were days when he talked about Mary but not often and Malcolm never knew whether it was for fear of upsetting himself or his son. And so Mary Grainger became a beautiful if vague memory to her only child who remembered the selfless love and care, the smell of lavender soap and the gentle touch of soft hands. Malcolm dearly wished he could have known her better. It didn't matter what she had done, only who she was, an extraordinary woman who loved her family passionately and did her very best for each one of them.

Chapter 21

Helen gazed around their new home at The Lawns with satisfaction. It had been a move prompted by necessity but it was turning out well with a certain comfort in being back in their home town, ending their days in the place they had begun. Life so often goes full circle. Shaking off the morbid thoughts which occasionally troubled her Helen determined to be positive, remembering that the best thing about their move was being close to Maggie once again.

'Can I do anything else before I go Helen?' Alan Hurst had been marvellous. Helen didn't know how she would have managed without him. He had willingly given up his rest days to tackle the small amount of decorating the place needed to freshen it up and make it feel like home and Helen was so grateful.

'You've been wonderful Alan, how can I ever thank you?'

'My pleasure, I like pottering but Sue reins me in somewhat at home so I've enjoyed it, really.'

Helen hugged him,

'You get back to your wife and lovely little daughter now, we'll be fine, I think Maggie and Peter will be round later.'

Alan left and after watching him go Helen returned to the lounge where George was looking puzzled.

'Everything's moved, was it that young fellow who did it?'

'It was, yes, but we're in a new house now George, it is different but we'll get used to it. Look, let's have another look round shall we?' Taking her husband by the hand, Helen led him into each room pointing out their own familiar bits of furniture and telling him where things were kept.

'It's a nice place isn't it?' George seemed to approve. 'How long are we staying before we go home?'

Helen's heart sank. 'We'll just enjoy being here shall we and see how things go? Maggie and Peter will be round later, time for a cup of tea and a sandwich first I think. You sit at the table here and then you'll see where things are kept, cheese or ham?'

Maggie and Peter arrived at six thirty.

'Gosh, you look as if everything's done Mum.' Maggie said.

'It's mostly down to Alan, he's so quick I hardly had time to think about where to put things before it was done.'

'That's Alan, we've often been grateful for his practical skills too and he's great company to have around as well. So what's left for us to do?' Peter asked.

'Well, the bedroom's sorted and the lounge, I just need to empty the last of these boxes into the kitchen cupboards. Perhaps you can do the high shelves while we do the bottom ones?'

Peter saluted and began to unwrap the glassware to store in the wall units.

'How's Dad been?' Maggie had been concerned for her father all day.

'Not too bad really. He's mostly followed Alan around giving instructions but generally okay. I'm not sure it's actually sunk in that this move is permanent, he seems to think it's some kind of holiday but it will take time.'

'Well we've always the option of a weekend in Scotland if ever you feel that would help.'

'I know and I'm so glad you're going to take it on Maggie. As soon as we're settled in I'd like to see a solicitor about handing it over to you and Peter. I'd also like to consider arranging power of attorney, with your

Dad the way he is I think it's wise to do it now while I can.'

Maggie knew her mother was right but it wasn't a pleasant subject to dwell upon. She and Peter had discussed it and knew it was the sensible thing to do but it seemed to be acknowledging that there would be a time when her parents would no longer be around, a sobering thought and one she did not want to think about at present.

'Come on, let's get these cupboards filled while we can, I know you'll never be happy until you have a fully functional kitchen.'

Twenty minutes later a tap on the front door interrupted the work and Helen opened it to find a neighbour holding a large tin and smiling broadly.

'Hello, I'm Nancy, your next door neighbour. I just wanted to welcome you to The Lawns and bring you these biscuits, I hope you like ginger?'

'Why thank you, that's so kind. Please come in and meet my husband, ginger is his favourite, you've made a lifelong friend already.' Helen took their visitor through to the lounge where George was trying in vain to tune the television. 'George, we have a visitor, this is Nancy, our next door neighbour and she's brought biscuits!'

George put down the remote control and beamed in Nancy's direction. She placed the tin on the dining table and offered her hand to him. She was a small, neat lady with short wavy grey hair, thick glasses and a welcoming smile and looked positively tiny next to George, whose hand clasped hers in a firm handshake.

'Delightful, thank you so much.'

'I hope you like ginger, my husband loved them. If there's any way I can help please just say, I've been here for six years now so know my way around pretty well.'

'Thank you Nancy. We've moved from Scotland but Fenbridge is actually our home town so hopefully we'll still manage to get around if the place hasn't changed too much.'

'Oh how lovely, returning home to retire! We moved all over the country but I have to admit this is the spot we chose to retire to, it's so beautiful and the town's big enough for all I need these days. Well, I shall leave you to it but please, do call any time, you're always welcome to pop in for a cup of tea, I'll look forward to getting to know you.'

Helen showed their visitor out before continuing her task. Nancy had been very kind and friendly, endorsing the feeling of this being a good move.

'Are these George's old slippers?' Peter asked.

'No, he was looking for those earlier, where did you find them?'

'Well, they were in the bin...'

Helen smiled it was another indicator of George's illness, sad but quite funny really.

'It could have been worse I suppose, he could have put them down the toilet!'

****

Frank sat back in the chair to admire his handiwork. 'Not bad at all old boy, especially for someone who flunked art 'o' level' he told himself. Sliding the finished results into two envelopes, he addressed the first to Malcolm Grainger at thirty four Acacia Avenue and the second to Kate Grainger, he didn't know her married surname, at forty Drakes Lane. He couldn't be bothered to find either post-code but had every confidence that the good old Royal Mail would deliver them to the correct recipients. Frank laughed softly to himself as he imagined the reaction of the Graingers and their daughter when the post arrived. This little campaign was proving to be quite amusing and he'd surprised himself at how inventive his imagination could be. If the photographs didn't produce the desired effect, he would enjoy thinking up new ideas to unsettle the family. Frank looked at the clock, the only adornment on the bland walls of the pokey room he was presently occupying. Two thirty-five, if he went out now he could easily catch the last post, perhaps he'd even splash out on first class stamps. Yes, he'd call at the post office first then on to the pub for a celebratory pint or two. The letters should arrive the next day when he would contact Grainger to see if he was feeling any more generous to his old school friend.

The letters were on their way and Frank walked the two hundred yards to the local pub, he'd earned a drink or two and of course he could stop drinking again whenever he wanted to, he'd done it before hadn't he? But for now, a couple of drinks would help pass the time and he had quite a thirst on by then.

****

Jenny's mood was more buoyant than it had been for days after meeting with Matthew. The family were her world and even the slightest division or hint of animosity between any of them was unwelcome. Matthew had agreed to call round to see his Dad and would be bringing Angie and the children too so hopefully things would be back to normal after this evening. She would bake a chocolate cake, Tom and Becky loved cake and they could sit with her in the kitchen while Matt spoke to Malcolm. So, almost everything in the garden was lovely, the only problem being that awful man Stokes but surely he'd got the message that they were never going to pay out to a blackmailer. Hopefully he would have gone home to Liverpool with his tail between his legs by now. He should be thoroughly ashamed of himself for putting them through such misery at a time when they should be enjoying their good fortune.

Malcolm was at home when Jenny arrived back and the kettle was boiling. She made tea and then began to mix the cake while Malcolm sat at the kitchen table watching.

'Matthew and the family are coming round tonight.' She told him.

'I thought the chocolate cake wouldn't be for me.' Malcolm smiled. 'I finished reading Dad's diaries this afternoon and I've left them out for you to look at.'

'Yes, I will. Are you okay love? It must have been upsetting to read about such a difficult time.'

'I can't say it wasn't but I'm okay. I think I'd like Matthew and Kate to read them too after you've finished. They need to know the truth about my early years and their grandmother. I'm only sorry I never told you all before but hiding it had almost become a habit and there never seemed to be a good time to bring the subject up.'

'It's alright Malcolm, I'm sorry too that I made such a big thing about it. I can understand your reasons, it was just a shock and especially finding out through a blackmail attempt. It made it seem so much worse. I'll read the diaries and pass them on to the children then we'll put it all behind us shall we? Hopefully that Stokes fellow won't trouble us again and we can start to enjoy ourselves as we intended.'

Malcolm stood up and crossed the kitchen floor to put his arms around his wife, so grateful that she had forgiven him. All the money in the world would mean nothing if he didn't have Jenny by his side.

For two hours Jenny sat quietly in the lounge reading through her father-in-law's diary, finding it very emotive and spilling tears onto the yellowing pages several times. The words were from the heart and deeply moving, this was a side to Bill Grainger that Jenny had never seen before. Yes, they had a good relationship but now, to read what he had suffered opened up a completely different aspect of the man she had thought to be a pleasant, quiet soul. The depth of his love for Mary came through on every page, equalled only by his love for Malcolm. It had previously occurred to her that Bill would have had a difficult time raising a son alone but now to read what he had gone through was quite harrowing. She could not begin to understand how he survived living through such a nightmare; Mary's diagnosis of cancer, Joan's death, the arrest, the publicity, Mary's death... however did the poor man survive? And yet he had come through those dark days to build a new life for himself and Malcolm. Jenny understood now why Bill had never re-married. It would have been nearly impossible for any woman to take Mary's place and in many ways Bill had remained married to Mary even after her death. The diaries stirred Jenny deeply. She felt the desire to cherish and love her husband in an inadequate attempt to make up for those arduous, formative years when Malcolm had needed a mother's love. And as for Bill, Jen knew without a doubt that she had underestimated the depth of the man. He'd been a good father-in-law, a good parent and grandparent but there was so much more to him than any of them had ever imagined. Jenny would view him with different eyes from now on, with more respect, love, and gratitude for what he had done for Malcolm.

'Matt will be here soon love.' Malcolm's gentle voice interrupted her thoughts. Laying the diaries aside she stood up and ran into her husband's arms, holding him as if she would never let go again. Eventually, pulling away she said,

'Thank you for letting me read these.' Jenny picked up the diaries and Malcolm nodded solemnly. 'Come on, we'd better get ready.'

Matthew, Angie and the children arrived as planned, bringing their chaotic presence and welcome laughter into the house. Matthew made straight for his father and hugged him, a simple gesture which was sufficient for them both and made words superfluous. Jenny witnessed the exchange with a sudden rush of love, thinking that surely things were going to work out for them now. Tom and Becky had already pulled out the travel brochures and were eagerly flicking through them.

'The pages marked in red pen are the ones we thought would be best, see which hotel you like.' Jenny suggested to the children who needed no more encouragement than those few words. While they were occupied Matthew asked his parents if they had heard any more from the blackmailer.

'No, at least I don't think so. There have been some strange phone calls, silence or a ticking clock and at all times of the day and night.' Malcolm explained.

'Do you think you should call the police in?'

'No son, if it was Stokes he'll get bored soon and move on to plague someone else but the calls might not have been him, just kids messing about perhaps.'

The conversation turned to the more pleasant subject of holidays and the children were eager to show the adults where they wanted to stay. Jenny smiled; a holiday was probably just the thing to take all of their minds off recent events.

Chapter 22

Alice seemed rather subdued at the next meeting with Maggie and readily admitted that she hadn't been sleeping well.

'Do you know why?' Maggie asked.

'Yes, I think so.'

A silent nod from Maggie encouraged Alice to share more of what was troubling her.

'I went out with a colleague from work last week, to the theatre. He had a couple of tickets and asked me to go with him. I said yes without really thinking it through and Joel seemed to assume it was a date. I then made a bit of a fool of myself when he reached for my hand. It's not as if I don't like him because I do I just don't want a romantic relationship. He's been rather quiet at work since then and I think I might have lost his friendship.'

'So, you agreed to go out with him on a platonic basis?'

'Well, I assumed it was only platonic but he seemed to have something more in mind.'

'And would that be a bad thing?'

'Yes, I decided a long time ago never to get involved in a long term relationship, I think I told you that before.'

'You did, yes. Would you like to tell me about Joel?'

'He's very nice, good looking yet not conceited with it. All the girls at work swoon over him and he could take his pick of them but I don't think he's been out with anyone from the lab.'

'Only you?'

'Yes, only me.' Alice was thoughtful and Maggie allowed space for those thoughts to develop without interruption before gently asking.

'And is it this situation with Joel that's been keeping you awake? The loss of his friendship perhaps?'

'Yes, no, oh I'm not sure. It bothers me that I might have spoiled our relationship. Not that he's been nasty in any way and is still pleasant when we speak but there's a cautiousness which wasn't there before and I don't want that.'

'Do you know what you do want?'

'I want to have the same relationship as before. Our visit to the theatre was great and I'd quite like to go out with him again, as a friend of course.'

'Could you perhaps have some kind of discussion about this?'

'I'd feel stupid asking for friendship when he might want something more. Oh Maggie, it's not surprising that I'm not sleeping, with thoughts of Joel and the situation with Mum... I honestly don't know where I am.' Again another silence prevailed as Alice gathered her scattered thoughts. The mention of her mother brought Caroline's visit to Maggie's mind. She would need to be careful in the light of the knowledge Caroline had imparted. It must not influence the relationship with Alice, but she was confident that this was possible.

'You are sometimes very hard on yourself Alice. Relationships are never perfect and there needs to be give and take on both sides. You appear to be fond of Joel. Do you know why you want to keep him at a distance?'

'It's not him personally, I don't want to get involved in a long term relationship with anyone, I'm not the type to settle down.'

'Sorry, I know you've told me that before but if you are losing sleep over Joel perhaps you are already involved to some degree? Have you thought how would you feel if you were never going to see him again, if he gave in his notice at work perhaps and was moving on to another area?' Maggie was challenging her client by being so direct and it had the effect of making Alice sit up, eyes wide as she gave the question some thought.

'Well, he'd be missed at work. Joel's very good at his job and a great supervisor.'

'But how would you feel, on a personal level?'

'Oh gosh Maggie... I really wouldn't want him to go!'

****

Kate Burton picked up the morning's post and smiled at seeing the name 'Kate Grainger' on the envelope. It was a long time since she'd been called that. Opening the envelope, and wondering who could possibly have sent it, her smile disappeared as two photographs fell from the envelope, one of herself and the other of Daisy. On her image someone had drawn a large red jagged line from the cheek bone to the chin. The one of Daisy was untouched, but the fact that her little daughter was looking at whoever took the photo and smiling, almost reaching out to them, sent a shiver throughout Kate's body. The red line was raised and appeared sticky, probably painted on with nail varnish, giving the effect and appearance of congealed blood. Kate felt sick at the thoughts it conjured up in her mind. Was this some idea of a joke? The background was easily recognisable as the mini-market where they had called for milk a couple of days ago. She hadn't noticed anyone taking their picture but juggling Daisy and the shopping had demanded her full attention. What did it mean? Was it some kind of threat? Mike had already left for work so she called his mobile number, her hands trembling while tapping the numbers. The phone rang out and Kate left a message asking him to ring as soon as possible. Daisy had finished breakfast and was demanding a playmate, oblivious to the fact that her mother didn't feel in the least like playing after such a shock. Kate tipped a box of toys onto the carpet for Daisy to rummage through and then called her brother's number. With no job to go to Matthew would be around and Kate needed to talk to someone she loved and trusted.

'I'm coming straight over!' Matthew's decision brought comfort and true to his word he was there in less than fifteen minutes.

'We should ring Mum and Dad. I think this might be connected to that blackmailer.' Matthew too had been appalled by the photographs and agreed that it was some kind of threat, or at the very least an attempt to frighten Kate.

'Should we call the police?'

'Not until we've talked to Mum and Dad, but don't worry, I'll stay with you until you get hold of Mike.'

They decided it would be better to go to their parent's home rather than talk on the telephone and as Matthew drove them over, Kate desperately hoped they would be at home. They were and soon the four of them were discussing the distressing situation.

'We received the same photos this morning.' Malcolm admitted. 'I never dreamt that Stokes would have sent them to you as well, which, assuming it is him, means he knows your address.'

'Which also means he's been following Kate!' Matthew was fired up. 'We need to go to the police Dad, this mad man's gone too far now.'

Jenny looked expectantly at Malcolm; she had said the same thing when they received the photographs that morning.

'Yes, you're right. Do we go down to the police station or ring them?'

'Perhaps we should ring to explain the situation and let them decide if they want us to go down?' Jenny spoke quietly, pleased that Malcolm was actually going to do something. The photos had made her feel physically sick and she was still in a state of shock. To her mind, they were obviously from that Stokes man and it now seemed clear that he was the one who had been making the strange phone calls too. There had been more calls at various times of the day and night over the last couple of days. Malcolm knew that this had gone far enough and picked up the telephone to ring the police station, his family anxiously listening for the outcome. After some explaining and being transferred to a detective it was arranged that a police officer would visit them as soon as one was available.

'It's probably better that they come to the house, we can all be here then and present a united front.' Matthew was satisfied now the police were to be involved. Looking again at the photos spread out on the kitchen table, he shook his head,

'The man's a lunatic, does he actually think he can threaten and scare us into giving him money?'

'Well, he's got me frightened that's for sure. He knows our address, telephone number and even Kate's address now.' Jenny admitted.

'And I don't like the fact that he's been following me, it's sort of creepy!' Kate added.

'Well, it's up to the police now, they can handle it. I'm sorry for all the trouble it's caused. Perhaps I should have called them in at the beginning.' Malcolm was saddened that his family had been put through such an ordeal. Kate moved over to hug him.

'It's not your fault Dad, we don't blame you. None of us expected this to happen but let's hope the police can put a stop to it now.'

Within an hour there was a ring at the doorbell and Malcolm opened it to admit the two police officers who stood with their ID badges visible for inspection. By then Kate's husband Mike had joined them and they made room for the officers to sit down. There was an atmosphere of nervous tension in the room. The

Grainger's had never had cause to seek help from the police before and were unsure of protocol. Having introduced himself as DS Alan Hurst and his colleague as DC Claire Whittaker, Alan asked if they would fill him in on the events leading up to their call to the station. Claire took notes while Alan listened intently, asking the occasional question for clarification. Malcolm was the natural spokesman but Matthew interrupted at times if he felt his father was missing anything out. By the end of the story Malcolm was almost apologetic for his past history which had brought the whole scenario about, and for involving the police.

'You certainly don't need to apologise Mr Grainger, it's not you who is in the wrong here. Do you have the photographs?'

Malcolm passed the two photos to Alan who looked at them then passed them on to his constable.

'These must have been distressing for you. This man's obviously trying to make a point here, a veiled threat even. Can we just confirm the name again?' He looked to his DC who repeated the name, Frank Stokes, to check it was right. Malcolm's agreement led them to ask if there were any other details about him that they knew of.

'Not really, I assume he's still living in Liverpool but that might not be the case. He was in my year group at school so I know he was born in 1959 or thereabouts.'

'That's fine Mr Grainger. It should be fairly straight forward to track him down, especially with an approximate date of birth. Now, you say he's been here twice? Do you think he might come back?'

'Well his parting shot was that we hadn't heard the last from him and assuming these photographs and phone calls are from him I think he'll probably be in touch sometime soon.'

'I agree. Stokes seems intent on getting something out of you. What we're going to do now is try to trace this man but if he makes contact with any of you, which is quite likely, I'd like you to ring me immediately.' Alan proffered a card. 'This has the office number and my mobile, you can ring any time but if there's a problem or he approaches you when you're out and about, don't hesitate to ring 999.'

'What will happen when you do find him?' Jenny was curious.

'We'll see what he has to say and in the meantime we'll begin to put a case together. I'd like to take these photo's for evidence and to test for fingerprints but presumably you've handled them too so we'll need each of your prints for elimination. What I will say is that this man's already made several mistakes in his attempt to blackmail you which shows he's not a professional but on the other hand he's an amateur and therefore unpredictable so I would advise caution. I'll keep you informed as to the progress we make but perhaps if I just ring you Mr Grainger as a point of contact and you can update your family?' Malcolm agreed and thanked the police sergeant for coming. When they had left, Malcolm returned to a solemn mood hanging over the family. Mike spoke first,

'Well I'm going to take some time off work to be with Kate and Daisy. I don't think any of us should go out alone until this man's locked up.'

'Good and I need to speak to Angie to warn her to be on guard and keep the children close by.' Matthew went off to phone his wife. Jenny and Kate sat quietly, pondering the last hour. Malcolm felt the need to offer reassurance,

'It will probably come to an end pretty quickly. Once the police find Stokes we won't have to worry about him anymore, we'll be able to put this behind us.' Even as he spoke, the words sounded hollow. They were all aware that if the police found a Liverpool address, Stokes would most likely not be there, he was probably still somewhere in Fenbridge planning the next move. All Kate could think about was that ugly red line painted onto the photograph and the image of Daisy smiling trustingly at a stranger.

Chapter 23

On 4th May 1982, an Exocet missile fired from an Argentinean ship hit HMS Sheffield eight feet above the waterline, tearing a gash four feet by ten feet in her side with the missile's burning rocket setting fire to the Sheffield, damaging the electricity generating systems and preventing anti-fire mechanisms from working. The water main too was ruptured in the attack and there was no way the fires could be extinguished, so evacuation was initiated. HMS Sheffield had only just relieved her sister ship, HMS Coventry, from defence watch when the missile hit. It was fired from a distance of only six miles, the equivalent of point blank range. The stricken vessel was towed away from the task force to prevent the assisting ships becoming a sitting duck target for Argentinean aircraft. Burns casualties were evacuated first and un-injured crew members waited helplessly on the deck watching and waiting for their turn.

Ronald Greenwood was one of the navy personnel who watched in horror from that deck as injured ship mates were helped into lifeboats. The screams and cries of grown men in agony from their burns could be heard above the rough seas as Ronald waited in turn, praying that the Sheffield would remain afloat until they were all safe. Faces of the injured were barely recognisable, burned and disfigured by the greedy flames and he wondered fleetingly if they would have been better off going down with their ship. He was later to learn that twenty men lost their lives that day, twenty comrades who would never return to their waiting families. It was a life defining moment for Ronald Greenwood, an event that would remain with him forever as if the flames had scorched some inner part of his soul, a part which was destroyed with his dead comrades.

Caroline Greenwood could procrastinate no longer and was at last sorting through her husband's papers. His birth certificate and discharge papers were stored in a metal box together with their marriage certificate, and now Ronald's death certificate. In the same cupboard, crammed with several years' worth of miscellaneous items which had been kept 'in case' they would be useful, were newspaper accounts of the sinking of HMS Sheffield. It had been an event which had changed Caroline's life too, although there had been an even more personal violation while Ronald had been away serving his country. The papers were spread over the dining room table as she studied each one, deciding which to keep and which to consign to the bin, when the doorbell rang. Alice stood in the porch, wrapped up warmly against the early November chill and dancing from one foot to the other to keep warm. She had not been expected.

'Why don't you use your key?' Caroline asked.

'I don't have it on me.' Her daughter replied.

On seeing the clutter spread around the room, Alice paused, 'Am I interrupting something?'

'No no, I've been putting this off for weeks. You can help if you like?' Caroline looked hopefully at her daughter.

'Are they Ronald's papers?'

'Yes, but most of them can probably be shredded now. I'd appreciate the help but its okay if you don't want to, I can finish it later.'

'No, I'll help, at least I can shred while you sort through them.' They sat at the table and Caroline began to look again at the documents and lifted a newspaper cutting with headlines about HMS Sheffield.

'Ronald was never the same after the sinking. He changed, I think part of him went down with that ship too and he could never talk to me about it. It must have been horrific, I can't begin to imagine.'

Alice took the cutting and began to read.

'How did he change Mum?'

Caroline was startled at the question, Alice usually avoided talking about Ronald.

'He'd been so full of life before the Falklands conflict. It wasn't always easy, him being in the navy but we managed and the times we did spend together were special, wonderful. He had quite a sense of humour too, which was partly what attracted me to him all those years ago. But after the sinking of the Sheffield it all changed. The world became somehow black and white to him after that, he was bitter. He thought of things, and people, as either good or bad and he couldn't accept any grey areas. I don't know why he became like that, maybe it was the life and death situation, I suppose I'll never really understand but he wasn't the same man when he came home.'

'And then I was on the way, which would most certainly fall into the 'bad' category I should think.' Alice's words had hurt and shocked Caroline.

'Well... yes, it was difficult for him to accept. We had arguments about it almost from the day he came home. It was a very distressing time.'

'Why did he stay with you Mum? I honestly can't understand why he didn't just up and leave, especially as you were determined to keep me?' Alice had an urge to find out as much as she could about that time and it seemed that her mother was in a particularly reflective mood but then to her astonishment, Caroline suddenly broke down and began to cry.

'What is it Mum? I'm sorry, I shouldn't pry!' Alice held her mother while she sobbed; she had never before seen her cry apart from a few restrained tears at Ronald's funeral. Both women were trembling.

'He stayed because he loved me.' Caroline eventually composed herself enough to speak.

'Even after you betrayed him?'

'I never betrayed him Alice, I loved him too!'

'But I don't understand! If I'm not Ronald's child you must have been with another man?' Thinking about her mother's words it suddenly dawned on her.

'You were raped!' The sudden realisation stunned Alice. 'Oh Mum, it wasn't an affair, was it? It was rape!' The colour drained from Alice's face and she felt faint as the enormity of the truth slowly trickled into her conscious mind. Caroline covered her face with her hands as the tears flowed. The room was silent except for the muffled sobs from Caroline. Neither woman spoke for several minutes until Caroline composed herself enough to speak.

'I never wanted you to know Alice. I'm so sorry, I shouldn't even have told you that Ronald wasn't your father, that was a mistake, I should have let things be.'

Alice could think of nothing to say. Her mind was active with all kinds of thoughts, most of them unpleasant. There were still things she wanted to ask but couldn't bring herself to do so. This unsavoury knowledge presented a whole new facet to everything she had thought to have known. There was such pity in her heart for her mother which felt like a fist wringing her heart and a greater understanding of Ronald too. But what about herself? She was the child of a rapist, how on earth could she ever come to terms with that?

Caroline pulled herself together and went into the kitchen to make coffee giving them both time and space to think. Returning with the hot drinks, Alice gratefully took the mug from her mother yet remained silent. It was apparent that Caroline would have to tell her daughter the full story.

'I rarely went out while Ronald was at sea but some of my old girlfriends were going to a dance and insisted I went too. It seemed churlish to refuse, one of them had a birthday and I thought it would be a good chance to catch up with them all, so I joined their party. There was a live band, quite a good one but I was content to listen to the music and watch the handbags while my friends danced. Mark approached me half way through the evening. I remembered him from school; he'd been a couple of years above me and was quite popular with the girls, a reputation which had gone to his head. I don't think he remembered me from those days but he'd apparently been asking about me that night. I refused his offer to dance, he already seemed half drunk and so he sat with me, only moving to refill his glass at the bar. I tried to be polite but made it clear that I was happily married, a fact he already knew as well as being aware that Ronald was away at sea. The drink made him more and more obnoxious and he began making lewd suggestions. Mark came from a wealthy family and was obviously used to getting what he wanted. I moved to another table, catching the eye of one of my friends who came over to see what was happening. I told her I was leaving and then quietly slipped away, eager to get home. It was a Sunday evening and the busses were infrequent so I decided to walk, it wasn't far and it was a fine night. I had no idea I was being followed until I reached home. As I opened the door, Mark appeared out of nowhere and pushed me inside, slamming the door closed behind him.

I don't need to go into details do I? He eventually left and I retreated to my bed, bruised and bleeding and cried myself to sleep. I didn't tell anyone what had happened I was too ashamed and embarrassed. A few weeks later I realised I was pregnant and had no idea what to do. By the time Ronald came home so much had happened to him that it took me several days before I felt able to tell him about the rape, although not that I was pregnant. I don't know what reaction I expected, he was outwardly sympathetic yet inwardly seething. I didn't dare tell him who it was, he'd have killed him for sure, so I told him it was a stranger. A few days later I told him about the pregnancy and he exploded. I'd never seen him in such a rage and he insisted I had an abortion. My refusal was probably the catalyst which changed our relationship forever.' Caroline paused, it was obviously difficult to revisit such a terrible time in her life. Alice had listened silently so far but the questions were stacking up in her mind and she was compelled to ask.

'Why didn't you go to the police?'

'Shame, embarrassment, I don't know. Somehow I thought it was my fault although I was certain I hadn't encouraged him. It would have simply been my word against his and his family had connections. Who was going to believe me?'

'But why didn't you have an abortion, surely I would have been a constant reminder of those events?'

'No, you never were and I don't want you to think that! You were the only good thing to come out of that dreadful time and you know my views on abortion. My marriage would never be the same again, my life had changed irrevocably but you were my only solace. Each day as I felt you growing within me, I loved you more and more. You were a comfort to me, a consolation. I don't care how you were conceived, Alice, I've always looked upon you as my child, my baby and I felt an enormous love for you which has remained and even strengthened over the years. Ronald however felt betrayed, as if I had chosen you over him, which in a way was true and I could understand those feelings although none of that was your fault. You were a baby, helpless and dependent, you needed me and my love for you was overwhelming. I know this must be difficult but never lose sight of the fact that you were and still are the most important person in my life.'

There was just one more question that Alice needed to ask before the subject was closed.

'Now I know that my biological father was called Mark, but you must know his full name, who is he Mum, Mark who?'

'If I tell you Alice, what are you going to do with the information?'

'I don't know, but surely its best that I know everything now you've come this far?'

'His full name is Mark Appleton.' Caroline lowered her eyes as Alice's expression displayed recognition of the name and the awful implications of it.

Chapter 24

Helen Price studied her daughter from across the room. Maggie had always been an attractive woman but seemed to be growing into her looks and appeared quite beautiful with rich brown curls framing the heart shaped face which was inherited from Helen's side of the family. Her brown eyes were warm and smiling, with an inquisitive twinkle as she became aware of her mother's scrutiny.

'What is it Mum, have I got food on my chin?'

'No, it's just so good to have you pop in like this, living closer to you again is certainly the biggest advantage of being back in Fenbridge.'

'And how are you settling in?' Maggie asked.

'Better than I expected actually. It really is like coming home in many respects. Of course I'll miss the friends I'd made in the village and Scotland's beautiful scenery but there are always new friends to meet and as I said, you and Peter are close by which is one very big plus in favour of being back here. Nancy next door has been a rock too. She's offered to sit with your Dad anytime I want to go out and has invited me to go to a ladies group at Church with her but that's not going to be possible, I don't feel happy leaving your Dad on his own at all now.'

'If there's something like that mid week that you want to go to Peter would be happy for Dad to stay with him, here or at our house.'

'Thanks love, that's good of you but you have your own lives to lead, I don't want to be a burden for you.'

'But that's the whole point of you moving here, so we can help. I've actually been wondering about a group for Dad to go to once or twice a week. There are all sorts of activities he might enjoy and it would give you a break too. I'll look out some leaflets at the health centre. I know there's an art class for Alzheimer sufferers which meets at the hospital social club, perhaps Dad might like to join that?'

'The only painting he's ever done is with gloss and emulsion, but I'll mention it, see how he reacts. He became quite frustrated this week when he couldn't find things in the kitchen. I'm getting a bit that way myself, it takes time to remember where everything is but Nancy suggested that I put labels on the cupboard door so I bought some of those sticky note papers and everything's marked now.'

'That's a great idea and if it helps Dad, even better.'

'Did I hear my name mentioned?' George Price came into the kitchen and kissed the top of Maggie's head. 'My two favourite girls together, how nice.'

'We were just talking about what you're going to do with your time now Dad. Ever fancied taking up painting? Peter finds it very rewarding.'

'That's not a bad idea. I was top of the class in art at school. In fact I might just give my old art teacher a ring, see if he's still teaching at the grammar school,'

Maggie and Helen exchanged glances, the grammar school had been pulled down years ago and any teachers who may still be alive would most certainly be centenarians by now, but the idea hadn't been rejected which was progress to Maggie's mind. Changing the subject she asked,

'We've got Peter's family coming over on Saturday. Its Rachel's birthday and we thought it would be nice to have a family gathering. You will both come won't you?'

'What a lovely idea, now what can I make to help you out?'

Maggie grinned, Helen was always doing things for other people but that was the type of person she was and it would be a good help if she would make something for the gathering.

'Perhaps a pan of your lovely broth would be appropriate, this weather's getting worse and it would warm us all up.'

'Broth it is then and a batch of homemade bread too.'

****

On his return to the station after interviewing the Grainger family, DS Alan Hurst had easily found an address for Frank Stokes in Liverpool with just a few clicks of the mouse on the computer. Stokes appeared to live alone and Alan made contact with the police force in that area with a request to visit and arrest him for attempted blackmail. When Stokes was safely in custody, Alan would make the journey to Liverpool to question him. He was not at all surprised the next day when his colleagues did not find Stokes at home and had been told by a neighbour that he was often away and they had seen him leave with a suitcase only a few days earlier. It was as expected; Alan had reasoned that if he'd sent the photographs from Fenbridge, which the post mark clearly showed, then Stokes would be staying somewhere local hoping to cash in on his scheme within a couple of days. It was most likely that the next time he surfaced would be to make contact with his victims. This was confirmed at lunch time when a frantic phone call from Jenny Grainger informed him that Stokes was at their door and Malcolm Grainger was about to let him in. Alan hurriedly gave instructions for them to play along with Stokes as if they intended to pay and he would get to them in a matter of minutes. Leaving a half eaten sandwich Alan dashed out to the car, calling for one of the uniformed men to assist.

Frank Stokes was very drunk. His ancient Triumph Dolomite, complete with silver duct tape which appeared to be holding most of it together, was parked at an awkward angle on the grass verge outside the Grainger's home and he had rung the bell three times before resorting to banging on the door with both fists. Malcolm was stalling for time and only answered when Jenny had had sufficient time to get in touch with the police. Stokes was leaning heavily on the door jamb looking more than a little dishevelled and smelling of whisky. Malcolm took it all in and felt that the inebriated state of Stokes would give him an advantage if things became physical, which he certainly hoped would not be the case. Frank tripped over the doorstep, Malcolm steadied him and they stumbled into the lounge where Stokes dropped heavily onto the sofa. Jenny entered the room, gawping at their visitor with disgust before nodding at her husband to signal the police were on their way. They wouldn't have to tolerate the man for much longer.

'We got the photographs.' Malcolm said quietly.

'What photographs?' Stokes attempted to laugh but it came out as more of a hiss through his teeth. He obviously thought he was clever and appeared to be enjoying this little game.

'We know they were from you!' Jenny's eyes flashed with anger, 'Just keep away from our family.' She would have happily hit him with the poker if they'd had one handy but the anger only earned a reproachful look from Malcolm and an even louder hiss from Stokes.

'So have you got something for me old pal?' The words were slurred and sounded almost comical. This version of Stokes elicited something akin to pity from Malcolm and revulsion from Jenny.

'Twenty five thousand eh?' Frank looked hopeful. Malcolm knew he needed to play for time and so, sitting down opposite the drunkard who was trying to blackmail him, attempted to open a dialogue.

'How did you get to this state Frank?' The tone was soft and the question sounded as if he genuinely wanted an answer. Stokes looked puzzled and tried hard to focus. Jenny too was unsure where Malcolm was going with this.

'Why is it that you really dislike me so much? Is it something I did at school because if it is I have absolutely no recollection of it? I seem to remember you were always on my case then too. What have I ever done to make you hate me so much Frank?'

Frank's eyes were misty but his demeanour had changed almost as if he was giving the question serious thought. Before there was time to respond, Jenny saw the police car pull up outside and raced towards the door to open it. Frank looked out of the window and saw DS Hurst and a uniformed officer hurrying down the path. Suddenly he was wild again, eyes flashing with anger.

'You bastard, I said no police! You'll regret this Grainger and that's a promise, you and your perfect little family, you'll regret it!' Stokes was in no state to try to run, he could barely stand up and Malcolm wondered how on earth he had managed to drive and still be in one piece. While the uniformed PC cuffed Stokes, DS Hurst cautioned him and he was half led, half carried out to the police car and expertly assisted into the back seat.

Alan considered it futile to try and talk to Stokes while he was so drunk so had him taken to an interview room and plied with black coffee for the next couple of hours before attempting to question him. After the coffee and dry biscuits had taken effect, Alan began to ask about his recent activities in relation to the Grainger family, questions which received only the briefest of answers from Stokes. He did not however deny approaching them for money, nor did he request the presence of a legal representative which would have been his entitlement. It appeared that Frank had decided the game was up and he had lost, although he was not prepared to concede every point. As his brain cleared slightly he began to twist the events in his own favour, even insinuating that it had all been a light hearted prank played on an old school friend. Alan pushed the photographs under his nose.

'If my wife and child had received these in the post I would consider them more than a prank. They're sick, menacing and there's no doubt in my mind that they were intended to intimidate. Coupled with the fact that you have approached the family for money it seems quite clear that this has been an attempt to blackmail.'

'Oh come on, that's a bit strong! Well yes, maybe I went a little too far but it was all intended to be a joke, I thought he could take it but obviously old Malcolm's lost his sense of humour.' Stokes was trying to trivialize everything but Alan wasn't going to release him without letting the man know how serious they were taking the whole affair and that they intended to proceed with the charge.

Alan left Stokes for another two hours before conditionally releasing him, by which time he had sobered up and was growing increasingly angry. When he was eventually released it was made clear that he was not to approach any member of the Grainger family or go within a hundred yards of their homes and was to report each day to his local police station until further notice. Before Alan left for home he rang Malcolm Grainger to update him on the events of the afternoon.

'Well that's a relief!' Jenny sighed when Malcolm relayed his conversation with Alan. 'So presumably if he comes here again we'll ring the police?'

'Yes and I mentioned his car. They were aware it's here and are sending someone to tow it away.'

'Thank goodness, so hopefully we won't see anything more of Frank Stokes.' Jenny took hold of Malcolm's hand. They could perhaps make plans now without this hanging over their heads. To her mind Frank was an idiot for ever thinking that he could make money from threats to expose her husband's past. It was so long ago and the papers were far more interested in which celebrity was taking drugs or which politician had been found fiddling his expenses to be in the slightest way interested in what had happened to an ordinary family nearly half a century ago.

'Let's go out to eat tonight.' She suggested, 'Just the two of us, to that nice little Italian place you like?' Malcolm smiled in agreement. It would be good to enjoy an evening without worrying what would happen the next day and from what DS Hurst had told him it would be several months before Stokes's case would come to court and all they needed to do before that was to go to the station to give formal statements.

As they began to get ready to go out, a sudden urgent banging on the front door startled them both. Running downstairs to see what was wrong, Malcolm was surprised to see Frank Stokes once again on the doorstep. Jenny had followed him down and when she saw who it was went immediately to the telephone to contact the police.

'Wait a minute love.' He stopped her and to her amazement invited Stokes in.

'What are you doing?' she asked, 'He's not allowed anywhere near us!'

'I know, but let's just give him a minute.'

They were pleased to see that Frank had sobered up from earlier in the day but he still appeared dishevelled and somewhat weary, his face was darkened by a sullen scowl.

'What do you want Frank?' Malcolm asked rather wearily, he had no fear of this man now but was curious as to why he'd come back. Stokes's eyes grew even darker as he moved closer, but Malcolm didn't flinch.

'To finish our conversation.' He snarled. 'You wanted to know why I hated you so much? Well I'll tell you! You were always the golden boy at school, good at this, good at that, teacher's little pet, first one chosen for the football team. And as if that wasn't enough you had the perfect home life too. I watched your mother walk you to school and pick you up every day, smiling and holding your hand. She would kiss you goodbye and smooth your hair. You always had clean clothes and a full lunch box. And there was daddy too, cheering you on at sports day, lifting you onto his shoulders, laughing, chasing you! And what did I have? Nothing, that's what! Absolutely nothing unless you count a mother who was a slut, a drunk for a father, a filthy home and never any food in the house. I got beatings instead of kisses, the old man didn't care who he took it out on, his wife or his son.' Spittle was running down Stokes' chin and his face was turning crimson. Jenny feared he might have some kind of heart attack, so intense was his mood as he continued,

'Oh yes, it might have been years ago but look at today Grainger. Here you are in your smart little semi, a good looking wife, two children... grandchildren, and you've even won the bloody lottery! Is that fair I ask you? And what have I got? A wife who left me for someone I thought was a mate, kids who won't speak to me, no job thanks to you, and no money. Where's the justice in that? Go on, tell me?' Stokes had tears of anger running down his face and he was trembling after pouring out so much venom, his warped and twisted logic blaming Malcolm for everything bad in his life.

'I can't answer that Frank because I don't know. Admittedly you haven't had it easy but perhaps it's how you deal with life's knocks that makes the difference. Yes, I've been fortunate but not in everything. Remember, I lost that loving mother when I most needed her. Now, if you've said all you wanted to say I think you'd better go.

If you leave now you'll be able to take your car before the police tow it away. I won't report you being here this time but if you ever come back be sure that I will.'

Stokes was silent, with a last hateful glare he turned to leave without another word, a lonely pathetic figure who had made a mess of any chances he'd ever had in life. Malcolm watched with a heavy heart then turned to Jenny.

'So this whole debacle has been about nothing more than jealousy. What a sad man, but he's right about many things isn't he? I might have had a difficult start in life but that's certainly been made up for by what I've got now.'

'Malcolm Grainger, you never cease to amaze me. You have a soft side to you that often surprises me and I love you for it. And of course I particularly agree with the bit Frank said about you having a good looking wife!' Jenny laughed then they finished getting ready to go out, hopefully to relax and simply enjoy being together.

Chapter 25

'Is this the same Mark Appleton who is Fenbridge's MP?' Alice asked. The shock of her mother's revelation was clearly etched into her face.

'Yes.' Caroline's reply was barely a whisper and she lowered her head, unable to meet her daughter's eyes.

'Mum, don't look away from me... you have absolutely nothing to be ashamed of. You've lived with the consequences of that brute's actions every single day and it's robbed you of so much happiness while he's built a career in public life and got away with this crime totally free!' Alice's anger at the injustice of the whole situation took over from the shock of learning that she was conceived in such a violent way. 'I think you should go to the police, even now. Why should he get away with it?'

'Oh Alice, no! It's far too late to report it now, the police wouldn't be interested. Let's just leave it alone shall we?'

'But Mum, Mark Appleton is a respected figure in the community with a role he doesn't deserve. Why should he not be brought to justice?'

'He has a wife and family, think how they would feel.'

'But what about you, how do you feel? And me too? I actually voted for him at the last election! I believed all that fancy talk about family values and being tough on crime; well it should perhaps begin at home for Mister Mark Appleton MP. What a first class hypocrite!' Alice was fired up and ready to take on the world. Caroline felt the need to bring her back to reality.

'It's an historic crime, don't think I haven't thought about reporting it over the years but I've looked into these things and all it would boil down to is his word against mine. Only six percent of all rape cases are actually proven in court and they are the ones with concrete DNA evidence, there's no way I can prove that he raped me now so long after the event.'

'But Mum there is evidence, me! A paternity test would prove without question that Appleton's my biological father.' Alice sounded triumphant and Caroline had to admit to never having considered that fact as evidence but then she had never intended telling her daughter the true circumstances of her conception. Had she made a mistake in doing so? Hopefully when Alice was over the shock of this revelation she'd see sense and let go of these ideas of justice.

'What good would it do now dragging it all back up? I couldn't do that just to get even or to seek some kind of revenge.'

'I'm not talking about revenge Mum but justice. Anyone who sets themselves up in public office should be beyond reproach. He's a liar and a rapist and not fit to represent us in Parliament. But... have you ever thought that you might not have been his only victim? If he got away with it once he could have gone on to do it again and still could in the future. People like him rely on fear stopping his victims from reporting the crime. You're playing straight into his hands by letting him get away with it.' Alice's words made sense but Caroline dreaded the whole episode being made public. So far she had managed to live with the consequences of that night but for it to come out in the open at this late stage terrified her. Was she strong enough? As if reading her mind, Alice went on to say,

'If you did decide to pursue it, you would be able to remain anonymous and the police are very sensitive about these things. You've suffered so much from this Mum and he really should be punished for what he did.'

'Okay, I might have suffered, as have you and Ronald but there is another side to this. If that night had never happened I wouldn't have you and you are the single most important thing in my life. I've loved you from the day you were born, no, even before that as I carried you in my body. I wouldn't have missed having you for the world. You're the best thing in my life.'

Alice was touched by such heartfelt words. The whole issue was such a complex one to grasp and she honestly wondered if she would ever understand it fully. Perhaps it was time to leave the subject until another day. She was exhausted and could see that Caroline was too. With a sigh Alice said,

'Well, you haven't got far with your sorting out have you?'

'No, but some things are more important. I never meant to tell you all this Alice. I only hope it doesn't distress you too much and you can come to terms with it all?'

'I can't say it hasn't been a shock but it explains so much about Ronald and why he felt as he did. It's probably not fully sunk in yet and I know it's not going to be easy working through the reality of it all but I will Mum, I'm sure. What about you, will you be okay or would you like me to stay here tonight?'

'Oh, I'll be fine on my own, I'm getting rather used to it and you have your cats to consider now, they'll need seeing to.'

Before leaving Alice hugged her mother with more love and affection than she could ever remember feeling before. Having pushed and pushed until Caroline finally told the truth, Alice wondered now what on earth she was going to do with that truth.

The following day Alice found it difficult to concentrate at work. Sleep had not come until the early hours of the morning after much tossing and turning with disturbing thoughts running through her mind as if on a continuous conveyer belt. When sleep eventually came it was fitful with dreams of being chased by dark shadows which, with legs barely able to move, were gaining on her, increasing the fear of being caught. When morning dawned the dreams were still vivid but Alice determinedly refused any attempt to analyse them, deciding firmly that they were only dreams and she would ignore them. She wondered if her mother had slept any better but would be surprised if she had.

It was a quiet day in the lab and all work was up to date. Alice would have preferred to have been busy, a hectic day always passed much quicker but she was finishing an hour earlier than usual that afternoon for an appointment with Maggie. Hopefully talking recent developments through with her counsellor would prove beneficial. While making coffee in the small rest room, usually referred to as 'the cupboard', Joel came in, stopping abruptly when he saw Alice. She smiled at him,

'It's okay, I'm just having a coffee, would you like one?'

'Yes please, strong and hot, milk and sugar.' He returned the smile then sat in one of the two easy chairs watching her make the drink.'

'You seem a little distracted today Alice, is everything all right?'

His perception surprised her and for a moment she didn't know how to answer.

'I wish things were all right.' Passing him a mug of hot coffee she sat down in the other chair, suddenly feeling the need of company. 'Since Dad died some things have come to light which are unsettling. I went to see Mum yesterday and she told me things that weren't easy to listen to.' Alice took a sip of coffee then raised her eyes to look at Joel whose expression held concern.

'Sorry, I'll not bore you with all my family problems, I'll get over it.'

'It wouldn't bore me in the least. If you do ever want to talk, I've been told that I'm a good listener?'

'Thanks Joel, I might just take you up on that.' They finished their coffee in silence and Alice found herself frantically trying to think of something to say to keep Joel in the room a while longer. She somehow needed his company but was frightened that their night at the theatre had ruined any chance of friendship that they had.

'I really enjoyed our trip to the theatre Joel. I've been playing my CD's from the shows ever since and I swear that even my cats know the words by heart now.' What was she thinking, rambling on like that, whatever would he think?

'Good, I enjoyed it too. Maybe we could go out again sometime?'

The suggestion delighted her. Next time she would try not to make a fool of herself. After the night at the theatre thoughts of Joel popped into her mind frequently and surprisingly in a romantic way. She wondered what would have happened if she'd responded differently, what it would be like for him to kiss her? Then she would remind herself of that resolution to stay single but were her reasons for that now invalid? Knowing the truth about her mother's marriage was throwing every certainty she'd thought to have away. Alice didn't even know who she was any more; surely this was a most inappropriate time to be thinking about a relationship. But her heart was telling her that she wanted to see Joel again, to have a second chance and it looked as if that might be possible after all.

****

Maggie's room began to work its magic on Alice who immediately felt so much calmer than she had been all day in the tranquillity of the warm and comfortable space.

Alice wanted to be honest with Maggie but was reticent to disclose everything she'd learned of late in case such knowledge would have to be passed on. Having wrestled with this for most of the day she eventually concluded that the only way to find out was to ask.

'If I tell you about a crime which was committed but never reported to the police, would that negate the confidentiality of our time together?' Alice had to know before disclosing the rape and the identity of her biological father.

'Well, I'm obliged to report any instances of terrorism and also any crime which may be about to be committed, or if any person is about to be harmed. So if what you want to share falls into those categories perhaps you need to think again. Otherwise what is said within these walls remains here.' Hearing this question, Maggie wondered if Caroline had disclosed the rape after all which she soon found out was indeed the case. Alice poured her heart out, revealing every detail of what Caroline had said and every thought of her own about the way to go forward. Maggie already knew some of the facts but not the identity of the rapist. With that extra nugget of information the reason why Caroline had never reported the incident at the time became clear. Mark Appleton came from a well known family in Fenbridge, they had money and power and like most people who had grown up there Maggie could remember Mark's parents being patrons of many local charities. He had ridden on the coat tails of that reputation, using it to secure a nomination as an MP and success in the subsequent campaign. Maggie too had voted for him but when she actually thought about the reasons for doing so, it had more to do with his family's good reputation than anything she actually knew about the man himself.

'It's not too late for Mum to report this now is it?' Alice asked, quite weary now from going over it all again.

'No, it's never too late to report a crime, but your mother would have to be certain that she really wants to do so. The process is long and certainly not an easy one and if it does go to court it can be quite a traumatic ordeal. Rape cases are notoriously hard to prove, historic ones even more so. It generally comes down to whose word the jury believes.'

'Yes but although there's no evidence after all this time, a DNA test could prove I'm his daughter wouldn't it?'

'It would, but then Appleton could always claim that the relationship had been consensual. Perhaps making a list of pro's and con's might help your mum to decide?'
Alice knew that this had to be primarily her mother's decision and although she herself was convinced it should be reported, Caroline would need to be sure that it was the right way forward for herself.

'I'll talk to Mum again and maybe we could do the list thing together.' Apparently needing to move on, Alice suddenly changed the subject and began to talk about Joel, describing the incident earlier that day which she seemed to interpret as a positive turn of events.

'I can't believe I was actually encouraging him. I was so certain before that I just wanted friendship but now I'm unsure. I enjoy his company and want to be with him but it's against every decision I've made for my future.'

'So your feelings towards him have changed?'

'Yes, I'm even regretting rebuffing that attempt to hold my hand at the theatre. Stupid isn't it?'

'Not at all. You gave Joel a message and now you wish you hadn't.'

'That's about it in a nutshell. But what about everything I'd decided for my future?'

'Mapping out the details of our lives in advance rarely works out. Things happen to change our views and opinions and what seems right one day might seem completely wrong the next.'

'That's just how it feels Maggie.' Alice was confused, thoughtful and by then very tired.

'Just remember Tara and your two little cats, a day at a time perhaps?'

Alice left slightly more upbeat than Maggie would have expected. It appeared that although obviously shocked by Caroline's revelation, Alice was focussing on getting 'justice' rather than the actual issue itself. This was perhaps a coping strategy, a way to avoid dealing with the facts of her conception, such unpleasant knowledge for anyone to have to grasp. But there would probably come a time somewhere along the line when Alice would have to work through the issue itself. In the interim, concentrating on justice was the prelude that would perhaps go some way to helping her come to terms with it. Alice's sudden change of heart regarding Joel could also help in easing the burden she was carrying. Their relationship, if it blossomed as Alice appeared to hope, would bring something positive and fresh into her life at a time when she most needed it.

Chapter 26

Maggie thoroughly enjoyed preparing for the family gathering. Rarely was there chance to spend much time in the kitchen and so she'd devoted Friday evening to putting together some deserts and Saturday morning in making up quiches, salad, sandwiches and a variety of cheese to serve after Helen's broth. The scene from the kitchen window brought a frown to her face. Both of Peter's daughters would be travelling that morning and the clouds looked ominously grey. Huge drops of rain began to splash onto the window and the wind was blowing the trees in the fields which their house overlooked. For a moment she stared, fascinated at how the trees bent away from the wind, swaying together like a well choreographed dance. Not only was it Rachel's birthday but she was bringing her latest boyfriend which Peter interpreted as a sign that this relationship was serious. As well as her parents, they had invited Sue, Alan and Rose who were every bit as close as family. The rain began blowing harder against the window panes in loud relentless splashes. Hopefully it would move away later in the day but whatever the conditions outside, the atmosphere inside would be warm.

Helen and George arrived first with the promised broth and a huge batch of fresh bread.

'I thought I'd make plenty so there'll be some left for tea time.' Helen grinned. Maggie kissed her mother and thanked her, the bread looked delicious and she doubted there would be much left at all. As well as plain loaves Helen had made fruit bread and a cinnamon spice loaf and the mouth watering smell was almost too much to resist and had certainly got Ben's attention. Rachel was next to arrive, holding firmly onto the hand of a young man as if the wind would snatch him away. Alec was introduced to Peter, Maggie and Maggie's parents, all of whom welcomed the young man warmly. He had striking red hair, tightly frizzed and rather unruly, freckles covered a pleasant oval face and his smile revealed even white teeth. The most striking feature was his eyelashes which were so fair they were almost white, framing bright green eyes. Alec was obviously as besotted with Rachel as she appeared to be with him, giving rise to speculation of a family wedding in Maggie's mind and thoughts of the expense of a wedding in Peter's. Jane's family were not far behind with Sue and Alan arriving later, an intended ploy to allow the family members some time together.

Sitting down to eat, justice was certainly done to a heavily laden table with everyone enjoying not only the food but the conversation too. George became slightly confused with so many people in the room and although smiling broadly, Helen knew that trying to remember the names was baffling and even more difficult was getting right which partner belonged to which person. He did however enjoy the company of young people and managed reasonably well in keeping up with the conversation. Alec had been seated in between Rachel and Jane with Peter opposite and at times Maggie felt obliged to rescue him from the barrage of questions being fired mercilessly from his girlfriend's sister and father.

When they had finished eating, Sue helped to clear the table giving Maggie the opportunity to ask a question, one to which she thought she already knew the answer.

'Is there something you want to tell me Sue?' Maggie asked mischievously.

'Like what?' Sue feigned innocence.'

'Like why you've refused wine today and drunk only water or orange juice instead?'

'Okay, you've got me! I'm not quite three months so was going to wait a couple more weeks before I said anything, but we're so excited! You mustn't say anything though, we haven't even told Rose or my Mum yet.'

'Your secret's safe with me, come here!' Maggie hugged Sue, delighted at such good news. Rose was three and the perfect age to gain the elevated status of big sister.

'How have you been?'

'Sick every single morning so far, but after that okay. I'll get round to telling them at work when I'm a little further on so you can tell Peter but no-one else, okay?'

Maggie gave a mock salute and they went back to join the others. Her pleasure was genuine; she had never been blessed with children of her own and therefore was delighted to be actively involved with Sue's family and with Peter's grandchildren. It was hard to keep the smile from her lips but the others interpreted it as pleasure at their company. Jane helped to serve coffee in the lounge, enquiring after George's health when she and Maggie were alone.

'He's settled in better than we might have hoped but I know it's not easy for Mum. It's a twenty four hour job watching him so she doesn't get much respite. I've been looking into some groups he could attend during the day which would be good for both of them.'

'I wish we could do more to help Maggie, it could prove draining on you and Dad too.'

'Thanks Jane, but we're very conscious of getting the balance right. Your Dad's not working as many hours as he used to so he's been a rock and I actually think he enjoys my Dad's company. Dad can have some very lucid periods when you would hardly know there was anything wrong, but even when he's on another planet it can be quite amusing, albeit sad.' As they took trays of coffee into the lounge, George was fast asleep in the armchair with Ben, chin resting on his feet, also asleep.

'Two old boys together.' Helen commented. George and Ben managed to sleep through the noise of the children playing and the adults firing questions at Alec in an attempt to get to know him better.

The afternoon passed all too quickly and after tea Jane announced that they had better get started for home. The children were tired and the wind and rain had abated a little so they said their goodbyes and piled into the car for the homeward journey. Helen too decided they should leave as did Sue and Alan and very soon there was just Maggie, Peter, Rachel and Alec left.

'Can I help you clear up in the kitchen?' Rachel offered.

'No, I can do it later, there's not much to do but thanks anyway.'

'Really, I'd love to help.' Rachel stood up leaving Maggie with no choice but to follow her step daughter into the kitchen. When they were out of earshot of the men, Rachel explained,

'Sorry Maggie but Alec wants to talk to Dad on his own, but I'll happily help you clear up if you like?' Rachel looked nervous. It dawned on Maggie what she meant.

'Oh Rachel, does this mean you're getting engaged?'

'Yes, it does, amazing or what?' She was radiant and Maggie hugged her in congratulations. News of a new baby and a forthcoming wedding was simply the icing on the cake after such a perfect day.

****

Maggie's first call on Monday morning was to Jenny Grainger. Having never met Malcolm Grainger she wondered if his wife planned the times of their meeting very carefully or perhaps kept him locked away in the shed? Smiling at the thought, she stopped herself from actually looking out into the garden to check on any activity near the shed. Settling down to give her client full attention Maggie was soon brought up to speed on the various happenings in Jenny's family. She began by telling Maggie of the rift between her husband and son.

'We've always been such a close family but Matthew was absolutely furious with his Dad for not having told us all about his past. He needed a couple of days to calm down before I persuaded him to come round and make up with Mal. We certainly need to be united at the moment, there's been such a lot going on, strange phone calls at all hours of the day and night and then some horrible photographs of Kate and Daisy. It was frightening enough to realise that she'd been followed and for him to know her address but he'd painted an ugly red mark on the photo, right down the length of her face. How on earth can people be so cruel?' It was a rhetorical question and Maggie didn't have time to consider a reply as Jenny continued like a tightly wound spring,

'This whole incident has made us look at things we've never even thought about before. Matthew has really surprised me with his attitude to what his grandmother did. He almost admires her for having the courage to assist in a suicide! I was quite shocked but then it's not the kind of topic you generally discuss with your children is it? Matt claims that he would want someone to help him die in that situation. Well, it's easy to say that now, but who knows how they would actually feel in such a position and who makes the final decision?' Jenny paused all of two seconds for breath before continuing.

'He seems to think it goes on more than we realise, doctors helping patients to die and that kind of thing. Strangely he seems quite knowledgeable about euthanasia in general and I was amazed to learn that some countries have legalised it in one form or another... and it's not limited to people with terminal illnesses either. Folk with disabilities and mental illness are included, supposedly having the right to die with dignity. Well, we can all say that's what we want for ourselves when we're fit and healthy but if we were actually in that situation who knows? I know there are cases in hospital when people are in their last few days and it's decided not to resuscitate them in the event of cardiac arrest, that's different isn't it?' Another rhetorical question.

'Quite honestly I don't know where I stand on the issue. Malcolm's Dad could be said to have very little quality of life but I wouldn't dream of helping him to pull the plug! He still enjoys visits from family, he and Mal regularly do crosswords together and he can communicate with the help of a keyboard, he reads quite a bit too. It's not much of a life but to my mind it's better than the alternative.' Jenny shuffled uncomfortably in the chair.

'It gives me the creeps thinking about it all. Matt seems to think that when a person has no dignity left in their life they should be allowed to end it if they want to but who defines dignity? It's not really surprising that Malcolm never told us about his mother is it?'

'It's a very emotive subject.' Maggie calmly listened to Jenny getting all these thoughts out into the open, not wanting to be drawn into a debate on this issue with her client but conscious that Jenny had been through a difficult time and had much to process. Eventually she moved on with her story.

'Anyway, after the photographs arrived Malcolm agreed to call the police. A very nice detective sergeant came round with his colleague and listened to all that's been going on with that Stokes character. He said to contact him if we heard from Stokes again, which we did, the very next day. The idiot turned up at the house drunk! He seemed to think we were simply going to hand over money and he'd be on his way. I called the police of course and they came and arrested him there and then, took him off to the station but that wasn't the end of it, oh no! Later in the afternoon he turned up again, not quite as drunk but in such a foul mood. Malcolm had tried to talk to him earlier, quite gentle he'd been too, but Stokes was full of hate and anger. He spilled it all out going back to when they were just boys at school. Do you know, he'd actually been jealous of Mal? He didn't have much of a home life and envied every good thing about Malcolm's family. Would you believe it, this whole thing has been about nothing more than jealousy?'

'Envy can be a powerful emotion. Did you call the police again?'

'I wanted to but Mal said no. He actually listened to that madman spewing all his hatred and jealousy out. Mal was quite calm and eventually told him to leave but not to come back as we'd certainly call the police if he did. I couldn't believe Mal's attitude after all that man has put us through, he was almost sympathetic.'

'Your husband sounds like a very gracious man.'

'He certainly is. I've seen a different side to him through all of this and the same with my father-in-law too. I read those diaries Maggie, they were heart wrenching. What he suffered during that time was shocking. I'd never realised it before but he's quite a man. Kate and Matt are going to read them too. I think it will do them good to learn how difficult it was for their dad and granddad. Anyway, we're going to have that holiday we've been talking about for ages. We've booked a hotel in Florida and leave in a couple of week's time. Things should be back to normal then, the police say it'll be months before Stokes goes to court so there's nothing preventing us going away. The only thing we have to do is go down to the station and give formal statements which they record on video, then give our fingerprints so they can eliminate them from the photographs to prove that

Stokes sent them. I almost feel like a criminal myself having to give fingerprints.

You've been really helpful Maggie and I'm so grateful for all you've done. Can I ring you when we come home from Florida? I don't know if I'll need to see you again but I'd like to keep the option open, would that be alright?'

'That would be fine but you've done all the hard work yourself really Jenny. It's been a difficult time and a holiday sounds like a really good idea, just the thing to get away and relax. You perhaps need to be aware that you may not feel like your old self again for a while. Sometimes when a particularly difficult time comes to an end we think we should be back on top of the world again but unfortunately that isn't always the case. Don't be surprised if you're feeling a little down at times, our minds can't just switch off when problems seem to be over. You need to look after yourself and that lovely family of yours and I hope you have a truly great time. I'll look forward to hearing from you when you get back.'

Leaving Jenny Grainger, a lady who knew her own mind, Maggie was confident that this client would move on enthusiastically with life to enjoy time spent with family and friends. Jenny had certainly had her share of changes to cope with of late but hopefully the negative ones were behind her now and she may not need to see a counsellor again.

Chapter 27

'Maggie suggested that making a list could help us decide what to do.' Alice was again seated at her mother's dining table attempting once more to encourage Caroline to go to the police.

'A list of what?'

'Pro's and con's about reporting Appleton to the police. Haven't you been thinking about it?'

'Oh love, I've thought of nothing else all week! But I really don't think I can do it and he might have changed, that could have been the only time he ever did anything like that so why drag it all up now?'

'But it might not have been the only time either Mum. They don't say 'a leopard can't change his spots' for nothing. He should be held accountable.'

Caroline sighed, her nature was that of a peace-maker, goodness knows she'd had plenty of practise over the years but Alice seemed intent on confrontation. During the last few sleepless nights Caroline had come to the decision that if her daughter could not be persuaded to drop the issue, it would be better to go along with whatever she did want. Perhaps this was the way in which Alice would cope with the stark facts of her origins. Caroline could not decide whether it was worse for her to have been raped, or for Alice to know that she was the child of a rapist. But if this was the way forward for Alice in order to come to terms with the facts then they would walk down that path together. At least they had regained some kind of unity now, a new closeness which had been sadly lacking in recent years.

'Okay, so let's do the list.' Caroline produced a pen and notepad from the dresser and pushed them across the table. With the purpose and concentration of a

General planning battle strategy, Alice drew a line down the centre of the first page and headed each column.

'Right Mum, what are the reasons for reporting him?' Caroline looked blank, having hoped that Alice would do all the thinking.

'Er, because he broke the law?'

'Oh Mum, we're not talking about a shop lifter, this was a violent, vicious crime which has had consequences on your life as well as Ronald's and mine.'

'Yes, sorry you're right. The first reason must be that Appleton is, or was, a violent man and needs to be accountable for his actions.'

'Good, that's better.' Scribbling the words down and adding... 'Also, he's in public office making decisions which affect other people, a position he attained by being a hypocrite.' Alice certainly had more conviction about this task than her mother.

'He's in a position of trust and might use such to repeat his actions?'

'Good one Mum!'

Their list began to take shape but there were reasons on both sides, the 'not to report' side coming mainly from Caroline.

'I'm just concerned that it might have been an isolated incident which he perhaps regretted afterwards. If that's the case then I'm going to feel really mean and petty going to the police now so long after the event.'

'I know Mum and that says a lot about your nature but reporting a rape is not petty. How about if we talked it over with the police without giving them a name? Do you think we'd be able to do that?'

'I'm not sure but I would certainly feel happier doing that than going for the jugular as it were. Are you sure this is the way forward for you Alice? It's as much about you now as me and I can live without this pursuit of justice, so I really need to know that you are certain you want to do this?'

'Absolutely Mum, I'm totally convinced about it.'

Alice was the one to ring the police station to find out the best way of proceeding and Caroline listened, holding her breath as her daughter was first transferred then spoke to someone, giving details in very general terms and finally made an appointment to see a detective the following day.

'But it's Saturday tomorrow, do they work weekends?' Caroline had not expected such a swift response.

'Of course they work weekends Mum and evenings too, they could hardly do their job only during business hours could they?'

'I suppose not, I just didn't think it would be so soon. Is it a woman we're seeing?'

'Yes, a Detective Sergeant Sandra Freeman, she apparently works solely on sex related crimes.'

'Poor thing, what an awful job to have to wake up to every day.' Caroline could only see the negative side of such a job but when she met DS Freeman those perceptions began to change.

Sandra Freeman was five feet two inches of attitude and sheer determination. Her elfin face was without make-up and her grey trouser suit and white shirt gave the impression of crisp efficiency. She greeted Alice and Caroline with a pleasant smile and a warm handshake. Apologising for the room, a bland boxy cubicle with no windows, she offered them coffee which both women declined.

'You're probably very sensible, it's machine stuff and quite revolting.' Sandra sat opposite mother and daughter and took out a pen and an A4 note pad. Leaning back in the chair she smiled again and asked,

'It was you I spoke to on the phone Alice?' A nod confirmed this. 'But the incident happened to you, Caroline, is that correct?'

'Yes, that's right but it was over thirty years ago, it's probably too late to do anything about it now?' Caroline half hoped this young detective would agree with her and send them away as time wasters.

'Absolutely not!' Sandra shattered Caroline's last hope. 'A rape is a very serious, violent crime and it's never too late for the perpetrator to be brought to account. Perhaps today you can outline the event for me and then we'll meet again at a later date and take a more detailed statement, one which will be recorded. Is that okay with you?' Alice nodded for both of them and Sandra continued, 'Caroline, are you happy for your daughter to be present while we discuss this, I'm sure she would understand if you wanted her to wait in the corridor?' Two pair of eyes turned towards Caroline who shrugged and replied,

'Alice knows all about it now and I'd like her to be here today, especially if we're not going to get into all the details.'

'Good, let's crack on eh? I know it happened a long time ago but can you give me any idea of the date?'
Mentally Caroline counted back nine months from Alice's birth and came up with the month and the year.

'That's great! We often don't have such a clear time frame to work with. And your daughter told me you knew the perpetrator, can you give me his name?'
Mother and daughter exchanged looks and Caroline spoke up.

'Well, we wondered about that. Is it possible for me to explain what happened without telling you his name and then for you to tell me if some kind of prosecution is viable?'

Sandra looked directly at Caroline Greenwood and raised one eyebrow.

'Caroline, if you are intent on bringing this charge then we need to have a name. I realise this is a historic case and quite honestly if you came in here about a rape so long ago by a complete stranger, I would have to tell you that it would be almost impossible to investigate. As you do know who this man is, we need to be told in order to investigate the allegation and if appropriate charge him.'

'Yes, of course.' Caroline suddenly felt very foolish. How on earth could she expect this girl to do her job without the facts? The enormity of what she was about to do sat uncomfortably upon her. It was decision time. She could procrastinate no longer and certainly didn't want to waste the detective's time. Looking at Alice for encouragement she smiled at her daughter's anxious expression.

'His name is Mark Appleton.'

A look of surprise crossed Sandra's face.

'Are we talking about Mark Appleton, the Fenbridge MP?'

'Yes, the very same.' Caroline's boats were burned and she was committed to making this charge. There would be no backing out now, for Alice's sake as well as her own and she would be as co-operative as possible with the police. On that gloomy Saturday afternoon in November, Caroline outlined the worst experience of her life while DS Freeman listened with trained ears and an expressionless demeanour. Thirty minutes later Caroline quietly asked,

'Could I have that coffee now please?'

Sandra left the room to fetch it, returning in just a couple of minutes and, as she had previously told them, it was quite revolting. As Caroline drank the scalding liquid, Sandra scanned quickly over the notes she had taken before saying.

'Thank you both for coming today, I know this has been far from easy. If it helps you to get through it I'd like you to know that I believe you whole heartedly. Not everyone who comes in with this kind of story is telling the truth but over the seven years I've been doing this job I have developed a very sensitive 'hogwash radar' which rarely lets me down. If you are certain you want to pursue this then I will be one hundred percent behind you and will work my socks off to bring this man to justice. What happens now is that I open a file and begin my investigation. This will take time, nothing in today's justice system moves very fast I'm afraid but when I'm confident I have a case, and the CPS agree, things will start to happen. I'll give you a card with a direct number on to reach me here and I'll put my mobile number on the back. Please ring if you have any queries or worries. If I'm not answering leave a message and I'll get back to you as soon as possible.'

Caroline took the card, 'Thank you, you've been very encouraging. Can I just ask a couple of questions?' Sandra nodded. 'You know now that Alice is Mark Appleton's daughter but does this have to be made public? Perhaps I'm looking too far ahead but that is my biggest worry and I would hate her to have to suffer because I've decided to go ahead with this.'

'I can't deny that this is going to be a problem. Alice's DNA is our only bit of concrete evidence. In due course we'll need a sample, a simple mouth swab will be all Alice, and then we'll collect one from Appleton as well. We will not at any time be disclosing to Appleton or his solicitor that you are his daughter, this is our rabbit out of the hat; we'll give him enough rope to hang himself and then, probably in court, reveal this detail. We will of course request that your name will not be given but because of who he is, there's bound to be media attention and leaks do happen. There's always the chance of course that

Appleton will hold his hands up and confess but he has a lot to lose so I don't think that's a realistic possibility. Let's see how I get on with the initial inquiries shall we? There will be dozens of questions you'll think of over the next few days and what I would suggest is that you jot them down and we can look at them next time we meet, how's that?'

'Fine, thank you so much, you've been very kind.'

'Now, the only other thing you can help me with now is a photograph of yourself from around that time, do you have one?'

'I can find one and drop it in for you.' Caroline offered.

'That's great. Now I will keep you informed of any progress, and hopefully I'll be in touch within a week, two at the most.' Sandra showed them out before hurrying off with a sense of purpose which instilled confidence in both Alice and Caroline who made their way back to Alice's flat. Both were physically drained but still craved each other's company and the chance to discuss the experience of the afternoon. Letting the cats into the garden was the first job followed immediately by boiling the kettle for a decent cup of coffee. Alice took a couple of pizzas from the freezer and put them in the oven. Comfort food, there would be ice-cream for afters.

'What did you think of Sandra Freeman?' Caroline asked.

'She's brilliant. I wouldn't like to come up against her, I'm glad she's on our side. Quite a feisty lady I think, probably just the right type to be doing that kind of job.'

'I agree. I liked the way she said she believed me. I hadn't actually said that I was worried no one would believe me but it was at the back of my mind, so she addressed that one for me. And if your name could be kept out of the proceedings I'll be grateful.'

'Mum, I don't want you to worry about that. If it comes out, so be it, it won't be the end of the world, probably only a seven day wonder and then people would forget. Getting a conviction is the most important thing now so please don't fret on my account. Sandra seems to be a tenacious lady who's quite passionate about the job. She reminds me of Gavroche in 'Les Miserable' when he sings that cheeky little song about 'little people' and what a big impact they can make. I'm hoping that DS Freeman will prove to be as effective as I think she'll be.'

Chapter 28

'Everything all right Alice?' Joel asked, concerned that her mood was still low and she again appeared distracted from her work.

'Yes thanks... I'm fine, it was just... a rather unusual weekend. Sorry did you want something?'

'No, well yes actually. I was thinking of going to see the Nicholas Cage film 'Captain Correli's Mandolin'. It's showing at the Art Centre tonight and I wondered if you'd like to come with me? Unless of course you saw it first time round and didn't like it?'

'That would be lovely, thank you Joel. I did see it years ago but it's such a lovely film, I'd enjoy seeing it again.' Alice surprised herself at the eagerness and genuine pleasure she felt at this unexpected second chance with Joel. He arranged a time to pick her up before going back to work, smiling. The invitation only served to add another distraction to Alice's task and she had to shake herself and blink several times before being able to actually focus on the slide in the microscope. The day dragged and it was a relief when it was time to head for home. Bumping into Joel again on the way out she felt a strange and exciting warmth in being able to say 'I'll see you later.'

Kefalonia was the perfect setting for such a romantic love story, set in the rocky northern coast and the gorgeous sandy beaches of the south, the film moved Alice every bit as much as it had the first time round and a desire to visit Greece was rekindled. Joel drove them back to her flat and she invited him in for coffee. He appeared rather nervous when accepting; there was certainly a shy side to Joel which Alice found somewhat endearing. Making the coffee she wondered how the rest of the evening would work out. They had discussed the film, its merits and location, on the way home and as neither of them wanted to talk about work, Alice tried desperately to think of a safe topic. Fortunately the cats came to the rescue and by the time the coffee was ready, Wallace had taken control of the situation, introducing himself and demanding Joel's full attention. In the light of Wallace's antics it seemed only natural to relate the story of how she became the owner of two cats, a story which included Maggie's little homily on the wisdom of living in the moment. Strangely, sharing with Joel the fact that she was seeing a counsellor also seemed natural even though she had told no-one else except her mother.

'Is it since your father died?' Joel's question was prompted by concern and not in the least bit intrusive. Before Alice knew what she was doing she had poured out the whole story, beginning with Ronald's death and the discovery of her origins and even the recent visit to the police.

'Now I know why you often seem a little pensive at work, you've had much to cope with of late.' Again Joel seemed in no way patronising or pitying, with an attitude of genuine concern as he asked. 'Will the police press charges?'

'It's too early to say. DS Freeman needs time to investigate, after which she'll approach Appleton and charge him or at least get his side of the story. Nothing's going to happen quickly and I think the CPS have the final say on whether to prosecute or not. I suppose I'm rather concerned that a man in his position will be able to pull a few strings and perhaps get away with it.' It had been much easier to tell Joel than she could have expected but Alice suddenly realised that perhaps she shouldn't have named Appleton. 'You won't tell anyone will you? I mean his name or anything?' Anxiously looking into gentle blue eyes, Alice saw nothing but compassion and immediately wished she hadn't asked the question. But she need not have feared. Joel was not in the least bit offended and quietly reassured her that nothing she had shared would be repeated to anyone.

'More coffee?' Alice wanted to change the subject.

'Thanks but no, I'll be awake all night if I drink any more. You must be tired too Alice, I'll go now shall I?' Unable to think of a reason to detain him any longer, Alice smiled.

'Thank you for a lovely evening Joel and for listening to me moaning on about my problems.'

'I've enjoyed it too and you weren't moaning. I asked and I'm pleased that you trusted me enough to share your concerns.' Joel stood up to go and Alice fetched his coat. Being in such close proximity sent a shiver through her body and when he looked directly into her eyes she smiled up at him. Very gently he touched the side of her face, his hand cupping her cheek and leaned over to kiss her very gently.

'Is this okay?' Joel asked tenderly. She nodded, not trusting herself to speak and he moved closer, drawing her into his arms and kissing her again, this time with a little more urgency. Alice's arms fitted perfectly around his body and relaxing into his hold wished the moment could last forever.

'I should go now.' Joel spoke the words but made no move to leave.

'Yes' Alice too remained in his arms, savouring the closeness and comfort of his lean, strong body. Eventually he did go, leaving Alice with something other than her parentage to dwell on, something good and unexpected, new and frighteningly fragile.

****

Fenbridge Police Station was behind the market square, a Victorian building with a sixties built annex which appeared to have been added on with no thought to aesthetics or even comfort. This annex was the main entrance to the entire building, its steel framed windows bleeding rust down the concrete exterior. An oblong hall housed a reception desk where the personnel on duty were protected by a full length plexi-glass screen. Plastic bucket seats lined one wall, most of which were discoloured with stains which were probably best left unidentified. Jenny was directed to sit on one such chair as she waited for DS Hurst to collect her and she could feel the damp draught from the window behind her. The only other occupant in the reception area was a heavily tattooed young man whose face was obscured by several piercings and a shock of greasy blue-black hair. Jenny sat on the opposite end of the row of chairs, feeling like a criminal as she waited to give the video statement and be finger printed. Kate and Matthew had been to do the same thing earlier that morning and Malcolm, who was visiting Bill, would provide his evidence later in the day. DS Hurst soon appeared and led Jen to a room already set up and waiting for them. Instructing her to try and ignore the camera, he switched it on and she once again related the events of the last couple of weeks in regard to Frank Stokes. An hour later Jenny had found herself furtively looking around on leaving the station, hoping that no one she knew had seen her and then chiding herself for being so silly. When Malcolm came home they were going out to eat, something which was becoming a regular feature in their lives. She would have to be careful, all this dining out was piling on the weight but it was such a treat. Perhaps after the Florida trip she would go on a diet, join one of those slimming clubs or something before it got out of hand. Jenny enjoyed getting ready to go out; the wardrobe was bulging, much like her waistline and she felt good in the new clothes bought with their lottery winnings. Not that they were extravagant, Jenny's idea of designer wear was still M&S or Debenhams; the only difference now was that she did not have to wait for the sales, or worry about the figures on the price tags. Hearing the front door open and then close, she called,

'Is that you Mal?'

'Who else are you expecting?' He replied. Jenny rushed downstairs, anxious to ask how he had got on and compare notes about their experiences at the police station. Mal was in the kitchen, his face already buried in the local paper.

'Well, how did it go?' She asked.

'I didn't do the statement.' Malcolm kept his face hidden by the paper, avoiding eye contact.

'Why, wasn't DS Hurst there?'

'He was but I decided that I don't want to press charges.'

'No! I don't believe you. Why on earth would you say that?' Jenny was horrified.

'Because it's true, I don't want to press charges.' He put the paper down and turned towards his wife who was sitting beside him shaking her head.

'Look Jenny, we've got such a lot going for us, a wonderful family, money, each other. And what has Stokes got? Nothing. Okay I know he did wrong and had us all worried for a while but is it going to make us any happier to see him suffer the indignity of a trial?'

'Yes, it will certainly make me feel better! He needs to pay for what he's done Mal. How could you do this without talking to me about it first?'

'Sorry love, perhaps I should have spoken to you but I was at the police station feeling unsure about what we were doing and I made the decision there and then. I'm sure when you think rationally about it you'll agree. I know you're not a vindictive person. Stokes has never had a decent break in his life, for all we know if either of us had had the same upbringing we might have turned out like him, or bitter in other ways. So I didn't tell you because I honestly only decided when I got to the police station.'

'Malcolm Grainger,' Jenny sighed, 'I don't think I'll ever understand you. This man bullied you at school, tried to blackmail you and scared your family half to death and you don't want to press charges? You'll happily see him let off? I don't know what Matthew will say but I certainly hope I'm not around to hear it!'

'Well it might not be as simple as that. DS Hurst said that they were still investigating and it was actually the CPS who bring the charges and they may still decide to go ahead. I got the polite lecture about how extortion is a very serious crime and that in the public interest Stokes needs to be held accountable.'

'Good, at least someone's got some sense. So what happens now?'

'Well if they decide to bring the case to court I'll have to give evidence and so will you. I think DS Hurst was disappointed and I do feel bad after he's already put so much work in but I honestly think sending Stokes to jail will serve no purpose. He'll be living at the tax payer's expense and a trial would be costly too. Being in jail might even turn him into a hardened criminal so what's the point?'

'The point is he put us through hell, why shouldn't the man be prosecuted?' Jenny was feeling a mixture of emotions, understandably angry with Malcolm but in another way quite proud of his forgiving nature. Shaking her head sadly she took hold of his hand.

'You never cease to amaze me. Will I ever know the real Malcolm Grainger?' Her tone was softer now, gentler and Malcolm knew her anger was already abating.

'DS Hurst said he'll keep us informed on any progress but, as we already knew, it could take a few months.

'You had better let me tell Matthew and Kate, we don't want any more rifts in the family caused by that awful man. I know you feel sorry for Stokes, he is a pathetic figure but he has done wrong and I for one will be happy if the police continue with the case. Anyway, I'm changed and ready to go out, so let's forget about Frank Stokes and enjoy our evening together shall we?'

Chapter 29

Sandra Freeman had been doing her research. Before an arrest could be made it was necessary to check out what sort of woman Caroline Greenwood was and as expected her digging had revealed nothing of concern. Caroline was exactly what she appeared, a law abiding woman who had lived with a terrible injustice which Sandra intended to put right as far as it was possible. Caroline's story had a ring of truth about it and was certainly believable, Sandra's instincts were usually spot on in this regard. The fact that Alice was conceived from the attack was indisputable evidence, with the only sticky bit as far as she could tell was if Appleton somehow found out about Alice and claimed that the sex was consensual. Fortunately that explosive little fact did not have to be revealed to Appleton or his legal representative and Sandra felt sure that he would deny all knowledge of even knowing Caroline.

Digging into Appleton's history also drew a blank. It would have been helpful to find a string of complaints from other women against him but Sandra's job was not going to be that easy. This was however only the start of the investigations but there was enough to arrest and charge him after which she would seize his laptop which often gave an insight into a person's character, such as which sites he visited, what images he downloaded. The tech guys would dig around into his cyber history and who knew what they might unearth? It was time to confront the man himself. His initial reactions would help to construct the picture Sandra was putting together. Being arrested out of the blue could shake Appleton into making mistakes, she would be watching very carefully.

The Right Honourable Mark Appleton was furious. Ward surgeries were never his favourite part of the job, some of the constituents were frightful and their expectations totally ludicrous at times but his agent and the party whips insisted on a minimum number of surgeries when the 'House' wasn't sitting. He'd just got rid of a particularly obnoxious little man who wanted him to intervene in a dispute he was embroiled in with his landlord, when the police arrived, two of them, both young women who hardly looked old enough to be out of school never mind police officers. His secretary, flustered and embarrassed showed them in before beating a hasty retreat. Mark would have to speak to her about this later. Then the blow struck. The officer who introduced herself as DS Sandra Freeman informed him that they were there to arrest him in connection with an alleged rape in 1980. Mark was stunned, that was over thirty years ago. His immediate instinct was to defend himself, vigorously.

'What the blazes do you mean? Do you know who I am?' The words came out before Mark had thought them through. Of course they knew who he was they had just addressed him by name hadn't they?

'What I mean is, surely this is a mistake? Who is it that's made this ridiculous claim?'

'I think it would be better if we went down to the station to discuss the details sir.' Sandra's colleague, a young detective constable began reciting his rights.

'You can't arrest me on the strength of some ancient allegation!' The MP's face was a picture of shock from the raised eyebrows down to the open jaw.

'We can sir and we'd appreciate your co-operation in this matter.' Sandra's face showed no emotion, the complete opposite to Appleton's angry demeanour.

'But I'm in the middle of a ward surgery, can't it wait until later?'

'Sir, we are arresting you and I'm sure you'd rather we didn't use the cuffs?'

Mark Appleton turned angrily at the mention of handcuffs and made for the door. His secretary sat in the lobby of their rented constituency office looking as if she would rather be anywhere but there. Appleton was fully aware that she must have heard every word.

'I'll have to cut the session short Lindsay. I don't know how long I'll be out but please cancel all of today's appointments.'

'Yes Mr Appleton.' Lindsay kept her eyes down not daring to watch her boss being accompanied from the building, while two bewildered constituents stared wide eyed at their respected MP being ushered from his office by the two young women they had heard identifying themselves as police officers only a few minutes previously.

In less than half an hour, Mark Appleton was ensconced in a bare, stuffy, interview room, the same room Caroline and Alice Greenwood had been in a few days earlier. DS Freeman however did not apologise for the windowless room or offer any coffee, disgusting though it might be. He had requested his lawyer and been allowed to make the call. They would have delayed their questioning until the lawyer arrived but he seemed to want to talk, so they let him.

'Look, I can assure you that whoever has accused me of this horrendous crime is lying! Being brought here like this is outrageous.' Appleton wanted to get things straightened out at the outset of the interview and went on,

'This kind of thing happens all the time to men in my position. Women try to make a name for themselves, or think they can cash in by selling their fictitious lies to the media. Can we just get this over with, I have places I need to be!'

'It's not as simple as that Mr Appleton.' Sandra began. 'We have a duty to investigate such a serious allegation but if you're prepared to answer our questions truthfully we will perhaps get through things a little quicker.'

'I hope you're not insinuating that I would lie about such a matter? I don't have to, I didn't do anything!' Appleton was getting angrier by the minute, his face growing darker as he scowled at the women sitting opposite him.

'I'd like you to tell me exactly about this 'allegation' so that I can get out of here and back to my work. I'm a very busy man!' Sandra, aware that his actions and words were designed to intimidate, decided to test his reaction by revealing some of what they knew.

'The incident happened over thirty years ago Mr Appleton, to a young woman called Caroline Greenwood.' The MP actually missed a beat and there was a moment's hesitation which Sandra picked up on before he replied,

'Never heard of the woman.' His tone was clipped, dismissive but Sandra could tell the name had registered no matter what he said. She looked down at the papers spread out on the desk, turning the top sheet over, pretending to read details from the file and allowing a few minutes of silence, just enough time to make him panic and hopefully give something away.

'I don't think I should say any more until my lawyer gets here.' Appleton raised his chin and focussed on a spot above Sandra's head, refusing to look her in the eye. She smiled slowly. In her experience when people clamped up and asked for their lawyer they were usually afraid. He might as well have just admitted it as far as she was concerned. His attitude had convinced her of his guilt, even though the interview had so far been short and he would say no more without legal representation. Sandra would fight tooth and nail for Caroline Greenwood and bring this arrogant man down. She would apply all her tenacity and training to ensure that Mark Appleton would pay for what he had done.

Appleton's lawyer arrived at the station within the hour. It seemed much longer to the MP who had eventually been given a coffee and left alone in the same interview room with only his thoughts and the accompanying dark mood to keep him company. When the lawyer, Mr Jenson, arrived he was given time to talk to his client alone before Sandra resumed the interview. The tape was again switched on and the people in the room identified before she asked again,

'Mr Appleton, you stated previously that you had never heard of Caroline Greenwood, nee Fraser, do you still maintain that you do not know her?' Mark sat with his arms across his chest, staring into space as if he had not heard the question.

'My client does not know this woman, now or at any time in the past and does not wish to answer any more of your questions. Much of his precious time has already been wasted, so, perhaps we can wind this up and Mr Appleton can resume his duties representing the people of Fenbridge.' Jenson seemed harassed and obviously would also like to leave quickly.

Sandra could play the ignoring game too and addressed Appleton again,

'Mr Appleton, could you take a look at this photograph please? This is the lady concerned, taken at around the time we're talking about. Perhaps this will jog your memory?' She slid the picture across the table where it could easily be seen by both men. Appleton glanced at Jenson who gave a small nod, then he picked up the photograph.

'Never seen her before.' The chin rose again and his focus returned to the ceiling.

'Are you certain?'

'Of course I'm bloody certain!' He was losing his cool. Sandra would help him along a little.

'Thank you. Before you can leave someone will be along to take a DNA sample...'

'What the hell for?' Appleton's lawyer placed a restraining hand on his client's arm and spoke to the detective.

'If this alleged incident happened thirty years ago as you said, why the need for DNA samples?'

'Mr Jenson, you know as well as I do that this is simply procedure after any arrest. And we have sent an officer to your home address Mr Appleton to seize your personal computer and also the one from your constituency office.' Sandra smiled sweetly, it was only procedure.

'This is outrageous. I demand to see your superior officer...' Appleton began. The restraining hand grasped his arm again.

'If that is all for today my client would like to leave now.' Jenson wanted out before Mark could really vent his anger.

'Certainly, after the swab has been taken...'

Appleton moved to stand up but Sandra snapped, 'Sit down Mr. Appleton. There are a few things we need to agree on before you leave.'

To the MP's annoyance, Sandra Freeman went on to list the conditions of his release, mainly in regard to Caroline Greenwood, not attempting to approach her and also to inform the police if he intended to leave town. He seemed to have at last got the message to let Jenson do the talking and simply glowered at the women until the PC arrived to take a swab and they left the room, leaving the two men to make their own way out. The final humiliation came in the form of two journalists waiting in the lobby.

'Mr Appleton, can you tell us why you're here today?' Appleton again averted his eyes and ignored the question, quickening his step to get out as swiftly as possible but not in time to avoid the flash of a camera.

Sandra had expected the first encounter with Fenbridge's MP to turn out the way it had. It was early days in the investigation and the purpose of approaching him so soon was to test his reactions and form some kind of opinion as to the man himself. That opinion was that Appleton was an arrogant man who thought highly of himself and probably thought his position made him untouchable. She had almost expected him to drop hints that he played golf with the Chief Superintendant or some such connection but perhaps he was saving that kind of threat for later. After a quick lunch in the station canteen, Sandra settled herself at her desk to work on the case, firstly ringing Caroline Greenwood to update her on the morning's events.

'Caroline? It's Sandra Freeman here, how are you?'

'Oh, hello. I'm okay thank you; have you some news?' Caroline sounded worried. The DS knew she would be on a roller coaster of emotions over the next few months, choosing to press charges against a rapist was a monumental decision and Caroline would need every ounce of strength and determination to see it through.

'It's early days still but I thought you'd like to know that we arrested Mark Appleton and during our initial interview he denied even knowing you.'

'No surprise there then, he was hardly likely to own up to what he did.' An audible sigh punctuated Caroline's observation.

'It's about what I expected but as I said, it's still early, hang in there Caroline, something will turn up and when it does, we'll have him!'

Chapter 30

At 8.30 am Caroline was preparing breakfast, still unused to making meals for only one and thinking how much life had changed since Ronald's death, when the doorbell rang. Wondering who could possibly be visiting so early on a Friday morning, she tentatively opened the door. Standing in the porch to shelter from the rain was a tall, well dressed woman of about forty years old. The hem of her tailored camel coat met the tops of expensive brown leather knee high boots and leather gloved hands clasped the collar of the coat in an effort to keep out the cold.

'Mrs Greenwood?' the woman asked.

'Yes ...' Caroline was curious.

'My name is Georgia Appleton. I wondered if we could talk?' Those two short sentences prompted a whole series of thoughts to dance through Caroline's mind; the first and most startling being the visitor's name, there was little doubt that this lady was Mark Appleton's wife. Should she invite her in or refuse to talk to her? What could this woman possibly want; to persuade Caroline to drop the allegation, to threaten or even bribe her? The sensible thing to do would be to send her away but something in Georgia Appleton's expression elicited Caroline's gentle nature and she stood aside to allow this unexpected visitor inside her home. The immaculately turned out MP's wife nodded in thanks. Her fine boned face held a degree of sadness with perhaps a little fear in her intense grey eyes.

'I apologise for turning up so early and unannounced but I thought if I rang in advance you might not agree to see me.' Georgia had certainly got that right Caroline thought. Leading the way into the lounge and switching the gas fire on to warm the room, she wondered whether to offer coffee but decided that it would be inappropriate until she knew the purpose of the visit. The fire began to warm the room and Georgia loosened the top buttons on her coat. Caroline remained silent, unsure and a little apprehensive of how the next few minutes would turn out.

'If my husband knew I was here he would be furious... so in many ways I'm in your hands and I hope you'll not let anyone know about this meeting?'

'I can't make any promises until I know why you're here.' Caroline spoke before continuing the silence, hoping this visitor would get to the point as she was beginning to feel decidedly uncomfortable. Georgia removed the gloves and focussed on smoothing them on her lap. A slight tremor was noticeable in her manicured hands before she clasped them together so tightly that the knuckles became white.

'What is it that you want?' Caroline was growing more anxious and beginning to regret allowing this woman into her home. Georgia raised her eyes and began to speak,

'I need to know if you are serious about continuing with this allegation against my husband?' There was a pause before Caroline answered.

'Yes, I am and if you have come here to attempt to persuade me otherwise then I'm afraid you've had a wasted journey.' She spoke boldly, surprising even herself. 'And how did you know my address?'

'It's very easy to find things out when you have the contacts Mark has, your address was a simple matter for him, but I haven't come to persuade you to drop the allegation Mrs Greenwood, I'm here to help you!' Georgia Appleton suddenly broke down in tears with huge sobs wracking her slim body. Caroline was stunned, what on earth could she mean? Motherly instincts kicked into play and she moved over to the sofa next to Georgia, sliding a comforting arm around the woman's shoulders and making soothing noises as she had so often done with Alice so many years ago. The sobs continued for several minutes as if years of pent up emotion were being released. Mrs Appleton had reached breaking point and the outpouring of these emotions seemed long overdue. Caroline moved quietly to the kitchen to put the kettle on and returned with a box of tissues. Georgia gratefully took a handful and attempted to pull herself together, mumbling words of apology which were dismissed as unnecessary. Leaving the visitor to compose herself again, Caroline went to make tea, returning with steaming mugs for them both, hot, strong and sweet. The room had warmed through and Georgia appeared flushed, her perfectly applied make-up ruined by tears.

'Why don't you take your coat off and you can explain what you mean?' She didn't want to rush matters when the younger woman was in such an emotional state but was intrigued and wanted to know what Georgia was talking about. It was to take two hours to learn the answer to all her questions, two hours which completely erased any doubt in her mind as to whether she was doing the right thing in attempting to bring Mark Appleton to justice.

Georgia's story was difficult to listen to and obviously painful for the woman to disclose. She had married Appleton when only nineteen, wildly in love with an attractive older man and dazzled by his wealth, ambition and charm. All plans for a career of her own were abandoned as she happily gave up the chance of a university place and a previously longed for degree to become a full time wife to a budding politician. In those days, Mark had not been an MP but was steeped in local politics, swiftly rising to the position of leader of the town council, the youngest in Fenbridge's history. With family money behind him, Appleton could provide a luxury home and a certain standing in the community for his wife, which brought with it a glittering lifestyle to captivate the young Georgia. During the first two years of their marriage, the new Mrs Appleton thought she was living in paradise. Mark encouraged her to spend money on extravagant clothes and seemed to enjoy showing her off at the many functions they attended. When his ambitions were eventually realised and he was selected to stand for parliament, Georgia did her best to support him but her best was no longer good enough. Canvassing for election proved to be stressful for them both. Mark persistently required more from her and she began living completely in his shadow, any needs of her own dismissed as trivial. After he was elected, she hoped their lives would settle down to some kind of normality but was to be disappointed once again. Georgia had always longed for children yet when broaching the subject, Mark ridiculed her, leaving no doubt that a child did not figure in the master plan of Mark Appleton's career. Depressed and feeling isolated, Georgia struggled to meet her husband's exacting standards and with no life of her own, became desperately unhappy. He was spending more and more time in London and only required his wife's presence for occasions when it was deemed appropriate to have a dutiful wife by his side. In time she began to long for him to be away from home and dread his return. When he was at home, Mark used her to meet his own needs showing none of the charm which had won her over. Georgia knew by then without doubt that he did not love her and probably never had.

'I hate my marriage... and I hate my husband but it's impossible to escape.' Georgia's face reflected the wretchedness of her situation.

'Don't you have any family who could help?' Caroline spoke softly, with a heavy heart at this poor woman's plight.

'It's too late for that now. I initially stayed in the hope that things might get better which they didn't of course. In reality I have nowhere to go and no way to support myself. I'm not qualified to do anything other than be an MP's wife. My parents are elderly now but even in the early days they were so proud that I was married to Mark that they could see no wrong in him. Most people only see the beautiful house, the clothes and the glamorous lifestyle but it means nothing, nothing at all and Mark can certainly turn on the charm when it's to his advantage.' Georgia could shed no more tears. Her face was gaunt and sad and Caroline's heart went out to her. Having known problems in her own marriage she could understand where this woman was coming from, but where was this all leading?

'I can see that you've had a difficult time but how can you help me? And why would you want to help me prosecute your husband for something which happened before you even met him?' The story so far had been a sorry tale of an unhappy young woman but how this was relevant to Caroline's situation was unclear.

'There are other things... other incidents which would demonstrate the kind of man Mark really is.' Georgia's eyes dropped again to her lap. 'After he was elected to Parliament his behaviour worsened. He'd always been aggressive in manner but this seemed to escalate into physical aggression. The work was more stressful than Mark had expected with long hours, social functions and the like which, as time went on he began to loathe. He'd never tolerated people whom he classes as below him but being an MP involved keeping constituents happy. They had elected Mark to represent them and rightly expected him to do so, a part of the job he loathed. So, each time he returned home he needed to vent his anger... physically and I became the target for his abuse.' Georgia had spoken the words with eyes averted from Caroline's as if ashamed and somehow responsible for her husband's violence.

'I was shocked the first time he struck me but put it down to a 'one off', until it happened again. There is never an apology afterwards. Mark simply acts as if it has never happened. I've been too afraid to try and talk to him about it but any kind of discussion would be futile, the beatings have become a regular feature of our marriage. You must think me very weak and pathetic but I've never known what to do. If time could be turned back I would have nothing to do with Mark Appleton, but of course it can't and I'm scared of what he would do if I tried to leave.'

'I don't see you as weak or pathetic, in fact coming here today is such a brave thing to do. But surely there are places you could go for help?'

'Oh yes. There's a shelter for abused women not far from Fenbridge, I actually opened it five years ago and Mark has encouraged me to become involved in fundraising for them. Can you imagine what he would say if I tried to take refuge there? I'm trapped in this sham of a life. To Mark everything is about image. Socially we pretend to be the stereotypical 'happy couple' but privately he treats me worse than he would a dog.' Georgia sighed; it had not been easy disclosing such personal information to a stranger.

'And I don't think it's only me he treats badly.' The eyes lowered again, 'I found some emails once when I was looking for an address. They were between Mark and his agent and I tracked the conversation. It appeared that there was someone, a woman, who was threatening to go to the police. I'm not sure what for, but I can make an educated guess. He instructed his agent to give her money to make sure she kept quiet. I don't know if such vague information would be useful to the police, but it might go some way to revealing his true character.'

'I honestly don't know what to say to you Georgia. If you really want to help me, it would certainly involve talking to the police and possibly giving evidence in court, are you prepared to do that?'

'I thought a wife couldn't give evidence against her husband?'

'We'd have to ask about that, but if you were to pursue your own allegations against him I suppose together we would have a stronger case.' Caroline could see possibilities but didn't want to speculate or raise her hopes until she knew whether Georgia was serious and exactly how far she was willing to go to help in the case against her husband. There were also alarm bells ringing due to the fact that Appleton knew where she lived. Sandra had assured her that he had only been released on caution with one of the conditions being that he would in no way try to make contact with her. But words can't protect and sitting here before her was yet more proof of just how violent a man Appleton was.

'I'll have to go, Mark will be back at lunch time, he'll want to know where I've been if I'm not at home.'

'But what happens next? Will you go to the police?'

'I'll talk to them, see what they say but please don't tell them I've been here, they might come to find me when Mark's around. If you have a number for the detective you mentioned I'll ring her when I get the opportunity.' Georgia noticed the worried frown on Caroline's face, 'I'll do it soon, today if I get chance, okay?'

'Yes, thank you. I'll wait until you've contacted her and we'll see what happens next.' Caroline gave Sandra Freeman's telephone number, as well as her own, to Georgia who left, looking exhausted, to return to her opulent prison.

Chapter 31

The weather had suddenly improved and all forecasts were predicting an Indian summer for the following weekend, a welcome occurrence for mid November. Maggie suggested taking advantage of the weather by having a couple of days in Scotland. Peter was agreeable and Helen thought it would be good for George and also wanted to check things out at their old home. They would travel in Peter's car so wouldn't have room for Ben and Tara, something which didn't present too much of a problem as Sue was always happy to look after them and Rose would be ecstatic. By Friday it appeared that the forecasts were correct and coats, jumpers and boots had been discarded in favour of lighter clothes as people began to enjoy what would probably be the last spell of good weather before winter took its hold.

On Friday afternoon the traffic was moderately light and the journey itself was an enjoyable start to the weekend as the scent of rich peaty heather welcomed them across the border. The unseasonal sun picked out the last remaining colours of summer as specks of gold, red and orange glistened among the thick browning heather. George had been quiet for most of the journey, disappointed to learn that Ben would not be travelling with them. He had formed a strong bond with the dog and enjoyed the times they spent together. The sight of their cottage however lifted his mood and he was first inside, touching the door and walls as if greeting an old friend. Helen too was pleased to be back, making straight for the kitchen to switch on the boiler and get the place warmed through. Maggie and Peter saw to the luggage and when everything was unpacked they sat drinking tea in the lounge.

'When we get back to Fenbridge Maggie, I'd like to see a solicitor about putting this place in your name and I've been looking into 'power of attorney' which I think we should go ahead with.' Helen was determined to get their affairs sorted.

'There's no hurry Mum, you've had a lot on your plate lately.'

'I know but we're well settled in now thanks to your help and Alan's contribution. Life's proving a little easier for me but I want to do these things while I'm still able. We never know what the future will throw at us.' Helen looked wistfully at George. Just twelve months earlier none of them could have foreseen how rapidly the Alzheimer's would take hold. Changing the topic to a more pleasant theme Helen suggested.

'How about a trip to the outlet stores at Gretna tomorrow and we could go to that lovely new garden centre for lunch. We were thinking of a few pots and troughs for outside the doors at home weren't we George?'

'Good idea. I'll get that lawn cut now and dig the borders over for the winter.' George made to go into the garden.

'Are you up to it love?' Helen asked.

'Don't fuss woman, I've been neglecting the garden and it needs sorting for the winter.' He continued into the kitchen and out to the garden.

'I'll go and help him.' Peter offered. 'He's right really, the lawn does need cutting even though we thought we'd done the last cut for the year. The price of this good weather I suppose.'

Helen and Maggie cleared the cups and began to make up the beds. There was enough furniture to make the house comfortable and as the boiler worked its magic each room began to feel warm and lived in again.

'Are you okay about being here Mum?' Maggie was concerned that being back in their old home there would be memories Helen might find painful.

'I'm fine, really. I've come to terms with your father's condition and I know that things will only get worse but we've made the right move and I can cope knowing that you and Peter are there if I need you. Dad seems to have accepted the move too but coming back here on occasions will help, at least he'll have the garden to potter in when he wants to.'

'We'll have to make some decisions about this place now. I wondered if you knew anyone locally who could keep the gardens tidy? This winter won't be a problem but from next spring when everything starts to grow we will need help. We don't want to be coming every weekend just to mow the lawns and keep the borders tidy.' Maggie was aware that keeping the cottage as a holiday home would entail some degree of work to maintain it. While they were happy to keep it on and enjoy it on occasions she was conscious that it could very easily become a burden.

'We could put a card in the village shop window, but in the spring perhaps? As you say it will be fine over the winter and at the moment your Dad's physically well enough to do some gardening himself so we'll let him content himself with that shall we?'

The drive to Gretna was pleasant. Again it was warm enough to open the car windows and they all enjoyed the rugged landscape. The sun was highlighting the rich purples and mossy greens of the undulating hills while sheep grazed at the roadside, ignoring passing vehicles.

'It really is very similar to the Yorkshire moors.' Helen noted, 'They're both beautiful in their own way.'

Peter and George had coffee while Maggie and Helen shopped before they loaded their bargains into the boot and made for the garden centre. Dinner consisted of soup and a ploughman's sandwich which would suffice them for the rest of the day. They didn't spend too long looking round the centre but Helen did find a couple of pots and a wooden trough which was lined with tin and would make an excellent window box. Peter carried them through the till as she paid for them and they headed back out to the car park.

'Excuse me!' A young man appeared from behind them, stopping them in their tracks. 'I wonder if you would accompany me back inside the store?'

'Is something wrong? Peter asked.

'Perhaps we could discuss it in the manager's office?' He motioned for them to go back inside where another member of staff was waiting.

'Not until you tell me what's going on.' Peter again asked. The young man looked at George,

'I have reason to believe you have some items on you which you haven't paid for sir.' He looked solemnly at George. Helen blushed and stared at her husband.

'Dad, did you pick anything up in there?' Maggie asked.

'Of course I did, I got some packets of seeds for potting in the greenhouse. It is a garden centre isn't it?' George pulled the items from his pocket. Maggie turned to the young man,

'I'm terribly sorry, my Dad's not been too well and it probably slipped his mind to pay for them.'

'Could we have this conversation inside?' The young man was insistent. Maggie steered her father back towards the store followed by Peter and a very embarrassed Helen. A few customers stood and stared at them aware of what was going on and flashing reproachful looks in their direction. As they followed the young man into the manager's office, they felt like criminals and could feel the accusing looks from staff and customers alike. George was becoming agitated and shrugged free from his daughter's hold.

'I thought we were going home?' He asked, 'I'm ready to go now, where are you taking me?'

'Please sit there Dad.' Maggie steered her father into a chair and Helen sat beside him. The manager looked at them over the top of his glasses, a deep frown creasing his brow. Peter moved towards the desk and with his back purposely towards his wife and in laws, spoke to the manager.

'We are suitably embarrassed now if that was your intention. My father in law has Alzheimer's and I apologise for the misunderstanding. He obviously just picked the items up and forgot to pay. I'm quite happy to pay for the goods now but I do think you could use a little discretion here. We have bought goods for which we've paid and you surely can't think we'd deliberately take a few packets of seeds?'

'I get all sorts of excuses from shoplifters but I must say this is a first. He looks okay to me.' The manager, who was not much older that the young male assistant, had adopted an arrogant tone and Peter was getting annoyed.

'Fine, so what are we going to do now? You call the police, arrest this elderly gentleman and then we'll get his doctor to confirm his condition. After all this time consuming, upsetting waste of time we'll then write to your head office to complain about your unsympathetic attitude. Is that how this will play out?'

It was the manager who blushed then. Straining to peer past Peter's shoulders and take another look at George, his tone softened.

'I don't think there's any need for that sir. My assistant was perhaps a little hasty but if you're happy to pay for the goods, we'll say no more about it.'

'What's going on Chris?' George addressed Peter, reverting to calling him Chris again, 'I thought we were going home?'

'We are George, right now.' Peter took a ten pound note from his wallet, more than sufficient to cover the cost, and put it on the desk then turning to smile at George said, 'Come on then, let's find the car.'

Maggie played scrabble with her father later that evening. They had turned the heating up; in spite of the Indian summer the darkness had brought a chill to the air. The scrabble tiles were in her father's favour and Maggie conceded after only half an hour. George whispered quietly to her,

'Why was Chris annoyed with that chap at the garden centre?'

'It's Peter Dad, Chris died a long time ago don't you remember? But he wasn't cross, it was a misunderstanding that's all, nothing for you to worry about.'

'Good, I think I'll turn in now then. Goodnight sweetheart.' He bent to kiss Maggie's forehead and squeezed her shoulder. 'Don't let that Chris upset you love, it wasn't you he was mad with.'

Helen was apologetic, unnecessarily so.

'Mum, you don't have to apologise for him, not to us nor to anyone.'

'But it was so embarrassing for you.'

'It wasn't, he's my Dad and it was just one of those things, no one was hurt so it's fine. I actually enjoyed seeing my husband assert himself.' She looked at Peter, who smiled,

'I quite enjoyed it myself too! The man's attitude was totally out of order, he just needed it pointing out to him.'

'Well thank you Peter, I was so glad you were there with us.'

'Always happy to help a damsel in distress!' Peter winked at his mother in law. They were all aware that no matter how much they chaperoned George there were going to be occasions when things like this would happen. It was a cruel disease which was slowly taking away the faculties and dignity of a man who had, in his time, been a strong, intelligent husband and father. The three of them fell silent, each reflecting on the uncertainty of the future and trying hard not to anticipate what else it could possibly bring.

Chapter 32

It was Appleton's worst nightmare. His picture was splashed across the front page of nearly every newspaper, nationals and local alike. Most of the photographs were library shots of him smiling and waving during some function or other but the local paper printed the one of him leaving the police station with Jenson, his arm raised to shield his face and turning away from the camera. He looked like a guilty man.

'Who the hell leaked this?' The question was directed at his wife but Georgia knew no answer was required. Perhaps he should have been more surprised that it had taken a couple of days for the story to break. He continued to vent his anger verbally and she made sympathetic noises, hoping that he wasn't going to become violent. The doorbell rang and Mark shouted,

'Don't answer that! It's probably reporters.'

'At seven thirty in the morning?'

'Yes, stay away from the window; let them think there's no one home.' Mark surreptitiously moved the curtain to confirm his guess. At the end of their drive several vehicles clustered close to their gate and journalists had actually positioned themselves along the drive, cameras at the ready. He could hardly go out and shift them and he doubted the police would help, it was their fault they were here. No, he would wait them out, they couldn't camp out there forever.

Georgia sighed wishing she wasn't enjoying her husband's discomfort quite so much. She didn't want to be driven by revenge but simply wanted out and this allegation could be her big chance. If he went to prison, and she was sure a guilty verdict would merit a custodial sentence, she would seek a divorce and move away somewhere to start a new life, somewhere Mark would never find her. Even knowing things were going to get worse couldn't prevent a swelling in her chest at the thought of freedom and a life without him. When he was around Georgia had to check herself, pretending to sympathise when she was inwardly smiling at the embarrassing mess piling up on her husband. The first thing she knew about his arrest was when the police arrived at the house with a warrant to take his computer and any documents they felt were pertinent to the charge. She had stood and watched in amazement as they searched his desk, using some kind of skeleton key to open the locked bureau. Again conflicting emotions had washed over her as she dared to hope that this was the beginning of Mark's downfall and her own freedom. Watching him now, banging about the house in such a foul mood, Georgia felt safe. Hopefully he wouldn't risk hurting her while journalists were so close, but the almost tangible frustration her husband exhibited was unsettling, like waiting for a bomb to go off. After two hours Mark could stand it no more and rang his agent Jim Barker, with instructions to drive to the street two blocks away and be ready to pick him up. Twenty minutes later without a word to his wife, Appleton left by the back door. Georgia watched with guilty pleasure as he clambered over the overgrown shrubs into the garden of the house backing onto their own, if it hadn't been so sad it might have been comical.

Georgia had been true to her word and had rung DS Sandra Freeman later on the day in which she had visited Caroline. After outlining the reason for the call, Sandra asked if they could meet. It was difficult as Mark was almost confined to home with the situation as it was, so she offered to ring DS Freeman again when he was out of the way. This could be the opportunity, it seemed improbable that Mark would come back soon while the media were camped on their doorstep so she rang Sandra in the hope that the detective would be free to come straight round.

'DS Freeman' The voice was clear and efficient.

'Hello, its Georgia Appleton here, I rang the other day?'

'Yes, hello Mrs Appleton, how are you?'

'Fine thanks, well, sort of. We seem to have the world's press outside the house. Mark's slipped out the back and I shouldn't think he'll be back soon so I wondered if you could come round?'

'I'm on my way.' The phone disconnected. Within fifteen minutes Sandra and the young DC were making their way through the journalists to the Appleton's front door. Caroline opened it only a fraction, allowing them to squeeze in without being seen herself. Cameras had clicked and flashed catching images of the police officers entering the house. No doubt they would be identified as police in the next edition of the papers but Georgia was getting to the point where she didn't care anymore. She offered coffee which was accepted gratefully before they settled in the dining room, keeping well away from the windows.

'You said on the phone that you wished to help in the case against your husband, is that right?'

'Yes. I went to see Caroline Greenwood...'

'Can I just stop you there a minute. How did you know where Mrs Greenwood lives?'

'It was the first thing Mark did when you released him. He rang his agent and instructed him to find out where she lived. Jim rang back later with the address which Mark repeated while he wrote it down.'

'Do you think he intends to visit Mrs Greenwood himself?'

'I don't know but I shouldn't think so. I wouldn't put it past him to get someone else to do it but he's not stupid enough to go himself.'

Sandra made a mental note to speak to Caroline about the possibility of staying with her daughter for a while.

'Thank you, please go on.'

'Mark is a violent man. I know that from personal experience. He's also very cunning, he targets the blows where they won't be seen, I think that's common practise among abusive men?'

Sandra nodded, encouraging her to continue while her colleague made notes.

'I don't know if I'd be able to testify against him, but I will if I'm allowed.' Georgia paused and sipped her coffee, in need of the hot sweet liquid.

'There's no reason why you shouldn't testify Mrs Appleton. Do you want to press charges regarding these incidents?'

'Oh, I hadn't thought of that but I will if it helps to send him away.'

Sandra was inclined to believe this woman but she needed to be absolutely sure that this was the truth and not simply a woman who wanted out of a soured relationship. She began to push for details, probing gently into the personal life of Mark and Georgia Appleton. The more the woman talked the more convinced Sandra became that she was genuine. Dates were sketchy but there had been a couple of occasions when Georgia had needed medical attention, once with a broken wrist and the other a badly sprained ankle. It would be easy to check medical records to confirm these instances. The icing on the cake however, came when Georgia began to tell them about the emails she had read about paying off a woman.

'Both computers are with our technical guys at the moment but we'll get them to search specifically for those. They should have something in another couple of days.'

Georgia had about finished all she could think of that might help the detectives and was about to ask one or two questions about how things would proceed when they heard the back door slam. A very angry Mark Appleton appeared in the doorway, slightly dishevelled from his fight with the shrubbery and obviously furious to find his wife having a cosy chat with the police. Georgia looked flushed and Sandra recognised the fear in her eyes.

'Good morning Mr Appleton. We'd hoped to see you to ask one or two more questions. Your wife very kindly made coffee but now that you're here perhaps we could have a few minutes of your time?' She seemed to have diverted attention from Georgia but would now have to ask Appleton a few impromptu questions.

'I suppose that lot out there took note of you calling.' The anger was apparent in his voice. 'Whatever happened to discretion and innocent until proven guilty?'

'Freedom of the press sir, a price we have to pay I'm afraid. Now, perhaps we could begin?' Sandra brought out the photograph once again, of the young Caroline Greenwood. 'Could you have another look at this sir, just in case you've remembered this woman since last time we met.'

Appleton barely glanced at it.

'No, I told you before I don't recognise her at all.'

Sandra went on to ask more questions, mostly the same ones he had already been asked. His patience was deserting him.

'Look, if you're trying to trap me by asking the same bloody questions all over again, it won't work. I've told you all I know. Perhaps you should put your efforts into investigating this woman whoever she is. She's probably deranged and needs locking up! Why aren't you interested in protecting innocent citizens detective?'

'Oh we are sir, believe me, we are.' Sandra stood to leave, thanking Georgia for the coffee and giving Mark a brief nod. They left by the front door, initiating a flurry of activity in the garden. Mark hardly dared to suggest that they slip out the back way as he had done. Appleton slammed the door then went back to his wife.

'What have you been saying?' He snarled
'Only the truth.' Her candour earned a sharp slap across the cheek before Mark turned and stormed out of the room. Blood trickled from Georgia's lip but she smiled at the thought that she didn't have to take this much longer. Mark Appleton's past was about to catch up with him and he was going to pay dearly for what he had done.

Chapter 33

Bill Grainger was reading a book on his bedside computer when his son appeared in the doorway. Malcolm joked that his father must hold the world record for the highest number of books ever read. It had been his passion throughout life and he always considered himself fortunate to work in a library, a fitting place for such a bibliophile. Books were his solace and his companions. The only way he could get out of the room he now lived in was through the pages of a book when he could be transported to far more exotic locations than Willow Dene Nursing Home. Reading electronically wasn't quite the same as a good old paper copy but in Bill's situation eBooks gave him the means to continue his passion when physically turning a page was almost impossible. He switched the reading app off to give his full attention to Malcolm.

'Ready?' he mouthed.

'Yes, we've packed everything bar the proverbial kitchen sink and I think Jen would take that too if she could.' He smiled, 'Will you be alright Dad?' It was a concern to Malcolm that the whole family would be away together. Usually when they took holidays, Matthew or Kate would be around to pop in and see Bill more regularly but this time they were all going to Florida together.

'Fine...enjoy.' Bill managed to say and Malcolm knew he meant it, his father was the most selfless person he had ever known with the exception perhaps of his mother whom he had not had chance to know for long enough.

'It's only two weeks and I don't think we'll be making a habit of it, it's been a nightmare arranging things to suit six adults and three children, I think perhaps we'll opt for quieter less hectic holidays in the future.' Malcolm took hold of his Dad's hand and the older man smiled.

'I've been thinking Dad. When we come home, Jen's set on looking for a new house. I know we said we wouldn't move, but we've rather changed our minds. It'll not be anything flash, just a nice modern place, a bungalow perhaps, with a bit more space. I wondered if you'd like to come and live with us?'
Bill squeezed his son's hand and shook his head.

'Hear me out first, please. We could find somewhere with enough space to build an extension, something specially designed to suit your needs and we could have private care for you, money's no object now Dad. I don't want you to answer now but think about it while we're away and we'll talk some more when I come home. What I don't want is you thinking we're doing it just for you. It's what we want too. Seeing your things in the attic just waiting for you to come home is what's given me the idea but I'd love for you to be out of this place. Don't wrinkle your nose like that.' He laughed at his father's comical, lop sided expression, 'I know it's been a good place and the staff are great and everything, but it's not home is it? Just think about it Dad, that's all I ask.'
Bill nodded, eyes glistening with tears. He was so proud of Malcolm perhaps he hadn't done such a bad job of raising him without Mary after all. Father and son began to tackle their usual crossword together and the time slipped swiftly by.

'Well I suppose I'd better go home and check that Jen hasn't sneaked anything else into the case, she started packing a week ago.' Malcolm kissed his father's forehead and left the old man to his beloved reading.

'What did he say?' This was Jenny's first question when Malcolm came through the door.

'At first he said no, I'm sure he thinks he'll be a burden but I talked it through with him and asked him to consider it while we're away. I hope he'll go with the idea.'

'Me too. You know I feel as if I know your Dad so much better now than when he was active and we saw more of him. That diary was certainly an eye opener. Still waters certainly do run deep in Bill's case. He's got a depth that I never understood before but then I didn't know the full story did I?'

Jenny saw a pained expression cross her husband's face.

'Oh love, I'm not getting at you. You did what you thought was best. It's just that knowing what you and Bill went through in those years has helped me to understand him better and you as well. I'm over the fact that you never told me, you and Bill are like two peas in a pod in keeping your thoughts to yourselves but I'm glad I know now.' She gave Malcolm a brief hug, then pulled back remembering something else.

'Oh I almost forgot DS Hurst rang while you were out. It looks like the CPS has decided not to bring charges against Stokes. I know you'll be happy but I'm not so sure, and I know Matthew won't like it.'

'Matt will have to live with it, yes, I am pleased. Stokes is more to be pitied than punished and he's lost his job over this so he's not got away with it completely.'

'Well, DS Hurst was going to ring Kate, apparently if she wants to carry on there's a possibility that they can get him on a charge of stalking. She probably won't go for it, she's inherited your soft centre, so he'll get away with it all won't he?' They had agreed to differ on the issue each knowing that the other would never change their mind.

'Now, I wondered if we should pack some extra towels, I think I could squeeze them into the cases, what do you think?'

'I think we've got everything we need. If not, you'll surely find a shop to buy them, we don't have to penny pinch anymore.' Malcolm grinned at Jenny. Life was good and he was looking forward to their holiday even if he was a bit old for Disney World

'Come on, we need an early night. The flight's at an unearthly hour so we'll have to be up before the larks.'

****

'Hello gorgeous!' Joel slid his arms around Alice's waist and kissed the back of her neck. Blushing she wriggled free,

'Not at work Joel, someone might see!' she chuckled.

'I've locked the door.'

'You haven't!' Alice blushed.

'You're right, I haven't.' He earned himself a playful punch. Alice couldn't believe how comfortable she felt with Joel. Their relationship was still very fresh and new but it was a magical time. He had brought a lightness to her life which she hadn't even realised was missing. Had she really never known how to have fun?

'Still on for tonight?' he asked.

'Can't wait. Are you sure you can cook because from a work point of view we can't both go down with food poisoning.' Alice teased. She was so looking forward to an evening with Joel.

'You'll be amazed. I've been cooking for myself for ten years now and I'm still alive and kicking.'

'Beans on toast doesn't count as cooking, though...'
Joel silenced her with a kiss and left the room before anyone else came in and discovered them. Alice felt the warmth of contentment sweep through her body. It seemed ironic that the worst time of her life, the discovery of her true parentage, should coincide with the

happiest time she could ever remember. So much was happening at the moment, supporting her mother to name but one, yet it all seemed bearable now that Joel was around. Not that she talked constantly about these problems; it wasn't necessary. They had slipped into an easy companionship and it was sufficient to know that Joel was there for her and would listen when the need arose. Tonight would be the first time Alice had visited his home and she was so looking forward to it. His claim to be a good cook would be put to the test, but it wouldn't take much to be better than Alice who regularly survived on beans on toast. She wanted Joel to meet her mother too. Caroline had been so pleased to hear about him and couldn't wait to get to know him. She too recognised how much Alice needed something good to offset the difficult issues which had arisen from out of the blue in the last few weeks, a romance would bring a more than welcome diversion.

Alice had so much to tell Maggie that afternoon, an hour would barely be enough time to get through it all. However, thoughts today were mainly positive, especially where Joel was concerned. The only exception being the rather disconcerting feeling that her previous resolve to avoid relationships had been so easily swept away by this unexpected strength of feeling for him. Maggie listened carefully to this outpouring, recognising the confusion Alice was experiencing. When Maggie met Peter the initial euphoria had prompted an inner struggle regarding the ethics of dating a man who had previously been a client. It had taken a dose of Sue's down to earth common sense to steer her in the right direction, for which she would always be grateful. Of course Maggie wasn't in the business of giving advice and could only help Alice to explore these new feelings and emotions in the belief that Alice would reach the right decisions for a happy future.

Maggie remembered fondly the time when Sue had almost bullied her into visiting Peter at a point in their relationship when he was trying to protect her by distancing himself from her. Having drawn strength from Sue's straight talking she was eventually the one to propose to Peter! Alice of course was not Maggie, but the younger woman did have a similar inner strength which would hopefully carry her through this difficult time. Perhaps Joel could be the light at the end of the tunnel as Peter had been for her, but Alice needed to reach her own conclusions about this new relationship.

'I keep thinking of your question last week about how I would feel if I never saw Joel again. I don't want to be in that position and the strength of my feelings is quite frightening. In such a short time he's come to mean so much to me and I've told him everything Maggie. All about my feelings for Ronald and how that led to the knowledge that he wasn't my biological father and even the circumstances of my conception.'

Maggie noticed that Alice rarely used the word 'rape' which wasn't surprising. It was one of those words which, although only four letters long, was difficult to verbalise. Alice did what many clients did and chose other euphemisms rather than the word itself. That was fine; it was a coping mechanism and meant that she was able speak about the rape without that almost electrical jolt that the word conjured up and the implications of the violence and cruelty held in such a small word. Joel was obviously becoming important to Alice and Maggie hoped that he could be the ballast to steady her throughout the difficult time ahead. It seemed that the focus of Alice's life recently had been the possibility of obtaining justice and her energy was concentrated on a future trial. When that was over, if indeed it ever went that far, she would be left with the reality of being the child of a rapist, not an easy fact to work through.

Perhaps with a new and positive relationship it would be easier to ride out the difficult time ahead and come to terms with who she really was. Alice was certainly more animated than on previous occasions and this new relationship was definitely something good to help offset the bad. But equally important to the young woman was her mother and the improving relationship between them. Using the last few minutes of their session to update Maggie on Caroline, Alice had another positive to bring a sense of balance to her life. Although there was still an uphill climb, it now seemed that she would not be facing it alone.

Chapter 34

Mark Appleton was suspended temporarily from his party pending the outcome of the charges brought against him. If he had expected colleagues to line up in support, he was disappointed. The reality was that Appleton was not a popular MP among his peers and even the leader of the party refused to comment other than to say that he had every confidence in the police to find out the truth of the matter. An ambiguous statement if ever there was one. Mark was left with nothing to do but idle the time away at home and couldn't even leave Fenbridge without permission from the police. Georgia was no comfort either, having changed in a way he couldn't quite put his finger on. There was a different air about her, more confident perhaps and she certainly wasn't going out of the way to placate him as had always been the case. Mark was furious at times and would like to put her in her place but the reality was that he was afraid to take the usual steps to control Georgia as they seemed to be living in a goldfish bowl of late. Thankfully the press had given up camping on their door step but Mark was reluctant to venture far from the house for fear of being recognised. Long discussions with his agent were the only times he had any kind of stimulating company but he didn't always like the line his agent took. Barker had never asked Mark if the allegation was true but he didn't know if that was because he believed Appleton implicitly, or he thought there may be a grain of truth in there somewhere. Either way Mark found it best not to discuss the incident and an unspoken agreement seemed to be in place as the two men talked around the issue a full three hundred and sixty degrees without so much as questioning the possibility of a guilty verdict. The future became a popular topic, planning for Mark's return to work and debating how he could best restore his good name. These discussions however became fewer as the time lapsed. Barker seemed to have other commitments which left him little or no time to devote to Appleton. The rest of the party continued as if he didn't exist and the only other person Mark had regular contact with was Jenson, his lawyer. Jenson had endless questions, prying questions which made Mark want to tell him to mind his own business but questions which he knew he would face in the witness box, if or when the case got to trial. Mark was still confident that all he had to do was keep denying that he knew anything about the woman and there would be no case to answer. It was all about evidence these days, DNA and that kind of thing. After thirty years there couldn't possibly be anything like that, he didn't know why they even bothered to swab him. Jenson said it was simply procedure but he knew they were also trying to intimidate him. Well it wouldn't work. Naturally Jenson had lined up an excellent barrister to defend him but at a very high price. Altogether it was a worrying time all round and one which seemed to take an age to resolve even though there was no way the police could tie him to the rape. They couldn't even pinpoint the date, other than the month and year, which was over three decades ago. Surely there was no one on the planet who could remember what they were doing that long ago? Caroline Greenwood was heading for a fall and making a complete fool of herself. Why couldn't she have kept her mouth shut and forgotten all about it as he had done?

****

Sandra Freeman was delighted with how the case was progressing. She had needed a breakthrough to counter the mounting pressure from the superintendent who was nervous about such a high profile case on his watch. The breakthrough had come from Appleton's laptop. The tech guys were amazing. She thought herself to be relatively computer literate, but the stuff they could find out was incredible. Deleting incriminating evidence simply didn't work anymore and most browsing history was in there somewhere, it was simply a matter of knowing where to look. Georgia Appleton had been helpful in directing them to emails between her husband and his agent, emails which had been recovered and were interesting enough to be able to approach Jim Barker and seize his laptop too. This provided them with a name, a woman who had been assaulted by Appleton at a hotel in London. Freeman's DC was working on that angle, trying to find the woman and hopefully get a statement from her. Appleton's browsing history was also pertinent in proving that he wasn't as squeaky clean as he would have the word believe. He frequently visited sites containing pornography and violence. Sandra was both disgusted and delighted to be able to show concrete evidence of Appleton's true character which served to get the green light from her superiors to proceed with building the case. It had become broader than simply the Greenwoods although they remained Sandra's chief priority and the picture of Caroline, distraught but trying to remain strong for Alice, spurred her on. She would make certain this case was watertight and a warning to other men who assumed their position gave them license to do as they pleased. Sandra Freeman slept well at night.

It was time to update Caroline Greenwood and Sandra was confident that the progress to date would be welcome. Having rung in advance she set off with a spring in her step.

'Hello, come in, please.' Caroline greeted the visitor warmly. 'The kettle's boiled, tea or coffee?'

'A tea would be lovely, thanks.' It took only a couple of minutes for Caroline to bring the tea and they were soon seated with conversation flowing freely. As expected Caroline was pleased that the case was pulling together and that Sandra was certain the CPS would have no problem in taking it to court.

'Appleton's wife has been helpful and is prepared to testify, even bring separate charges of assault which we will probably go for even though I think we already have enough to lock him away for a long time already. He's maintained that he doesn't know you and never has. Trying to make out that this sort of thing happens all the time to men in his position and he's the victim here. His denial will be his downfall and I rather think that when we're finished with him he'll get sympathy from no one at all. The press will have a field day. Of course our biggest weapon is Alice. The DNA is a match but Appleton and his legal team won't hear of that until during the trial. It's good then that he's denied knowing you so vehemently, he's incriminating himself and his lies will ultimately send him down.'

'Any idea of when this will come to court?' Caroline naturally longed for this to be behind her.

'Well, it's nearly December now so I'd like to think we can get it into crown court by August or September next year.'

'As long as that?'

'I'm afraid so. The judicial system never moves very quickly but at least it gives us plenty of time to make doubly sure that everything's in place. The plea hearing could be in January. That's when the charges will be read and Appleton will have to enter a plea. If he's of the same mind as he is now, that'll be not guilty. Then he'll be bound over until the trial, with the same conditions he's under now, mainly not to approach you.'

Caroline nodded. Having hoped things would be over sooner than that she was a little disappointed but Sandra's positive attitude was encouraging.

'It's as well that I didn't go to stay with Alice if it's going to take so long.'

Sandra had on a couple of occasions suggested this as a safety measure but Caroline had been adamant that Alice needed her own space, particularly with Joel now on the scene.

'I've had Georgia Appleton on the phone a couple of times.' It seemed right that Sandra should know.

'Really! What did she want?'

'Just someone to talk to I think. She seems quite isolated.'

'Typical in an abusive relationship. They isolate their partner until they're dependent solely on them and rely on fear to maintain control. Appleton's certainly one loathsome individual. You haven't mentioned Alice to her have you?'

'Only in that she knows I have a daughter, she has no idea her husband is Alice's father.'

'Good, it's best not to tell her. I know she's helping us but she's still living with him and something might slip unintentionally.'

'Yes, I thought it was best not to say anything.'

Sandra's phone rang. She looked at it then apologised,

'Sorry, I'll have to take this.'

Caroline cleared the cups away, remaining in the kitchen until Sandra had finished her call. The detective had to leave,

'Something's come up but I think we'd about finished. If there's anything else, just ring, okay?'

'Yes thanks, but I think we've covered everything for now.'

Sandra hurried out, unable to stop a smile playing on her lips which Caroline thought most peculiar.

****

There were two patrol cars outside the Appleton house as Sandra pulled up, and another car arrived at the same time from which a local reporter appeared, almost tripping over himself to speak to her before she disappeared inside.

'DS Freeman, can you tell me what's happening here?'

'Obviously not, as you can see I'm just arriving too.' Sandra walked briskly away heading for the front door. A uniformed officer let her in and she followed the sound of heated voices coming from the lounge. Mark Appleton was in the process of being cuffed by a young constable and was shouting at his wife who sat on the sofa, head in her hands, holding a wet dish rag over one eye. Sandra glared at Appleton who quietened at the sight of her. She sat beside Georgia, asking what had happened. Georgia sobbed quietly and the constable spoke first,

'Mrs Appleton called 999 from upstairs as her husband was apparently threatening her. We found her still barricaded upstairs with Mr Appleton trying to get to her.'

'I keep telling him there's no need for you to be here, it was just a misunderstanding, something and nothing between my wife and I so please go away!' Mark shouted angrily.

Georgia lifted her head and Sandra could see a large bruise beginning to develop above her right eye, with the area around it so swollen that Georgia's eye was beginning to close.

'It doesn't look like a misunderstanding to me.' Sandra remarked. Mark glared at his wife and shouted,

'Tell them Georgia, tell them how you fell!'

'My husband struck me DS Freeman. I told him that I intended to leave and he lost his temper.' Georgia was determined never to cover up for Mark again.

'Do you want to press charges?'

'Yes, I do.'

'Take Mr Appleton to the station will you constable and book him in.' Sandra enjoyed saying those words. As the constable endeavoured to lead Mark away, he continued to shout, claiming his wife was lying and it was all a conspiracy to bring him down. Georgia sighed.

'I'm going to take you to A&E now and you can tell me all about it on the way.' Sandra said.

'That's probably not necessary; I've had worse than this without any treatment.'

'Maybe, but we need to get you checked out. When you're feeling a bit better I'll take a statement and we'll get some photographs of that eye.' Sandra couldn't believe how stupid Appleton had been. He was handing them evidence on a plate, a photograph of his wife would go a long way in proving to a jury just how violent this man could be.

'Where were you going to go Mrs Appleton?'

'To the women's refuge initially, I don't have anywhere else.'

'Well I think we can do better than that for you. There's no reason why you should be forced to leave your home, we'll arrange to get the locks changed and when your husband's released later today we'll have a court order to prevent him from coming back here.'

'Can you do that?' Georgia was amazed.

'Just watch and see.'

Chapter 35

Florida had been a great success with the Grainger family. Whoever would have thought that winning the lottery would be such a stressful experience? The holiday however had gone a long way to relieving that stress with little to have to agree on other than where they should eat their next meal or should it be a day of rides for the children or relaxing around the hotel pool. Family unity was once again restored and although Matthew had spared no words in telling his father exactly what he thought of the idea of dropping charges against Stokes, a part of him admired Malcolm's forgiving spirit. Kate had decided to take her father's lead and not pursue charges of stalking. It seemed to them that Stokes was just a sad man and probably not dangerous after all. He was certainly not a particularly successful man and had even bungled the attempts to blackmail and intimidate them, leaving a trail of evidence to incriminate himself. Another factor which had somehow changed the family dynamics was the diaries of Bill Grainger. All the adults had read them and each one had been moved by the story they told and the emotion they held. When considering the difficulties Bill had faced and eventually overcome, their own problems seemed trivial and life too short to worry over petty issues. Certainly their financial worries were over and as they enjoyed the luxury the money had brought them, they also took time to discuss how the same money could be used to help others. As charity begins at home, they were unanimous in supporting the plan to bring Bill home to live with the family after all he was the family hero now. Naturally the decision lay with the man himself, but they hoped he would decide to go with the plan; Jenny had mentally already designed a suite to suit his every need. But the consensus was that the money should be used to help others going through difficult times and they agreed on a trust being set up which Matthew could oversee rather than looking for another job. Already the list of what they wanted to do was increasing. Jenny had a passion for helping children overseas and wanted to direct money there to provide better living conditions, health care and education. Matthew's wife Angie was a cat lover and had already identified several shelters for cats which needed finance and their children, Tom and Becky, wanted to open a donkey sanctuary. It would take time and research to look into these ideas and Matthew would certainly have his work cut out in suiting everyone.

Although the holiday had been a wonderful experience, Jenny was happy to get home. One of the first things she did was to make an appointment to see Maggie. At times her mind hummed with all the different aspects of the lottery win and she felt in need of someone to talk to about some of the issues it presented. They arranged for Maggie to visit a week after they had arrived home from Florida. The week was spent catching up with correspondence, the inevitable bills, which were thankfully not a concern these days and Jenny decided to get stuck in and sort everything out as soon as possible. This would also free her up to begin looking for a new home for her and Malcolm and hopefully Bill.

A week after the Grainger's had returned from Florida, Maggie rang the doorbell for what she knew would be the last time. Christmas carols rang out their message of cheer, reminding Maggie that Christmas was only three weeks away. Jenny's doorbell always brought a smile to her face.

'Come in Maggie, come in!' Jenny was quite animated. Once inside, the cold December weather shrugged off, Maggie asked about the holiday.

'It was amazing! Disney World certainly isn't just for children, I actually think Mal and I will go back again on our own. We didn't get to see all there is, it would take much longer than two weeks.' Jenny said little more about the holiday and switched the subject to Frank Stokes.

'Malcolm decided not to give his statement about Stokes. He doesn't want to press charges.'

'And how do you feel about that?' Maggie asked.

'At first I was rather angry but the more I thought about it the more I could see where he was coming from. Apparently Kate could have brought charges of stalking because of those horrid photographs but she's decided not to as well. There's more of her Dad in her that I knew. We chewed it over while we were away and I think we're all happy about it now. For a while it looked as if the police might have gone ahead with a prosecution anyway, but there was a letter waiting when we got back to say the CPS don't think it's in the public interest to go ahead with the charges, especially as Mal has withdrawn the allegation.' Jenny looked thoughtful.

'You were angry at first, have you got over that now?'

'Yes, I have. I found something else too when we got home. The credit card statement had arrived and I checked everything off like I always do. There was quite a lot on it this month too, but I found a large payment which I couldn't understand. It was for nearly three thousand pounds. We've never had amounts that big before and I didn't recognise the company name, it was the Bainbridge Foundation, do you know it?' Jenny asked.

'I have heard of it, isn't it a clinic for treating addictions?'

'Got it in one Maggie. When I asked Malcolm about the payment he went all sheepish on me. It turns out that he has actually paid for Frank Stokes to be treated there for his alcoholism! Can you believe it?' It was quite difficult to believe, Maggie thought but then Malcolm Grainger seemed to be a very unusual man.

'So, you've got over your anger at Malcolm withdrawing the charges against this man but now you have found out that he's paid for this treatment?'

'Yes, but actually I'm quite proud. Not many men would help out someone like Stokes especially after all he's done to our family. Malcolm says that any of us could have turned out like him if we'd had the same life experiences but I'm not so sure. I don't think I'll ever understand my husband fully, I think I know him and he surprises me with something like this.'

Jenny went on to tell Maggie of some of their plans for using their money. It seemed as if the Grainger family were now of one accord and it was heart warming to hear about some of their plans. Perhaps Jenny and her children were more like Malcolm than she thought they were.

While Jenny spent time with Maggie, Malcolm Grainger was visiting his father. Naturally he'd visited the day after they returned but found then that Bill was leaning towards refusing their offer of living with his son and daughter-in-law. Malcolm was having another shot at persuading him otherwise.

'I don't know what to say Dad to make you realise how much we want you to come and live with us. We wouldn't have asked if it wasn't what we wanted so I don't want you to refuse because you think we don't really want you.'

Bill reached his arm up and began to tap at the keys on his bedside computer. *'Too much work for you.'* It took several minutes to write so much.

'No Dad, not at all! We'll get help, proper professional help. I'm not daft enough to think there's not a lot of work involved in caring for you but it's no problem. We've already been looking at houses on the internet and

Matt's been looking at specialised equipment which we can have installed. You'll be able to have a much bigger room than this, one with a view, that's on our wish list as well. You can see the kids when they come round and really be part of the family again.' Malcolm stared at the old man, he looked tired and worried. 'Dad, will you answer two questions for me, answer them honestly?'
Bill looked apprehensive but nodded his agreement.

'Is it because you're so happy here that you don't want to leave this place?'
Bill smiled and shook his head as best as he could.

'Would you like to see more of Jen and me and the children?'
Another smile, Bill knew he was defeated as he attempted a nod.

'Okay then, I don't see the problem so here's another question...honesty remember...do you want to come and live with us?'
The nod continued and the smile on Bill's face grew wider than Malcolm had seen it for years. He hugged his father.

'That's settled then, as soon as we find a place and make the alterations, you'll be coming home to us!'

Chapter 36

Neither Caroline nor Alice had been inside a Crown Court before and could think of several other things they would rather be doing on such a beautiful August morning. DS Freeman had offered to drive them there for the duration of the trial which could run into three or four days. They gratefully accepted and an hour before the trial was scheduled found themselves cradling weak tea in a small ante room while Sandra tried to find the CPS barrister who was to represent them.

'I couldn't have done this on my own.' Caroline whispered.

'Well, you don't have to and we don't need to whisper either.' Alice squeezed her mother's hand. They were both nervous although they had been warned that if there were any delays it could be that they would not be needed to give evidence until the following day. The second hand on the wall clock sounded like a time bomb, one that appeared to move in slow motion.

'I can't drink this tea, it's too weak and I'll need to go to the loo if I finish it.' Caroline put her cup beside Alice's untouched one on the low table and stood to walk around the tiny square room. Sandra eventually came back accompanied by a tall, rather attractive lady dressed in a black gown with her wig swinging in her hand.

'This is Emily Blackett, she'll be representing us today.' Sandra sat down and Caroline followed suit. The barrister shook hands with both women, smiling confidently as she too sat down. The room was beginning to feel slightly claustrophobic. Emily crossed her long legs and opened the file on her knee. Her wig slid to the floor and a nervous laugh escaped from Alice.

'Archaic thing but all part of the system...' Emily smiled and retrieved the wig, 'Now, I know we haven't had the opportunity to meet before but I am familiar with your case. Sandra has been keeping me informed and I must say we're in a very strong position. We are trying Appleton primarily for rape but also with assault, the incident at the end of November last year being the specimen charge. Georgia Appleton should be here somewhere.'

'She's with my colleague in another waiting room.' Sandra spoke up.

'Good. Hopefully if everyone for the defence is present we'll get a prompt start. Caroline, you'll be the first witness. I know this is an ordeal for you but it's almost at an end. Please try not to be nervous and if I or the defence barrister asks anything you are unsure about just say so and we'll re-phrase the question. If you stick to a simple answer to each question without too much detail I'll ask for more if necessary, okay?'

'Yes, what about that woman in London, is she appearing as a witness? The question was more for Sandra who answered,

'The woman in London turned out to be a prostitute who actually took money for her silence therefore an unreliable witness but I don't think we'll need her.'

Caroline nodded then addressed Emily,

'I'm a bit worried about the defence questions. Will he try to trip me up or confuse me, that kind of thing?'

'No, you don't need to worry about that. That type of clever narrative only happens on the telly, we're much more boring in real life and we stick to the facts. If he does try to confuse you, I'll be on my feet complaining before he finishes his sentence.' Emily was smiling again and came over as confident but natural with it. Caroline liked her already.

'Alice, we'll be hearing from you after your Mum's given evidence but having said that, you may not be needed. When we pull our rabbit out of the hat as Sandra so beautifully puts it, the DNA match, I'm expecting the defence barrister to call for a recess. If he does, Appleton may be advised to change his plea. So it could all be over today or it could take the full three days scheduled. You have both been extremely brave to come forward with this, I know how difficult it must have been and I admire you for it. Now, have you any more questions?'

When Caroline was eventually called, after lunch, she entered the courtroom with a pounding heart. She worried that she would be unable to hear the questions as the pulse in her neck was throbbing so loudly, there was a hollow ringing in her ears. In any other circumstances she would have stood back to admire the room. It was a large square area, beautifully panelled in a warm golden wood. The courtroom was divided by different seating areas, the highest for the judge at the front and directly opposite an enclosed space for the defendant with steps leading to the cells below. The jury sat on benches along one side with a good view of the whole courtroom and the witness box towards which she was directed was facing them. It was a beautiful room and would have made a stunning Church but the purpose of this room was nothing akin to worship in a Church, in fact quite the antithesis. Entering the box she was aware of Appleton in her peripheral vision but purposely didn't look at him. Caroline took a deep breath; she'd made it into the witness box without tripping over and making a fool of herself, now to give evidence. Exactly as Emily had said the questions were straight forward and easy to understand. It crossed her mind that they were all speaking very slowly with lengthy pauses, not at all like 'Law and Order UK' but then perhaps that was because someone was writing down every word which was spoken. A strange feeling took over Caroline's senses, as if she wasn't there but observing the proceedings from a height, outside of her own body.

Carried through in this manner she managed to answer the questions, difficult though some of them were. Emily led her through the whole event, recollections of which were painful but handled sensitively and when it was his turn, the defence barrister was actually very kind too, phrasing his words in a straight forward manner and being nothing other than polite and considerate.

Caroline lost track of time and when the judge called for a break, she had no idea how long she had been in the witness box. It was good to get back to Alice who naturally wanted to hear every detail, yet unfortunately her mother could barely remember anything as she still had that spaced out feeling as if not really there at all. More tea was offered and declined but they did try to eat something from the canteen, it was well past lunch time and they hadn't been able to face food before. Emily and Sandra left them alone to attend to other business which in a way was a relief.

'It wasn't as bad as I expected, it's all handled with polite civility. Ironic really when rape is anything but civil.' Caroline half heartedly nibbled a sandwich, it must have been difficult for Alice too, waiting and not knowing what was going on. Sandra Freeman came trotting in.

'They're bringing everyone back in now. Appleton's up next so this is where we hit him with it!' Professional or not, the detective was enjoying this. 'After his testimony will be when you'll be called Alice, unless of course his barrister calls for a recess. Fingers crossed.' She jogged out again and the two made their way back to the waiting room.

The courtroom buzzed with an undercurrent of excitement. All public seating was occupied, mainly by journalists from all the national papers. The first day of a trial against an MP was big news and the journalists were hoping for something shocking to happen, hopefully sooner rather than later to meet their deadlines. The only face Appleton could pick out as a supporter was his agent, Jim Barker, but the man had been distancing himself more and more over the long months of waiting. For the first time in his life Appleton felt lonely. He was isolated by the high wooden rails around the stand which he had entered from the steps which led directly from the cells below. Lonely or not, he maintained an arrogant expression. Caroline Greenwood had caused him such grief over one foolish prank over thirty years ago. Well, his moment had come, he would stick to his story and the prosecution wouldn't have a leg to stand on. A voice broke into the hum of a hundred whispers,

'Please rise!' Every person stood to their feet while the judge entered his courtroom. The Right Honourable Mark Appleton was called to take the stand and he walked forward, head held high. Emily was every bit as polite and considerate to him as she had been to Caroline. She began by asking him if he knew Caroline Greenwood, nee Fraser.

'No I do not.' Mark spoke clearly, emphatically.

'Perhaps if you looked at this photograph you may remember differently?' Emily smiled and passed the photo to the clerk; the judge and the defence team each had a copy. Appleton sighed and looked at the same picture he had seen several times before.

'No, I do not know the woman.'

'That was how she looked thirty years ago, at the time of the alleged rape. Are you sure Mr Appleton?'

'Yes I am sure. I do not know this woman now, or any time in the past.'

'Then do you also deny that you had a sexual encounter with her, in fact you raped her in September 1980?' Emily's tone remained even, friendly almost.

'I most certainly do deny it!' Mark's eyes grew dark, his face reddened.

'Mr Appleton, do you remember when DS Freeman first arrested you and you provided a DNA sample before you were released from custody?'

'Yes, it was an outrage. How can people make these accusations and put a respected MP such as myself through such humiliation...'

The judge broke in.

'Mr Appleton, will you please confine your remarks to answering the question only.'

'Sorry Your Honour, it won't happen again.' Mark thought he had made his point and mentally notched a point to his defence.

'Mr Appleton,' Emily smiled, 'Would you please examine these documents which are in regard to that DNA sample?' The clerk repeated his moves and Appleton put on a pair of reading glasses to scrutinise the documents. At first it didn't sink in. The document seemed to be matching his DNA with that of someone else, a Miss Alice Greenwood. Emily gave him more than enough time to read the few words on the paper. Everyone in the room seemed to be holding their breath, conscious of something monumental about to happen. Mark looked over at his barrister whose face couldn't mask his anger, then at Emily who maintained her polite smile as she said.

'This proves, categorically, that you Mr Appleton are the biological father of Alice Greenwood who was born on June 6th 1981.' There was an audible gasp from the jury and the public gallery and all eyes fixed on The Right Honourable Mark Appleton MP. After a lengthy pause, Emily asked,

'Do you still maintain that you do not, nor ever have known Caroline Greenwood?'

Marks face had lost its previous colour in fact he looked quite ill and had to grasp the rail in front of him for support. His former bluster had deserted him and he couldn't think straight enough to form a coherent answer. Fortunately his barrister was quickly on his feet.

'My Lord, may I request a recess to confer with my client?'

The judge paused for a moment. He was quite enjoying the proceedings but granted the defence request and called for a recess of thirty minutes.

It was just over an hour before Caroline and Alice heard anything. Both women had brought books but couldn't concentrate enough to read. Eventually Emily and Sandra joined them looking very pleased with themselves.

'He's asked for a recess, half an hour.' Sandra was smiling. 'I wish you'd seen his face. Having so arrogantly maintained that he had never seen you before and trying to make you out to be the bad guy, he was like a burst balloon! He didn't know where to look or what to say. Second only to his shock was his barrister's surprise. No barrister likes to be confronted with evidence as incontrovertible as that. He's not a happy bunny!'

'So what happens next?' Caroline turned to Emily.

'Well, if he was my client I'd be advising him to change his plea. If he doesn't he's quite frankly stupid. If he does then he'll still have the charge of assault to answer to and we'll proceed with that.' Emily was confident both for the outcome of the rape charge and the assault. If he pleaded guilty for the first charge, his character would be sullied by his own admission and it wouldn't be difficult to get a guilty verdict for the assault against his wife, especially with Georgia's testimony.'

Sandra spoke again,

'There's nothing more certain now than Mark Appleton's political career being at an end, any ambitions for a move to number ten are scuppered that's for sure.'

'You seem to be enjoying this Sandra, I get the feeling you don't like our local MP?' Alice asked, 'What's he ever done to you?'

'What he's done to your mother is enough for me to dislike him but to be honest with you, I actually voted for him at the last election, the toad! I was taken in by his 'family values' sweet talk and I don't like to be taken in by anyone!' Sandra actually blushed at this admission, the others witnessed her discomfort. More than half the population of Fenbridge would be feeling the same way soon. An usher appeared at the door, tapping gently before coming in,

'They're back Miss,' he informed Emily. Caroline and Alice found themselves waiting yet again, the hands on the clock moving slower than ever. Would the day never end? Twenty minutes, which seemed much longer, was all it actually took. Sandra's face was animated as she almost ran to tell them the outcome.

'He's pleaded guilty to rape...and to the assaults on his wife!' It was almost too good to be true. Caroline and Alice hugged each other, it was over, life could move on.

'I don't understand, why would he admit the assault charge?' Alice asked Sandra.

'His barrister would have advised it. He'll then be able to ask for a more lenient sentence on the grounds that Appleton spared his wife the stress of having to testify. It sometimes works. But now we're free to go, it's over ladies.'

Mother and daughter both thanked Emily warmly. She was the first barrister they had met and hopefully the last but had left them with an excellent impression of her profession and they would always be grateful. Sandra drove them home and they thanked her too although the detective was so obviously experiencing job satisfaction, thanks were hardly necessary.

Alice rang Joel to tell him the outcome and he promised to come to her mother's later to help them celebrate. Caroline rang Georgia. Appleton's wife was experiencing a variety of emotions, primarily relief and shock. Although she had never doubted that Mark had raped Caroline it was a shock to learn that Alice was his daughter. Georgia was also dreading the media attention, a circus which would almost certainly begin as soon as the verdict was made known and unlike Caroline and Alice, she had no anonymity to protect her from the certain onslaught.

'I have a spare room.' Caroline offered. 'Not what you're used to I know, but you'd be very welcome.' Such a generous offer made Georgia weep. Once Caroline had convinced her that the offer was genuine, she accepted and after packing a few items arrived a couple of hours later.

It was a bittersweet victory. Mark Appleton had been responsible for so much unhappiness of those three women and who knew how many more? He would pay for his crimes but his victims would always carry the scars, invisible scars, the most difficult of all to heal.

Epilogue

Eighteen months later.

Mark Appleton was serving eight years for rape with six years running concurrently for assault. Many thought he had got away lightly. There was no possibility that he would ever resume a role in public life, even after serving his time. Such high profile disgrace added considerably to his punishment and being a well known politician proved to be quite a draw back in the prison community. He had reaped his just rewards.

Georgia Appleton stayed with Caroline for a month and the two became firm friends. A divorce was granted in due course and a generous settlement which also gave Georgia the house. She would not stay there however; it was too ostentatious and held too many negative memories. Something smaller and more manageable would be better, away from Fenbridge. Perhaps a country cottage where she could build a new, more peaceful life and begin the healing process, she longed for a simpler life. Georgia also enrolled on an Open University degree course in social care, determined to carve out some kind of useful life, the days of being a trophy wife and a battered wife were over for good.

Alice and Joel married in June, a wonderfully happy day which did much to lift the spirits of them all. The wedding preparations had been a welcome distraction for both her and Caroline and when the excitement of that was behind them Joel remained a solid platform for his wife to begin building a new life. There was still a long way to go in working out the issues around her parentage but generally she was happy and functioned well. Black days did descend unexpectedly, taking her by surprise and robbing her of any peace she may have achieved. Self loathing too was occasionally a problem, casting the shadow of doubt as to whether she was worthy of Joel's love but his patient understanding could lift her above these moods and he never ceased to tell her how much she was loved, exactly what she needed to hear. Alice's visits to Maggie continued, becoming an important part of the recovery process as she talked through her feelings in an atmosphere of comfort and security. They would continue to meet as long as necessary and Joel of course went a long way to boosting Alice's happiness.

Malcolm and Jenny Grainger designed their own new home, or at least instructed an architect to do so with some very specific requirements. The plot they purchased sprawled over the edge of Fenbridge with magnificent views over the valley below. Jenny loved the idea of space and being able to incorporate all the features she had only previously admired in the property programmes she watched on television. Malcolm worked closely with the architect to provide an area which would meet the needs of his father and Matthew had researched some amazing equipment which would improve Bill's life considerably. There was a new computer which could be operated by blowing into a tube, great for those days when his hands failed him. They purchased a wheelchair which was angled in a way to support the whole body and which was operated by a simple knob on the arm. Bill's room would be an annex at the front of the house with tall windows allowing him to appreciate the glorious views. A fully equipped bathroom with an air bath and a hoist would be for Bill's sole use. Malcolm and Jenny were thrilled when it was finally ready and they watched Bill's face as he saw it for the first time. Considering they had both retired Malcolm and Jenny were busier than ever administrating the various projects they had become involved in. This was what having money was truly about, making it work, not only for themselves but for their family and the wider community. Maggie was thrilled every time she came across a snippet in the newspaper about what the Graingers were doing and wished them a long and happy 'retirement'.

Frank Stokes had been utterly stunned by Malcolm Grainger's generosity, not only in dropping the charges and getting him out of serious trouble with the police but also in paying for him to receive help for his alcohol problem. The Bainbridge Foundation had an excellent reputation and Frank grasped the unexpected opportunity, determined to engage fully with their regime and turn his life around. Every day he spent there he had questioned Malcolm's generosity, constantly asking himself why? Why would someone whom he had treated so badly go out of his way to help him and to pay for such expensive treatment? It was beyond his comprehension but he would always be grateful. After the spell in the care of the foundation Frank had written to Malcolm to thank him and to apologise for his terrible behaviour. He couldn't believe that he had actually been so warped and consumed by such jealousy and greed that he had caused the Graingers so much grief. His bungled attempts to blackmail and threaten them shamed him when he thought about it and the fact that Grainger had actually helped him after all this, humbled him, giving cause to re-evaluate his life. He never heard back from Grainger which was no surprise, he knew that they would never become best buddies and grateful though he was, it was probably best left at that. He had been sober for over a year, a regular attendee at AA and had actually begun to write that novel which had previously been nothing more than a dream. Channelling his emotions into writing proved a much better way to handle them than attempted blackmail and who knows? One day he might write a best seller.

George Price passed away peacefully in his sleep in May, just a few short months since he and Helen had moved to Fenbridge. They had celebrated Christmas in their new home with Maggie and Peter and although George's condition was noticeably worse, they had enjoyed the festivities with their usual traditions and exuberance. During the cold, bleak days after New Year, George's physical health began to fail as well as his state of mind. There were several stays in hospital which he took badly too and seemed to contribute even more to his deterioration, saddening those who loved him. They did however manage a few weekends at the cottage in Scotland when George seemed to come alive again, walking through his garden and making plans which were never to be executed. Helen was grateful for her daughter and son-in-law's support, glad now that they had made the move from Scotland, a decision which had given Maggie so much more time with George than would otherwise have been possible. Mother and daughter were close, geographically now as well as emotionally, a closeness which offered Helen great comfort. Life as a widow took some getting used to but she was making friends and had begun volunteer work at the hospital a couple of mornings each week, manning the coffee shop in the out patients department. Helen's neighbour, Nancy proved to be a great friend and support and the two were planning a holiday together, just a coach tour to the Cotswolds but it would be a welcome diversion for them both. Maggie was so pleased to have had her parents close by during such a difficult time. She had made a point of taking her Dad out for a drive for an hour or two each weekend, to give Helen a break. Peter too had been wonderful. He had enjoyed George's company, often inviting him round to ask his advice on the garden or to sit in the office and share a coffee and chat whilst enjoying the view over the Yorkshire countryside. George would be missed for many reasons but Maggie would always remember her mother's words shortly after his death.

'Alzheimer's is such a cruel, unpredictable disease. I lost your Dad a long time ago when it first took hold of him, slowly stealing him away. It's like death by instalments; I wouldn't wish it on anyone.'

A summer wedding went a long way in bringing a degree of happiness back into the family. Rachel, Peter's youngest daughter, married Alec Russell. The happy couple were radiant and settled down to married life in York, a distance easily travelled for visits from both directions.

Sue and Alan became the proud parents of a baby boy. Once again Maggie and Peter were called upon to fulfil the role of Godparents, a role they looked upon as both an honour and a privilege. The decision to call him George brought such happiness to Maggie and Helen and he was known as 'Little George' but the way he was growing meant that this would not last for too long.

Peter's health remained stable thanks mainly to Gilenya, a drug which seemed to suit him well and certainly eased the symptoms of the MS. He devoted much of his time to painting while continuing to work part time at RBL Architects, and Maggie, try as she might, never quite managed to cut down her hours to match Peter's. There were always new clients to help but their life worked well and they were happy with Maggie continuing the work she so loved.

Each time Maggie visited Helen she was drawn to the portrait Peter had painted of George, which hung prominently above the fireplace. Peter had captured her father's likeness perfectly after hours spent working on the portrait while George had been happy to pose. The old man sitting quietly, wore a wistful, contented expression, as if deep in pleasant thoughts of days gone by. A shaft of sunlight brought warm shadows to his face and at his feet Ben curled up in the same pool of sunlight. It was exactly how Maggie liked to remember him and the first thing she looked for on each visit to Helen. George may have left them in body but his spirit lived on in the hearts and memories of those who loved him.

The End

Other books by Gillian Jackson

'The Counsellor'

The unexpected death of Maggie Sayer's husband shatters her perfect world. Struggling to make sense of her grief, a complete change and a positive focus seem to be the only thing which will help Maggie to carry on with life. Training as a therapeutic counsellor provides this focus, bringing her into contact with people who desperately need help.

Julie and her children are living in fear of an abusive husband, Janet is crumbling under the weight of a secret she has kept for over forty years and Karen has never recovered from her mother's violent death.

Maggie is drawn into each client's problem as she seeks to empower them to move on with their lives. And then she is faced with an ethical dilemma when she meets Peter...

Sensitively written, poignant and compelling, 'The Counsellor' is the first book in the 'Maggie Sayer' series by British author Gillian Jackson.

'Maggie's World'

Ellie Graham wakes from a coma to a strangely different world than the one she remembers. Sarah is a newlywed, whose fairytale romance and marriage is turning into a nightmare, causing her to doubt her sanity. Ruth, desperately longing for a child of her own is sinking beneath the weight of a long kept secret.

Therapeutic counsellor Maggie Sayer is no stranger to grief herself and uses her skills to help these three young women. But Maggie's own life has its complications too, her new husband is suffering from a degenerative illness and a past client returns to her door with problems she is unable to solve.

Maggie uses every possible approach to give the very best to her clients, but not every story can have a happy ending.

'Pretence'

For Rae Chapman the months before her wedding should be the happiest time of her life but the same troubling nightmare that disturbed her sleep in childhood has returned once more. Could something from the past be trying to re-surface? Are they only dreams, or long lost memories? Rae begins a journey to find out more about her past and discovers a family secret which throws her world into turmoil.

Lydia appears to have led a life of ease and privilege but now has a decision to make, one she has put off for nearly forty years and one which will shock her family and friends. As time is running out she turns to Maggie Sayer for help but is it already too late?

Linda thought she had escaped an oppressed life when her husband left, but has she simply exchanged one difficult situation for another and how can she support and protect her only child but still do the right thing?

As always, therapeutic counsellor Maggie Sayer seeks to give her best to these clients but is shocked by an unexpected turn of events in her friend's life and finds that her support is needed much closer to home.

www.gillianjackson.co.uk

Twitter @GillianJackson7

Facebook; Gillian Jackson Author

Lightning Source UK Ltd.
Milton Keynes UK
UKOW05f2123110814

236768UK00001B/15/P